GOTHIC NOVELS

GOTHIC NOVELS

Advisory Editor:
Dr. Sir Devendra P. Varma

THE FATAL REVENGE;

OR,

THE FAMILY OF MONTORIO

A ROMANCE

Volume 2

CHARLES ROBERT MATURIN

("DENNIS JASPER MURPHY")

New Foreword by Henry D. Hicks

New Introduction by Maurice Lévy

ARNO PRESS

A New York Times Company

New York—1974

Reprint Edition 1974 by Arno Press Inc.

Special Contents Copyright © 1974
   by Devendra P. Varma

GOTHIC NOVELS II
ISBN for complete set: 0-405-06011-4
See last pages of this volume for titles.

Publisher's Note: This volume was reprinted
from the best available copy.

Manufactured in the United States of America

————◆————

Library of Congress Cataloging in Publication Data

Maturin, Charles Robert, 1780-1824.
   The fatal revenge.

   (Gothic novels II)
   Reprint of the 1807 ed. printed for Longman, Hurst,
Rees, and Orme, London.
   I. Title. II. Title: The family of Montorio.
III. Series.
PZ3.M4375Fat5 [PR4987.M7]   823'.7   73-22767
ISBN 0-405-06018-1

FATAL REVENGE ;

OR,

THE FAMILY OF MONTORIO,

A Romance.

―――――

BY DENNIS JASPER MURPHY.

―――――

IN THREE VOLUMES.

Ἐβυλόμην δὶ ὺ πόλιιϛ, και όρη αὐτὰ μόνον, ὼσπιρ ΄ιν γραφαῖϛ ὁρᾶν,
ἀλλὰ τὺϛ ανθρώπυϛ αὐτὸϛ, κὰι ἁ πράτἰυσι, καὶ οἱα λίγυσι.
LUCIAN, Ἐπισκοτῦντιϛ.

I wished not merely to see cities and woods, as one can see them in maps;
but men, and what they do, and what they say.

═══════

VOL. II.

═══════

LONDON:

PRINTED FOR LONGMAN, HURST, REES, AND ORME,
PATERNOSTER ROW.

―――

1807.

C. Stower, Printer, Paternoster Row.

FATAL REVENGE;

OR,

THE FAMILY OF MONTORIO

CHAP. I.

Why do I yield to that suggestion,
Whose horrid image doth unfix my hair,
And make my seated heart knock at my ribs,
Against the use of nature?

MACBETH.

DURING the day Annibal gave to Cyprian some papers, which contained an account of what had recently befallen him, after briefly sketching to him what was first necessary to be known, viz. the subject of his former correspondence with Ippolito. Where this is deficient, said he, at the close, I can supply it by narrative. It was written

in solitude and durance; you must therefore expect a simple detail of lonely individual feelings; variety was precluded
by the barrenness of utter solitude, and
embellishment by the absence of all solicitude about a manuscript, which I thought
would never become visible till its writer
was no more.

It was on the second night after Palle-
rini's arrival at the castle, that I took the
resolution Filippo had suggested to me,
of visiting the tower. When I look back
on the expectations I had formed of this
circumstance and its consequences, and
compare them with what has actually befallen, I can scarce be assured of my
own identity. I can scarce think that
the being then, whose mind was but
partially tinged with fear and curiosity,
whose expectations were balanced by incredulity, and whose credulity was again
alarmed by experience—who was in that
suspended state in which fear is not too
powerful,

powerful, nor solicitude too severe, can
be the being now, whose mind is made
up, whose feeling is tense, and the terrors
of whose fate have appeared to him
without cloud or shadow, without mitigation or medium—whose knowledge is
without bounds, whose fear is without
hope—who has no relief of human uncertainty, no shelter of natural obscurity.
On that night we supped in the great
corridor; it was intensely hot. I observed the Duke and my father deeply
engaged in conversation, and quitted the
table unnoticed. I went to my apartment, where I expected Filippo would
soon join me; but he was there already,
his dark eyes full of something. I had
often seen them marked with curiosity
and wonder; never before with fear. He
anticipated my questions—" Oh, Signor,
strange things are doing within these
walls to-night—things that would never
come into the thought of man are pass-

ing near us, frightfully near us: (drawing close to me and whispering,) you will scarce believe what I have seen, Signor." "What have you seen, Filippo," (said I, laying down the light,)—" The confessor--the confessor, Signor! I knew it long ago—I told the Count—would to heaven the inquisition had him—would to St. Agatha the Primate Cardinal of Naples had to deal with him. There was an old Carthusian in the village where I was born, who would feel the presence of a spirit before a taper had burned blue; and banished from his convent a stubborn imp who had defied holy water, and even Latin ever so long. Oh! would he were but to meet this monk, I warrant he would find him other employment than lurking in vaults, and mingling with the dead, and" ... "Filippo, you must be composed; if you have any thing to relate, relate without wanderings and exaggeration: the time is a solemn

solemn one; nor do I wish my mind to be disturbed from the object I have fixed it on." " Signor, I will not exaggerate; I will tell you what I have really . . . but forgive me if I tell it with many starts of fear. Remember it is midnight; and that I am speaking of things fearful to think of, even at noonday; and forgive me . . . You know, Signor, how suspicious I have been of that father Schemoli, as he calls himself, though all that ever knew him say, they never saw father, or mother, or relative, or any one that owned him; but that, a few years back, when he took the vows in the Dominican convent in Gaeta, they talked of his having been first seen by some wrecked fishermen, after a terrible storm, all in a blaze of lightning, perched on a crag of a little desolate island in the Grecian sea; but this is nothing to the purpose." "I wish you could have remembered that, Filippo." " Well, Signor,

nor, I have always watched and feared him; and, after I saw him last night, visibly pacing down that passage to the north tower, I felt assured that he was connected some way with the strange noises and strange reports I had heard of that tower. So, Signor, all day I sought him through the castle; for I have a strange desire, Signor, to look into the eyes and face of one whom I suspect of any thing: I always think I discover something by it; but all was in vain. At length I bethought myself, and it was a bold thing, for some of the people of the castle would as soon enter the hole of scorpions as approach that room; I bethought myself of going to his chamber. I knew the partitions and doors there were crazy; and I thought, through some chink or crevice, I might get a sight of him, perhaps, strangely employed. Now, Signor, you have learning, and could perhaps explain your feelings better;

but

but I had a strong thought, an audible
voice, as it were, in my mind, that
seemed to tell me, if I went it would not
be in vain : it was as plain as if one of
those pictures spoke from its frame to
me : it was strange to me, and yet it
gave me courage.   I went about mid-
day, when most of the family were asleep
I stole softly along, holding my breath,
and looking round me, though there
was no one near me ; yet when I came
to the very door, I could not help
glancing behind me, to see if he were
close to me ; for I had a feeling, as if
he had been stealing along with me the
whole way, and would just gripe me as
I came to his door.   All was quiet ; the
passage empty ; the door closed.   I heard
a little noise in his room, often ceasing,
and often repeated, as if the person within
was engaged in something that he would
every now and then quit to prevent being
overheard.   I tried a thousand places to
get

get a convenient view of the room; at length I fixed on one behind an old picture, in a waste recess; for all that part of the west turret is waste and dreary; and they say he therefore chose it for himself. I had a full view of him; he sat with his cowl thrown back:—never, but in my dreams, the time I had a fever, have I beheld such a face. One arm was extended, and I saw by his whole frame, that he was talking with earnest, and, as it were, angry gesture, (as he might do in the confessional, when reproving a penitent,) though I believed him alone. I changed my posture at the crevice to spy who could be with him; and I saw— yes, Signor, with these eyes I saw" . . . "Hush, hush, Filippo; more than me will hear your information."—"Then, Signor," creeping to me on tip-toe, "you must let me whisper, for I feel I shall shriek telling, if I do not." "Tell it any way, only proceed. —"I saw, blessed mother, a skeleton seated

in

in a chair opposite to him, plain and
erect, and with all that horrid quietness,
as if it was the ordinary visit of a companion. My eyes grew dim. I had rather
have seen him rending and abusing those
dead bones, as they say the men of the
unholy art do; for to sit face to face, in
broad day-light, as man sits with man,
with the decayed remains of the grave,
with an object so loathsome to the eyes
of flesh . . . Oh! it gave me a more
ghastly thought of him than the night I
saw him in the vaults of the old chapel.
I could not bear to behold him. I stole
away again and as I went, there came a
hollow clattering sound from the room, as
if that strange object was in motion. I
hurried on, and scarce thought myself
safe till I had got down the great stairs,
and saw, at a secure distance, the little
narrow oratory window, like a hole in
a wizzard's den."—" It was indeed a
ghastly sight, Filippo; but what is this

to our present purpose ; light that other
lamp, and follow me." I was hastening
away : " Stay, stay, Signor, this is not all ;
Oh these are fearful things to pass so near
us, and to pass unnoted too ; to think that
we are in the next chamber to a being
whose dealings are with the dead ; for
to-night, Signor, to-night again I saw
him." " Forbear those gestures, Filippo,
they tell of worse things than your story."
" Oh ! it was just so, Signor, I felt my
arms raised, and my teeth grinding, and
my very eye-brows stretched up to my
forehead, when I saw him to-night coming along the passage from his room."
" Why do you throw yourself thus in his
way, if the only effect is fear ?" " I could
not help it, Signor ; I felt I could not help
it ; I wished myself far off, but I could
not move ; he came on slowly, as if he
were encumbered ; he saw me not, those
high windows give so little light, and I
had shrunk just under one of them. I
3   thought

thought, as he passed, I heard other sound
beside his steps : I looked after him, and
under his garments the dead feet were
peeping out. Oh! he is a creature, in
whom are so strangely mixed, what belongs to the living, and what to the
dead, that we know not who it is we
see when he crosses us, nor what he will
prove while we are yet looking at him.
I followed him, though I scarce knew
whither I was going, nor felt the floor
under me. He went down some steps to
the left, where you know, Signor, there
is supposed to be a passage that has been
long shut up, but where the wall is as
blank and solid as this. Then I thought I
should see something that would last me
to tell of all my life, that the wall would
open to receive, or the floor sink under,
or a huge black hand be held out to
him, or at least there would be a smell
of sulphur as he disappeared."—" Well—
well—but what did you really see?"——
"I

" I followed still, Signor; I know not
how I felt; but I followed, when, suddenly turning on me—blessed saints!—it was
not the monk:—a skeleton head stared at
me—a bare decayed arm beckoned me
backward. I retreated fast enough; but
I dared not turn my back, while it was
in sight least it should pursue me. It is
more than an hour since I saw it, yet I
see it still—every where—on the walls,
on the ceilings; when the light falls
strong, even I see it. I see it when I
close my eyes; the deep, dark hollowness
of the empty brow will never leave me."
—" Filippo, is this your preparation to
accompany me; to talk yourself into terrors about an object which, whether supernatural or not, has no connection
with us, nor with our purpose to night?"
—" Will you go to the tower to-night,
to-night, Signor?"—" I am going Filippo." I rose and took the lamp; for I
knew

knew it was easier to work on fear by shame than by argument; and I felt a rising disinclination to going alone. Oh! we are all, in every state of existence, in every stage of intellect, the slaves of an inward dread of futurity, and its beings. The wisest of us, in the very pith and pride of our wisest moods, will suddenly feel himself checked and oppressed by an influence caught from the remembrances of childhood, the dream of sickness, the vision of night or solitude; from the story, the monition, the bare hint of the menial, or the crone, the humblest inferior in rank and in intellect, at the strength of which he laughs, shudders, and submits. Filippo followed me in silence, ashamed to repeat his fears, yet displeased they were put to another trial. Ippolito, (for to you I address these pages, though doubtful you will even ever see them,) you must yourself feel the hushed step, the stifled breath, the

the suspicious and lowered glance of eye
that accompanies these movements, before their effect can be described to you.
We came to the door of the passage;
we tried, and found it open. At another
time this circumstance would have struck
me with surprise; but I was now so occupied by strange expectation, that I re-
garded it merely with that blind satisfaction which one feels at an object being
unexpectedly facilitated to them. As
we entered the passage, however, an
unpleasant sensation arose within me.
The first, and the last time I had trodden
it before, poor old Michelo had been
my conductor; the unfortunate old
man, whom either my curiosity or my
fear had actually killed. With an involuntary motion I raised my lamp to Filippo's face, to discover if my companion
was changed; for I had felt a change in
my own perceptions, that would prepare
me for, and justify any strange appearance

ance at the moment; and twice or thrice, not unconsciously, yet unwillingly, I heard myself call him Michelo.—" Do not call me Michelo, while we are here, Signor ;" and I was angry and disturbed at his mentioning the name, though I had uttered it first, and giving him the pain he only wished removed.

With many such crossings of mind, sometimes resisted, and sometimes resisted in vain, we reached the apartments. The doors were open there too; but I endeavoured to withdraw my mind from every lesser notice, to still the flutter and variety of my thoughts, and fix them singly on the search of the apartments, and on the discovery of any circumstances that might attend their being opened and visited the preceding night. I passed through both apartments slowly, looking around me, but discovering nothing I had expected to see. Filippo followed still slower, with the lingering of fear,
                                    holding

holding the lamp high, and confining
his eye to that part of the room where
the light fell clear. But in the second
apartment I perceived the pannel removed. The circumstances of my last
visit rushed on my mind: I moved mechanically towards it; but Filippo, when
he saw me actually entering it, could contain no longer.—" Ah, Signor, how well
you seem to know all these fearful places;
and will you indeed go down that passage, that looks like a passage to the
grave? (he shuddered,) If I entered it,
I should think the door would close on
me, and shut me into that dark cavern-
hole for ever. I should think (holding
the light over it with a shaking hand,)
to find the decayed bones of some poor
wretch, whose end no one ever knew,
thrown in one of those dusky nooks."—
I was disturbed at his unconsciously re-
viving every image I wished to banish;
for I felt that if I suffered my mind to
pause

pause over every fearful suggestion of
memory or fancy, my resolution would
be exhausted, and the moment of trial, if
one was approaching, find me unprepar-
ed.

I took the lamp from him, and bidding
him wait in the apartment, began to descend the steps.—"Pardon me, Signor,"
said he, following me eagerly; " if there
be danger, you shall not encounter it
alone." I easily persuaded him to stay,
however, for I had no wish that he should
witness all I had seen, or know all I
knew. His mind was too quick and tenacious to see the object I had formerly
seen there, without drawing conclusions,
perhaps too strong; and I felt in the
sense of his being so near me, a sufficient
balance for dreary and utter loneliness.

I went down the passage alone; my
lamp burned dim in the thick air. I
would have hurried through it, without
suffering my eye to glance beyond the
limits

limits of the light I carried ; but I was
come to search, and I felt myself impelled to do it. The opening of the pannel-
door and the passage could be ascribed
to no common cause. I soon found the
place where I had discovered the skeleton ; it was open and empty ; the cavity remained in the wall ; the rubbish
appeared to have been lately scattered
about ; but there was no vestige of its
former tenant.

I felt myself fixed to the spot. The
current of my thoughts ran like cross-set
streams, dark, and disturbed, and thwarting, and each perplexing me with brief
predominance. I was yet hanging over
the spot, indulging in doubt and fear,
yet believing that I was dissolving them,
when I saw Filippo above bending over
the steps, and beckoning to me. I could
not soon disengage myself, for my mind
was intensely occupied, and I resisted his
impatient motions, as the sleeper resists
                                    the

the effort to awake him; but before his
fear could become distinct, I heard
feet approaching, and saw other lights
above. The steps were light and quick;
I felt this was no spectre, and hastened up
with a thousand feelings and intentions.
They were driven back, crushed, silenced,
in a moment. I beheld my father and
his confessor already in the room. Oh,
how many thoughts were with me in
that moment's pause. My own situation
and fears were forgotten. Michelo's
hints, our joint discoveries, my father's
character and habits, the well-watched
secrecy of those bloody rooms . . .
Ippolito, you are my brother; my suspicions have since been but too well justified, or I would sooner perish than
write thus. But what have I known
since? what have I yet to tell?—Though
these thoughts were so busy so remote,
yet I felt my eyes involuntarily, and
even

even painfully fixed on his; their expression was terrible,—the monk was
behind, holding up a taper in his bony
hand; his face was in the shade.—" Annibal," said my father, with the broken
voice of smothered rage, " why are you
here?"—I was silent; for no language
could relieve the tumult of my thoughts.
—" Wretch, rebel, parricide," bursting
out, " why are you here, and who conducted you."—I was roused by his rage.
—" Why, is it a crime," said I, " to be
here!"—" That you shall know," said he,
fiercely, " by its punishment, at least."—
He turned round, and turning, saw Filippo, seemed to start into madness, and
drew his sword, and rushed on him with
a force, which the other scarce avoided
by a sudden bound ; but the motion was
so vehement, that the sword stuck in the
wall, and remained fixed. Though dis-
armed, he again flew on him, and but for
the monk and me, would have dashed him
                                        down

down the steps, or strangled him against
the wainscot.   Oh! it is horrible to hold
the straining arms, and look on the blood-
shot eye, and blue writhen lip, and hear
the hoarse roar of a man rendered a
fiend by passion.—" Villain," said he,
foaming, and scarcely held, " 'tis to such
as you I owe my being thus persecuted,
suspected, slandered—that my castle seems
like a prison, and I tremble to meet the
eyes of my own servants.   You crouch
over your fires, hinting treason to
each other, till every owl that whoops
from my battlements seems to call me
murderer."—" Hush, hush, this is madness," said the monk, in a peculiar accent.   " Follow me," said my father,
resuming his sullen state.—" Where is
my sword?"—His eye fell on the place
where it was fixed; the light which the
monk hastily held up, fell strongly on
his face.   For millions I would not have
had within my breast a heart that could
                                                        hold

hold any alliance with such a face as
his for a moment became. The sword
was fixed in the wall where the stain of
blood was so deep and strong. With an
eye (which he seemed unable to withdraw or to close) terribly fastened to
the spot, twice he said, faintly and inwardly, " Will no one give me my
sword? will no one approach that wall?"
The monk drew it out, and gave it to
him. He turned away with the effort of
one who would raise his head, and dilate
his chest, and stride proudly forward; but
his step was unequal, and his whole frame
was shaken. He bid us follow him, sternly, and quitted the apartment. I had no
means of resistance, and was so lost in
thought, that of myself I thought not at
all. The monk, who bore the light,
lingered a moment, as if to see us quit
the room. When my father called from
the passage, " Come quickly, Father;
I am in darkness, I am alone; Father, I
                                    say,

say, come quickly." His voice gradually
rose, as if something he feared was rapidly approaching him; it almost became a shriek. The monk hurried out,
and we followed him. My father placed
himself in the midst of us as we descended the stairs. I can give you no
account of my feelings at this time—
they were dark, mingled, strange. I believed there was danger impending over
me; but what it was I could neither
measure nor calculate. Ippolito, will you
censure, or will you wonder at me? If
I can recollect the state of my mind at
that time the predominant sensation was
pleasure; pleasure indeed of a doubtful,
gloomy character, but certainly pleasure.
The discovery I had formerly made, seemed so fully confirmed by my father's pursuit of us—his rage—his terror—and a
thousand other circumstances I had re-
marked with the keenest local observation, that whether it was from pride in
                                    my

my own sagacity and perseverance, or
from the resistless satisfaction that accompanies the final dissolution of doubt
and perplexity, or from some other secret spring within me, I certainly was
conscious of pleasure in no mean degree. Amid all this terror and danger,
whatever I then felt was about to be terribly interrupted. We had come to the
foot of the stairs without a sound but
that of our steps. I turned involuntarily
to the left, where the passage communicated with the castle. My father and
the monk stopped. I read a consultation of blood in their dark pause. I
turned to them. The lamp, held high,
and burning dimly, from our swift motion, did not shew me a line of their
countenances to read compassion or hope
in. I grew deadly sick.—" This is the
way," I faltered out, " from this tower,"
and pointed to the passage.—" It is a
way," said my father, gloomily, " it will
be

be long ere you find." I heard his words
in that confusion of sense that retains
the full meaning, though it mixes the
sounds. I felt that danger was threatened to me, but I could not conceive either
its degree or direction. My father went
a few paces to the right, and, with difficulty opening another door, motioned
me to enter it. I obeyed with a stupid
depression, that left me even no wish
for resistance. There was such a kind
of dark alliance between him and this
tower, that I felt him as the lord of
the place, and of the time, and followed the waving of his hand, as if it were
some instrument of power. In a moment the door was closed on me. The
human faces were shut out. Their very
steps seemed to cease at once; door
after door closed at successive distances;
but I did not feel myself alone till the
echo of the last had utterly died away.

When I looked around me all was dim

and still. The morning light soon broke, and shewed me a large desolate room, so buried in the dust of long neglect, that walls, and windows, and roof seemed to s'eep in the same grey and mingled tint. No part presented a change : you might gaze till your eyes grew as dim as they, before the objects would refresh you with the least inequality : all around was dark, heavy, still. I had soon completed my comfortless survey. My thoughts turned inward on myself; I strove to drive them forth again ; there was nothing to invite or to receive them. The sun rose, and the long, long day came on without object or employment for me. " Man went forth to his work, and to his labour," and I sat in cold stagnation. The monk's coming to me with food, relieved me from a thought that visited me with a sting of agony the moment before. He also brought preparations for a couch; and so miserably

serably anxious is the mind for the relief of variety in such a moment, that I
looked at them with a most desolate
eye. The very thought of changing the
place of my confinement, which I now saw
there was no hope of changing, had been a
latent comfort to me. He went and departed in silence, which no adjurations
could break, nor even procure from him
a look that intimated a wish or future
purpose of speaking. He went, and left
me alone. Solitary confinement !—may
I experience any sufferings but such
as those again! any other affliction
supplies the power of its own resistance.
There have been beings who have sung
in the fires, and smiled on the rack ; but
the nerveless vexation, the squalid lassi-
tude, the helpless vacancy of solitary confinement, when time flows on without
mark or measure; when light and darkness are the only distinctions of day and
night, instead of employment and repose ;

c 2   when

when, from the torpor of inexertion, man feels himself growing to, and becoming a part of the still senseless things about him, as the chains that have eat into his wasted limbs, have begun, from cold and extinguished sensation, to feel like a part of them — that —Oh—that to beings of thought, of motion, of capacity---what is it ?—the uneasy consciousness of life, without its powers—the darkness of death, without its repose.

When the first tumult of my mind had subsided, and I felt I was really left to myself, I began to inquire what resources I had ; for I shuddered at the idea of total vacancy. I had no books, no pen, no instrument or means of drawing. All I could do was --to think, to examine into my mind, and live on the stores of acquirement. I had read and thought more than young men of my age usual y do ; and the exclusion of outward things, I endeavoured to think, would rather assist than

impede

impede my efforts to plunge into the
depth of thought. But a short time convinced me how different the employment is, that is sought for amusement,
and the employment that is wooed for
relief. *I could not think.* Whatever train
of thought I tried to weave, whether
light or solid, became immediately tasteless, and declined into absence. A monotonous musing that yet had no object, no
point, nothing to quicken reflection, that
hung sullenly on the objects around,
without drawing image or inference from
them, succeeded to every attempt at mental exertion. Here all extrinsic relief
was precluded. He that is weary may
throw away his book, or change his companion, or indulge meditation without
the fear of vacancy ; but *I* could not.
My labour must be without remission or
variety, or my dejection without hope.
How long I strove, and how sadly I desisted:—I even tried to form an inward
conference,

conference, to raise objections, and to
construct answers ; but my powers of reasoning sunk within me.   I endeavoured to
interest myself in the subject, to taste
pleasure where I was conscious I had felt
it before ; to believe important what I had
often contended for as so ; but all was
cold, shadowy, remote.   I could bring
nothing into contact with my mind ; yet
I felt that what interposed, I was interested in keeping as remote as I could.   At
length I spake aloud to myself, in hopes
of forcing attention and interest.   I tried
to assent, and object, and interrupt, with
a sickly affectation of the warm and vivid
debates of society.   The accents faltered
involuntarily on my tongue ; and while I
was apparently talking with eagerness, my
eyes and mind were mechanically fixed on
the door and windows, whose height was
so remote, so unassailable.

By design, I am convinced, the monk
visited me but once a day ; but once a day
                                had

had I the satisfaction of seeing even that
cheerless face, of hearing even that slow,
unsolacing tread. There is no telling with
what delight I waited even that, and how
I listened to hear the rusty wards long
resisting the key, that I might longer feel
the presence of a human creature (as I
believed) near me!—how I protracted the
preparations for the meal he brought, that
I might compel him to continue longer
in my sight!—how I multiplied questions,
hopeless of answer, merely because it was
more like human conference, to see the
person you spoke to!—how I rose from
my untasted food to watch even his departing steps, and to pause, with piteous
sagacity, whether it was the echo of the
last, or the last but one I heard! But
all this was tranquillity to what I underwent at night. During the day, I had
the power of ranging through every part
of my mind, and examining its gloomiest
recesses without fear; but the first shadow

dow on the deep arches of my windows,
was the signal for my shutting out every
idea, wild, and solemn, and fantastic;
every thing that held alliance with such
feelings as the place was but too ready to
suggest. I measured the narrow circle of
my thoughts, with the fearful caution of
one who steals along a passage with the
apprehension that an assassin is about to
rush on him at every turning. When the
dark hour came, which no aid of artificial
light, no lingerings of grateful shade made
lovely, then I ceased to look around me;
for the dim forms so fixed by day, began
to move in the doubtful light, and often
I threw off my mantle, as I was wrap-
ping it round my head, lest some other
noise was couched in its rustling; but
though the darkness around me was ever
so deep, I felt there could be stillness
without repose, and oppression without
weariness. I could not sleep: I lay a-
wake, to watch my thoughts, and to start
with

with instinctive dread when any of them
declined towards the circumstances of the
last night. When I did doze, the habit
was communicated to my sleep, and I
started from my dreams when those
images recurred in them. After the experience of the first night, I determined to
earn sleep, at least, by bodily fatigue.
The limits of my room admitted of many
modes of exercise, and I, you know, am
strong and active. At every hour, then,
as nearly as I could guess, I rose to take
exercise; and Oh! how dreary was it to
rise to a solitary task! No stimulus of
competition, of elastic spirits, any object
proposed, or any prize held out, desired
and contended for by others. I *did* rise
and work myself into a fever of motion.
I perceived, however, when I was in that
tumultuous and bounding state, in which
the movements are in a manner involuntary, that mine all tended to climbing.
Once I had scrambled up the rugged wall

with

with amazing tenacity; but I quitted my
hold as soon as I was conscious of it, for
of such a means of escape I knew there
was no hope. But when I ceased, (the
motion given to the spirits and blood, by
violent exercise, seems communicated to
other objects; and after it the performer
looks around him, a consciousness of
cheerfulness, that every thing else seems
to partake—trees and fields dance and
wave to the eye;) but when I had ceased
there was no cheering voice. The echo
of the noise I had made moaned long
and heavily among the passages; and the
walls looked so still, so dark, so unmoved,
as if they scowled contempt on the puny
effort to escape even the thought of their
influence, to make the movements of
health and freedom in a prison. I looked around me dismayed. I almost expected to hear a burst of ghastly laughter break on my ear. I almost expected
to see the forms of those (if there be
                                    such)

such) who love to haunt and watch the
miseries of a prison, to scare the short
sleep of the captive,—to shape to him,
in the darkness of his cell, forms that wait
for the hour of rest to steal on him,—to
send to his grating, the faces and whispers of those he loves,---and, when he
starts from his straw, to thrust to the bars
some mis-shapen visage that makes mock
at him. Oh ! how pregnant with fearful
imagery is solitude ! At length, I bethought myself of the resources I had read
of others employing in lonely durance.
The thought of the little personal application with which I had read them was
bitter to me. But, on the third night, I
began to notch a pannel in my door with
my knife, with the number of days I had
been confined; but when the thought of
my being thus utterly a captive, of my
being so soon compelled to the very habits
and movements of those who have wasted
years in the sickness of deferred hope, the
                                    lingering

lingering death of protracted solicitude,---
the knife fell from my hand, and I burst
into tears.   Oh! let none talk, henceforth
talk, of the powers of which the mind
becomes conscious in solitude ; of the
utility of seclusion, and the discoveries
which an inward acquaintance delights us
with. Solitary man is conscious of nothing
but misery and vacancy ; it is the principle hostile and loathsome to nature, the
lethargy of life, the grave of mind.

Such was the general state of my feelings
during my confinement. On the eleventh
night, when they supposed me subdued by
weariness, or impatience of confinement,
as I was composing myself to rest, I thought
I heard a step.   I started up in hope and
fear ;---it came near. No words can tell
the state of mingled feeling with which
I heard it certainly approach—saw light
through the crevices of the door—heard
the key turn in it—and its hinges grate.

Freedom

Freedom could hardly repay me for such a moment—it was my father !

He approached with a slow, and, I thought, a timid step, holding up the light he bore, and glancing his eye around wistfully and intently. I thought I saw others without. When he spied me, he bore up proudly, and *I* endeavoured to rouse myself to the conference. " Annibal," said he, setting the light down, and fixing his eye on me, " you find I am not to be provoked with impunity." " I find," said I, " you can at least punish without provocation, or wherefore am I here?—For visiting a part of my paternal habitation ? For going where I could neither intrude nor alarm ?" " That it was my will these apartments should not be opened, should have been enough for you. From whom can I expect obedience, if my own children bribe my servants to transgress my orders ? And what," said he, after a pause, " what have you gained

gained by your rebellion? What have you
seen or done that was worth risking my
displeasure? Now, is your curiosity gratified? You have seen nothing but dust
and decay—nothing but what any other
ruin could shew you." There was such
an unnatural calmness in his voice, that
I was roused from my sullen negligence.
I looked up. His eye was bent on me
with a look so peculiar, as recalled at
once his last words, and unfolded their
meaning. I conceived at once that these
questions were suggested to discover
what I had seen and done, and discovered; whether I had found any thing which
other ruins do not always conceal.

The discovery, that he was come, not to
pity or to liberate, but to sift and examine
one whom he believed confinement had
tamed and enfeebled, at once depressed and
strengthened me. My whole mind was roused and revolted by this treachery. He appeared to me not as a father, but an assassin,

sassin, taking every advantage of a dis-
armed victim ; and I determined to resist
him with every remaining power, and send
him back, abashed and defeated. Nor was
I without hope of retaliating on him ; for
I had often heard of discoveries which it
was the labour of thought to conceal, being
made in the sudden confusion of rage, or
the answer to an unexpected reply.

" Whatever discoveries I made," said
I, " I should at least suppose your lordship was not interested in, and therefore
could not suppose them the cause of your
displea ure." "You have then made discoveries," said he, impatiently, "and why
is it presumed that I am not interested in
them ?" " I should at least hope you were
not," said I, with malicious pleasure ; " but
as your lordship has informed me there
were no discoveries to be made—that I
could see nothing more than what other
ruins might contain, I must imagine that all
I beheld was either an illusion or a trifle,
and in either how can you be interested ?"

Ilis

His eye kindled, and his lip shook.
" Insolent wretch, you mock me ; you
exult in rebellion, because you imagine my power of punishing exhausted ;
but you are deceived. I have other terrible means—others that you dream not
of. Drive me not to resort to them.
Remember they will not be temporary,
for they are not employed to extort confession, but to punish obstinacy. No ;
I need not your confession, foolish boy—I
know every thing you can know, and an explanation of them which you do not know ;
but I wish you to confess, that I may have
an excuse for forgiving you, and remitting your punishment. Tell me, therefore, how often you went with that lying
dotard, whom death has fortunately sheltered from my resentment—tell me what
he said to you, and what he shewed you—
tell me"———

He stopped, as if he was betraying
his expectation of too much. The im-

l   pulse

impulse I felt at that moment I could not resist. I sat up, and fixing my eyes on him, " If I told you," said I, " you would either aggravate my confinement, or place me where there is a quiet exemption from all pain." But when the impulse was gratified, I felt that what I had said was dangerous and foolish; and I withdrew my eyes from him in confusion, " If," said he, in the voice of one determined to sacrifice his passions to his object, " if I am thus formidable, why do you not fear me? nor would you fear me in vain. Reflect how extensive my power is, and reflect you are within it. The resistance you have hitherto been enabled to make, you falsely ascribe to an imaginary strength of mind and principle, which, you conceive, no trial can subdue. Believe me, it is only owing to your trial having been not yet severe: (my heart sunk within me) you have been nursed in luxury, Annibal, and in the

the indulgence of a romantic spirit of contemplative seclusion. For you, therefore, solitude has no pains, while unaccompanied by those privations that ought to mark it as a state of punishment. While your food is plenteous and palatable, and your means of rest and warmth commodious, solitude will be employed to subdue you in vain. But if these stimulants of fictitious courage be withdrawn; if light, and warmth, and ample space, and liberty be denied you, you will find the courage which you imagined the permanent offspring of principle, the short-lived dependant of local causes, too mean to enter into the account of the high motives of a hero in chains."

My heart sunk within me as he spake. How keenly true was his remark! how superfluously cruel his irony! Oh! it is easy to resist those who are armed only with the common weapons of infliction; whose blows can be calculated and averted; who strike

strike at parts that are exposed to and prepared for common and daily assault. But when the torturer approaches you, armed with a superior knowledge of your nature; when he knows exactly what nerve will answer with the keenest vibration of pain; what recess of weakness you most wish guarded and concealed, what are the avenues and accesses to all the most intimate and vital seats of suffering in your nature—then, then is the pain—then is the hopeless fear—the despairing submission. Such I felt, yet such I still wished to conceal.

" I know you," said I, " to have great power, and I believe you to have no mercy. Yet still I think I am not destitute of resources. My mind is yet unbroken, my resentment of oppression is inveterate, and my conscience is void of offence. This is my great stay and grasp. I will not declaim about the delights of innocence in a dungeon; 'tis ridiculous, and unlike nature.
I shall

I shall probably undergo much ; but what I shall undergo will, i am convinced, be rendered tolerable by the great aids I have mentioned. I will not sleep better on flint than on down ; but, till my health is destroyed, I shall sleep calmly ; nor will I be afraid, as long as my dim light lasts, to look into the nooks and hollows of my dungeon, rude and dark as they may be ; nor, when I lie down, to listen to the changeful moanings of the wind, through its passages ; to me it can tell nothing worse, than that the night will be dark and cold." As I spoke, a hollow blast shook the door, and made the light blaze bickering and wide.

"Will that be all ?" said my father, in a voice that struggled to be free, " Are you sure of this ?" " I will look around me," said I ; for my impulse to speak was strong and elevating, " even with sport on the fantastic things which darkness and my weak clouded sight will shape

shape out on the walls of my prison—
perhaps my grave." The images were
with me as I spake, and I wept a few
tears, not dejected, but sad and earnest.

"Fantastic," he murmured inwardly,
"do you call forms like these fantastic?"
"What forms?" said I starting in my
turn. I looked up. His eyes wandered
wildly round the chamber. He extended
his arm, and again drew it back. He re-
ceded on one foot, almost shrinking within himself, and declining till he pressed
on me. "What is it you watch," said I,
"with such gesture?" bending forward
with strange expectation. "Have you
eyes, and do not see it? 'tis you have
done this; you have brought it here. Why
will you talk of these things; their mention always does this." He reached his
hand backward to grasp my arm, not for
observation, but support—pointing with
the other, and carrying it slowly round
wi h the visionary motion he beheld. I
was chilled with horror. It was the first
time

time I had ever truly beheld a being labouring under the belief of the actual
presence of a spiritual nature. My eyes
followed his involuntarily, but I could see
nothing but the dark hollow extremities
of the room, darker from the dimness
that came over me at that moment.

"Beckon not thus," he continued to
murmur; "this is not the spot—no—you
cannot shew it—here, in this room, I am
safe."

Something too ghastly to be called
a smile, was spread over his face. "In
the name of all that is holy, whom
do you talk too, or what do you point
at?" "Who is near me," said he? "Ha!
Annibal, why do you grasp my arm thus?
What is it you look at so fixedly? there is
nothing there—nothing, believe me." "I
see nothing," said I, "but your language
has amazed me." "Then look another
way—you see there is nothing—I stretch
out my arm, you see, and nothing meets
it; but the shadows of these old rooms
will

will often shape themselves into strange array." He passed his hand once or twice over my forehead. " Annibal, when my spirits are thus wrought, I will sometimes talk wildly. You must not heed me, or if you do, set it down to the account of the anxiety you have caused me ; and let that operate with other considerations on your compliance. Annibal, disclose to me what you have seen and heard."

I was amazed and even incensed at a mans thus turning from the fearful punishment of guilt, to secure its concealment by the most abject wiles. I I could not conceal my indignation. " I have seen and heard," said I, fervently, " but now what confirms all my former discoveries." These strong words roused him at once from his ghastly abstraction. " Dare you," said he, sternly, " dare you persist in this mockery of suspicion and insult : mockery it must be—you impose on your own credulity—you falsify your

own

own convictions, that you may persecute
and slander me:—you have no proofs---
what you have seen in the tower would
not be admitted as such by any but a
wild and wicked mind, that would sooner
accuse a parent mentally of murder, than
want food for its frantic rage for discoveries."   "You accuse me unjustly,"
said I, amazed at the distinctness of his
references, but willing to avail myself of
his apparent wish to expostulate : "what
I have discovered was revealed to me by a
train of events which I could neither
control nor conjecture the issue of.   By
Heaven, I followed the pursuit with shrinking and reluctance, with more than the
fears of nature, with a gloominess of
presage and conviction, that I fear its
consequences will verify on my head.
The sights I beheld"————" Sights !"
he interrupted, " there was but one---
curse on the folly that tempted me to
expose even that one. But who could
                                   have

have thought that cursed prying dotard
would lead you to the very spot." All
this was said with such involuntary quickness, I am persuaded he no more imagined
I heard him, than a man does, who accidentally answers his own thoughts aloud;
but every word came to me as loud and
distinct as if he had been bent to force
their meaning on me. I believe he saw
horror in my face; for starting back, he
said in a rage, " Your aspect is horrible
to me; you would blast me with your
eyes if you could. There is an expression in them, worse than those that glared
on me just now. What matters it, that
you and they are silent, when ye can look
such things. But you are not as they are.
No, you I can lay hold on, and compel to stay, and to suffer. And remember,
in this contest of persecution, you will
fare the worst. I have means of infliction
beyond all thought, beyond all belief.
The spirit that resisted darkness and soli-

tude,

tude, may be bowed to scorn and debasement.—Wretch, you know not half my power. You know not that I am in possession of a secret, the disclosure of which would send you forth a vagabond and a beggar, without name, and without portion; scorn hooting at your heels, and famine pointing your forward view: that I have no tie to you, but a foolish one of habitual compassion: that to-night I might thrust you from my doors to want and infamy." "To want you might, but not to infamy. I would to heaven you would avow this secret, and thrust me out, as you threaten. Infamy may attach to me while bearing your name, and living in your crested and turretted slaughter-house; but were I suffered to make my own name, and establish my own character, I would ask only my honest heart, my strong hands, the sword you have deprived me of, and this precious picture, to animate me with noble thought."

thought."—In the enthusiasm of speaking, I drew the picture from my breast, I kissed it, and my hot tears fell on it. He bent over to see it, carelessly I believe; but, heavenly powers, what was the effect! The visage with which a moment past he had beheld, or imagined he beheld, the form of the dead, was pleased and calm, compared to the expression of mixt and terrible emotion! The horror and wild joy! The eagerness, and the despair with which he gazed on it for a moment, and then tried to tear it from me!—"Where!—How, by what, what spell, what witchery, did you obtain possession of this? Give it to me. I must have it.—'Tis mine. Wretch, how did you dare?—You kept it to blast and distract me. Struggle not with me, I would rend it from a famished wolf." "You shall not rend it from me," said I, holding it tenaciously; "it has been my companion in freedom and peace, it shall

D 2   not

not be torn from me in prison; I care not who sees it, or knows how I obtained it; I copied it from a picture in that tower; the original is in my heart; the chosen and future mistress of it. I have vowed to seek her through the world, and I will keep my vow, if ever I leave this place with life." " Miserable boy, miserable, if this be true, you know not what you say." He smote his hands twice or thrice with a look of distraction, and spoke evidently without fear and restraint. " My crimes have cursed the world. The poison flows down to the skirts of our clothing. Beings of another generation shall lay their load of sin on my head. Annibal, Annibal, hear my words; you have sunk my soul within me ; who but you has seen me thus humbled ? I speak not in passion or revenge; such revenge as your ill-fated passion might prepare for me, I shudder to think of. I do not wish to plunge your soul into utter condemnation.

tion. Annibal, should you ever see the original of this picture, fly from her, from her abode, her touch, her sight; should her thought ever visit you, banish it as you would the hauntings of an evil spirit, as the tempting whisper of Satan himself; when it besets you, go to some holy man, and let him teach you penance and prayer of virtue to drive it utterly from your—remember this is the warning of him, who warns you in no weakness of love." He paused, for he was hoarse with eagerness. "Annibal, let me look on it, I pray you, let me look on that face, Annibal, 'tis but once more. I see it so often in flames and horrors, I would fain see it in peace, with the smile of life on it." He spoke this with the dreadful calmness of habitual suffering. I held it to him with a cautious hand. "Poor Erminia," he murmured inwardly; and looked at it with that piteous and anguished tenderness, with which we look

on

on those, whose likeness recals their sufferings. " Poor Erminia," he continued
to exclaim and to gaze. In the interval,
I recovered my breath and my thoughts.
"If," said I, scarcely hoping an answer,
" the original be no more, what have
I to dread from one who but resembles
her? The original is dead, and in her
grave; and I am to fly from her shadow." " No, no," said he in a low voice,
" she is not in her grave." Again I perceived his eye fixing with that nameless
and horrid vacancy, that bespeaks the presence of an object, invisible to the common organs of sight! Again, my blood
ran cold. " I adjure you," said I, rising
and holding him firmly, " I adjure you,
be not thus moved again; I cannot bear
the sight of it. Your attendants are
without; go hence, before it overcomes
you. I cannot bear it. I am a captive,
a lone, fearful being.—Your ghastly face
will be with me in every corner; it will
be

be in my dreams." I could not move him.
His limbs appeared stiffened and wound
up; and the strong fixedness of his eye,
nothing could turn away. He appeared
to talk with earnest gesture to something that stood between him and the
door; but his words were lost in inarticulate murmurs as he attempted to speak.
My eyes followed his to the same spot;
but though sharpened with fear almost
to agony, they could distinguish nothing.
"Aye," said he, in that low, peculiar voice,
" I see it well enough ! Ye are not of this
element ! But now ye rose from under
my feet; and now ye muster round that
door !—Not gone yet—nor yet !—No,
they are larger—darker—wilder !" He
paused, but his terrors did not remit, nor
could I speak. Then he added, in a
deeper tone, with solemn enthusiasm, " If
ye indeed are real forms, that come with
power, and for a definite purpose, stand,
and I will meet you ; will meet you as I

D 5   may

may; for this hollow nodding and beckoning cannot be borne! Stand there,
and bear up to me visibly; and I will try
whether ye are truly as ye seem. I will
meet you!—Now!—Now!" He seized a
light in each hand, and rushed furiously to
the door. "Gone, gone! I will gaze no
longer, lest some other shape rise up before me." As he retreated, he said, "By
heaven, they hear me without—they
laugh at my folly—and you laugh, too, re-
bellious wretch! 'Tis you have brought
me to this; your unnatural persecutions
have subdued me to this weakness." He
quitted the room, leaving with me a conviction that the plans of guilt are often
frustrated by its terrors; and its cowardice
is an abundant balance for its malignity.
But all the use of this lesson was lost in
the fearful recollections that accompanied it. If the purport of his visit was
to punish, it was indeed fulfilled. The
terrible spectacle of a being writhing
under

under the commission, or the consciousness of a crime, oppressed my mind, almost as if I had been an agent in it : every
wind that night brought to my ear, that
low, strange voice in which he talked,
as he believed, with beings not of this
world; his wild, pale face was with me
when I shut my eyes, when I opened
them, it glided past me in the darkness;
when I slept, I saw it in my dreams; but
" joy came in the morning ;" such joy,
as no morning had brought to me since
my confinement. Under the conduct of
the monk, I was removed from that dreary
room, and placed in another, in the same
tower I conjectured, but more light and
spacious ; and, for greater indulgence,
to my continued importunities, I received
for answer, I should be supplied with
books.

When he departed to fulfil his promise,
I felt as if a new sense had been communicated to me; a new light of hope had

5   fallen

fallen upon life. There is no telling the
freshness and novelty of my joy on the
possession of this long-withheld resource,
which I wondered I had ever thrown aside
in neglect, or in vacancy, or in caprice;
which I wondered any one could believe
himself unhappy, that was permitted to
possess; which, above all, I wondered I
had never felt the full value of, till that
moment. During the hour that the
monk delayed, I was too happy to glance
at the probability of disappointment. I
experienced a thousand glad and busy
feelings. With the benevolence of joy.
I wished I could communicate my frame
of mind to the loungers, who yawn over
untasted libraries, to those whose eyes
wander over a book, without a consciousness of their contents. To me, my approaching employment seemed inex-
haustable; I remembered the time,
when I repined if I had not several books
to make a selection from; but now, *one*
appeared

appeared sufficient for the occupation of
the whole day.

I can pause, said I, over every sentence,
and though its meaning be nothing new,
or peculiar, to think on it will waken some
corresponding train of thought within
me; I shall arrive at some discovery, some
new combination, or resemblance in objects
unnoticed before; at least, the pursuit
will amuse me. I shall be intently, delight-
fully *employed*; and when I turn from my
excursion of thought, to see I have yet
so many pages to read; yet such a strong
aid to interpose between me and the feelings of solitude, and the hour of darkness.
Though reading had never been attended
with such consequences, still my perceptions were so new, that I was confident I
would enjoy all this, and more, on the possession of this new treasure, and I determined to husband my store with judicious
economy, not to suffer my eye to wander
over a single page carelessly; I determined

ed to pause and to reflect, to taste and to digest with epicurean slowness. I almost wished my powers of intelligence were slower, that I might be compelled to admit more tardily, and to retain longer. At length, it came—the treasure—a single book—it was a library to me; I scarcely waited to thank my grim attendant. I opened the book, and the delusion vanished. So vehement was my literary appetite, and so long had been my famine, that I could no more restrain it, than the flow of a torrent; I hurried at once into the middle of my scanty repast, and found myself nearly half through it, before the execution of my deliberate plan would have permitted me to travel over a page. When all was finished, (early in the day) I reflected I had yet to read it over again; and I began again, but soon found that my pleasure was diminished, even beyond the power of repetition to diminish it; the uneasiness of a task was over me; I

felt

felt that I must do this to enjoy tranquillity. I could not raise my eyes with the
happy vacancy of one, who knew he
was not helplessly bound to a single resource; I knew what I was doing, I
must persist doing, even in default of attention and pleasure, and therefore, I did
it irksomely Besides, as darkness was
coming on, many passages of a visionary
tendency, on which in the tumult of my
first pleasure, and in the broad light of day,
I had dwelt with peculiar satisfaction, I
did not like venturing on now; and they
presented themselves to me on the opening of a page; I scudded over them with
a quick, timid eye, as if I feared they
would assume some stronger characters
while I viewed them.

On the whole, I even felt my positive
pleasure less than I expected; my ideas
were too confused and rapid for pleasure.
I went on with blind admiration, and
childish giddiness, swallowing passage after passage, without pause or discrimination.

tion. But even to reflect on this, afforded me employment, and employment was
my object; of this I had abundance; the
confusion of my ideas would not permit
me to sleep; I turned from side to side ;.
still I was repeating to myself passages I
had read, and still I observed that those
recurred which had interested me least.
In a short time, all recollections became
weary and tasteless to me from my feverish restlessness, and I heartily wished it
all banished. When the castle bell tolled
twelve, I listened with a momentary relief to the echoes, to the long deep echoes
as they died away; the very recesses of
my chamber seemed to answer them, and
as they rolled off, I seemed to feel them
spreading above, below, around; I listened to them, till my own fancy filled up the
pause of sound. Would that it had never
left my ears. At that moment, a voice, in
strong, distinct human sounds, shrieked,
murder, murder, murder ! thrice, so near,
                                    that

that it seemed to issue from the very wall beside me. I cannot tell you the effect of this
cry; whatever disposition I might have felt
to assist the sufferer, to shout aloud in a voice
of encouragement, to lament my confinement, and to tell them a human being who
heard and pitied them, was so near, was
al lrepelled by a sudden and inexpressible conviction, that the sounds I heard
were not uttered by man. Whence this
arose I could not explain, I could not
examine; it would not be resisted, it
would not be removed. It chained me
up in silence; I could neither communicate, nor inquire into it. I could not
even speak to my warden about it; I felt
all day like a man, upon whose peace some
secret is preying. I looked in deep oppression around me, on the walls and windows, and dark corners of my room, as if
they possessed a consciousness of what
they had heard; as if they could pour out
and unfold the terrible sounds they had
swallowed.

swallowed. In the midst of this dejection
I recollected my book; I took it up, and
with diligence that deserved a better reward, I read every syllable of it again,
and paused over the very expletives with
a superstitious minuteness, that made me
smile when I discovered it. But it would
not do. All power of feeling pleasure
had ceased. I was like the vulgar, who,
when they are affected with any malady,
complain that it is lodged in the heart;
all the attention I could bestow still left
a dull sense of inward uneasiness, which
I could not remove, and feared even to
advert to. But long before night, I had
finished even my book; still I was resolved not to be " tormented before the
time ;" I resolved by every or any act of
exclusion, to keep the idea of what I had
heard away, till midnight, till I could
keep it away no longer. Oh, you have
never known the sickly strivings of solitude! to dispose my scanty furniture in
                              a thousand

a thousand shapes, the most distinct from use that can be conceived; to endeavour to walk up and down the room, confining my steps to one seam in the flooring; and when they tottered from its narrowness, to look behind, lest some strange hand was pushing me from my way; to trace the winding veins in the old wainscot, that amused and pained me with a resemblance to the branching of trees and shrubs; to follow them where they could be seen, and feel them where they could not—these were the wretched resources of a situation that demands variety, yet deprives the spirits of all power as well as means to exercise it; and these wretched resources were a relief in the horrible state of my mind; nor could even that relief be long enjoyed.

The hour came. For many minutes I remained silent, gasping, as if I was watching for the sound I dreaded. My book was open before me. I did not see a word

word in it. I felt the slow, yet progressive motion that brings you nearer an object of horror. I felt my hairs rising up. I felt my pores open, and the cold, creeping consciousness of the thing we cannot name, spreading over me. I heard a hissing in my ears. My eyes were involuntarily distended. I felt as if all the dark powers were invisibly, but perceptibly close to me—just preparing to begin their work—just in the intense silence of preparation. The hand of a little timepiece, that had been brought to me, moved stilly on. Worlds would I have given for a sound when I saw it just touching on the hour. The castle bell tolled. It was but a moment; for I could have borne it no longer; and the voice again shrieked, murder! It was, if possible, more horrible than the preceding night; there was more of humam suffering in it —more of the voice of a man who feels the fingers of a murderer on his very throat

throat; who cries with the strength of agony, stronger than nature; who pours all his dying force into the sound that is the last living voice he shall utter. Even he who hears such a sound feels not what I did. Man, the actual sight of man, in the most dreadful circumstances in which man can behold or imagine him, is nothing to the bare fear, the suspicion, the doubt, that there is a being near you, not of this world. Between us and them there is a great gulph fixed, on the limits of which to glance or to totter, is more terrible to nature than all corporeal sufferance. Of this mysterious sensation it is impossible to describe the quality or the degree. Its darkness, its remoteness, its shapelessness, constitute its power and influence. Whether my mind was wearied by its own motions, I do not know; but I soon fell into a deep sleep. I know not how I was awakened; but I recollect it was so suddenly and thoroughly

roughly, that I started up as I awoke, and became sensible in a moment. The monk was sitting opposite me. He sat at the table, on which stood the time piece and the lamp. His head rested on his hands, and he watched the time-piece in silence. My recollection came to me at once, and fully. I felt that at such an hour, such a visitor could have but one purpose. Oh! who can tell the gush of horror that comes to the heart of the being that, lone and helpless, is wakened at midnight, and sees around the hard blank walls of his prison, and, beside him, the face of his murderer, pale with unnatural thought, by his dim lamp-light.

I sat up with the impulse, but not the power of resistance. I gazed on him earnestly. He neither raised his head nor spake. I was amazed by his silence. It seemed to cast a spell over me. I had no power to break it. I could not speak

speak to him; yet my eyes remained
fixed, and my thoughts seemed rapid in
proportion to my inability to utter them.
A thousand causes for his silence were
suggested to me. He might be waiting
the arrival of some assistant, who was to
overpower my struggles, or help to thrust
my corpse into some dark, remote hole,
where no search would ever follow or
find me; where the foot of a brother
might tread over my dust, without a suspicion of my fate. Perhaps he was a-
waiting a signal to rush on me ; perhaps,
till some new and horrible means of
death should be brought in, and admi-
nistered to me; perhaps—that was the
worst of all—some such means had already been applied, in my food, or while
I slept; and he was come to watch its
operation, to witness the bitterness of
death, the twisted eye, the writhing feature, the straining muscle, without giving

ing the aid which all that retain the shape of man alike expect and afford.

While these thoughts were yet in their height, the hand of the time piece pointed to one. The monk extended his hand to it—it touched it—and he raised his head. " Now I may speak," said he, fixing his large heavy eyes on me. My former suspicion recurred. " Then," said I, " I shall know my fate. Oh! I feel that you are come to announce it; I feel that you are come to murder me." He waved his hand with a melancholy motion. I had but one construction for all his motions. " Speak," said I, " I conjure you; your eye is dark, and I fear to read it, or look into it. What is your purpose?" " Death," said the monk:— " Then I am to be murdered, murdered in this dark hole, without a chance, or struggle, or straw to grasp at for life? Oh! merciful Heaven, Oh!" " What is

it

it you fear?" said the monk rising:—
" my business is death; but not yours.
What do you fear ?   Look at this hand;
years have passed since it held a weapon; years have passed since blood has
flowed in its veins." I looked at his hand.
I involuntarily touched it.   It was deadly
cold.   I was silent, and awaited some explanation of his appearance or his words.
" My business is death; a business long
deferred, longun finished. Under its pres-
sure I have been called up, and kept wandering for many years, without hope, and
without rest. I have had many pilgrimages
without companion or witness: no one
knew me, or sought my name or purpose.
But my term is closing, and my task
will soon be finished; for now I am
permitted to come to you, and speak to
you." He spoke so slowly that I had
time to collect myself. I marvelled at
his strange language. " I know not what
it is you mean, nor to what business
                                    you

you allude," said I. " If my senses are not impaired, you are Father Schemoli, the companion of my father." " I am," said he, in a peculiar tone, " I am your *father's constant companion.*" " I know you well; you look pale and strange by this dim light, yet I know you. But what is the purport of your appearance at this hour, or of the words you have uttered, I know not." " And do you only know me as Father Schemoli? Have you seen me under no other appearance? Do you remember the last time you saw me?" " I remember it well: it was in the west tower; you bore the light; you accompanied my father; I remember you well." " Had you never seen me there before?" " Never; whatever I suspected, I never saw you there before." " Beware—beware. What spectacle did you behold there, buried and mouldering in one of the passages?" " I saw a terrible sight there," said I, shuddering;

shuddering; " but it was removed on
my last unlucky visit to that place."
" No; you saw it, though in another
form---saw it as plain as you see me
now." " I know not what you mean.
Your voice chills me, but I do not understand you." " You will not understand
me ; look on my eyes, my features, my
limbs," said he, rising, and spreading himself out, " the last time you beheld them,
they were fleshless, decayed, and thrust
in a noisome nook; yet still the strength
of their moulding, and shape, and character, might strike an eye that was less
quick, and gazed not so long as yours."
As he spoke—was it fancy, or the very
witchery of the time and place ?—his
eyes, his mouth, his nostrils, all the hollows of his face became deeper and
darker; as the sickly glare of the lamp
fell on the skin of his shorn head, it looked
tense and yellow, like the bones of a skull,
and the articulations of the large joints of

his up-spread hands, seemed so distinct
and bare, as if the flesh had shrunk from
them. I swallowed down something that
seemed to work up my throat, and I tried
to resist the effect of his words and appearance; for it outraged my belief and
my senses to a degree that no local terrors, no imposition, or fantasy of fear
could justify. " Is this mockery or frenzy?
Is it my ears or eyes you would abuse?
If I understand you, you mean something
that could not be imposed on the belief
of a child, or of superstition itself. You
would make me believe, that you, whom
I have seen exercise all the functions,
whom I have seen going in and out a-
mongst us, are a being who has been dead
for years—that you now inhabit another
form—that the flesh which I felt a moment past is not substantial. Do you
think that durance and hardship have de-
based me to such weakness? Do you
believe my mind cramped and shackled
like

like my body? Or, do you believe, even
if it were, that my senses are thus enfeebled and destroyed—that I cannot
hear, and see, and feel, and judge of the
impressions objects ought to make on
those senses, as well as if it were not
now midnight, and in this dark hold, and
by this single dim light? Away! I am
not so enfeebled yet." He heard me
calmly. " You, who wish to judge only
by the evidence of your senses, why do
you not consult that of your hearing
better? Have you never heard this voice
before? and where have you heard it?"
" Yes," said I, with that solemnity of
feeling which enforces truth from the
speaker, " Yes, I feel I have; but whether my perceptions are confused by
fear, or my memory indistinct, I cannot
recal when. I hear it like a voice I have
heard in a dream, or like those sounds
which visit us in darkness, and mingle
with the wind; yet I feel also it is not

the

the voice with which you speak in the family."

I was gazing at him while I spake, as if I could find any resemblance in his face, that could assist me to recal the former tones of his voice. He fixed himself opposite to me—he turned his eye full on me. " What voice," said he, " was that which bore witness to Michelo's fears in the west turret, that your father's *vengeance was terrible?* What voice passed you on the winds of darkness, when you watched at the tomb of Orazio? What voice rung in the ears of the dying man, ' Woe and death,' when you knelt beside his bed? What voice shrieks, ' Murder,' every night, from a depth never measured even by the thought of man since these walls were raised? Is it not the voice which speaks to you now?" His voice had been progressively deepening till its sounds were almost lost; but in the last question it pierced my very sense with

with its loudness. His form was outspread,
and almost floating in the darkness. The
light only fell on his hands, that were
extended and almost illuminated. All the
rest was general and undefined obscurity.
I was lost in wonder and fear, such as can
only be felt by those who suddenly find
their secrets in possession of another;
who find all that they had thought important to acquire or to conceal, the sport
of another, who sports with it and them.

"Blessed Virgin! who are you? where
were you concealed? how did you follow
me? who uttered these sounds, or if it
was you—?" "You cannot admit things
that would outrage the credulity of an
infant, or of superstition; you cannot
believe that I have assumed other forms
than that I now bear; you are prepared
with your reasons, and your answers, and
your arguments, physical and sage, and
able to solve all appearances and objects
you may witness." He pursued derisively—

"You

" You can tell me, then, what form
every night visits the burial-place in the
old chapel? Whom did you behold when
you ventured into the vault? Whom did
you see in the passages of the west
tower? Who waved the shadowy arm,
and pointed the eye of life from the dead
wall on you? Who shut, and you could
not open, the door of the vault? Who,
when I discovered your pretence for
breaking into the secrets of the dead,
was but a weak and unhallowed curiosity
—who removed with steps not unseen,
from that tower, to the dark and unblessed lair, from which my cry every
night reaches your ears? And if you cannot tell this, what is he who can?"

When I heard these words, fear, and
every other sentiment they might have
inspired, were lost in the prospect they
opened of satisfying my doubts, my
wonder, my long, restless, unsated curiosity. I cannot tell you the effect this
                              enumeration,

enumeration, so distinct, so well-remem-
bered in its parts, produced on me. The
predominant feeling of my nature revived
and arose within me. Images so remote,
so obscure, never recalled without perplexity and doubt, were now with me
as if just bursting into light. A hundred
inquiries were on my tongue, a hundred
wishes were in my heart. I was all restless, glowing expectation. Who, to see
my ardent eyes (for I felt them kindle
in their sockets) and out-spread hands,
who could have believed I was addressing
such a being—a being formed, in his most
favourable aspect, to repel, not to at-
tract; and now arrayed and aggravated
in the mist, and dimness, and shapeless
terrors of a supernatural agent.

" Have you indeed this knowledge?
Are you indeed the being Michelo's suspicions pointed to, and my own hopes,
and fears, and doubts have so long been
seeking? Can you make these rough
places

places, I have wandered on so long, plain
to me? Shall my feet stumble on the
dark mountains no longer? Will you tell
me all—all I wish to know— all (you
can discover) I want to know? If you
can do this, I will believe you, I will
worship you, and revere you. Take me
but out of this house of darkness, and
durance, and guilt; give me but to know
what it has been the torment and the
business of my existence to know; let
me learn if I am the dupe of fear and
credulity; or, as a better confidence has
sometimes whispered, set apart for something great, and high, and remote; let
me know this, and I will bind myself to
your service, I will, by all that is sacred,
I will bind myself by some tie and
means so awful, that even you, with all
your awfulness of character and purpose,
shall hold it as sacred, and tremble to hear
it."

In the eagerness of speaking, I did not
perceive

perceive my declining lamp. I was drawn to it by his eye. "You do not speak," said I, "my lamp is going out. Oh! speak before it goes out; for then, perhaps, I shall tremble to hear your voice, and wish you away; speak, I conjure you: it is a dreadful thing to be left in darkness with such feelings stirred within me; satisfy them before you depart: are you going? or does the dying light deceive me?"

I could only see his eyes and his hands, that beckoned with a fitful motion in the flashing light. "That lamp warns me away. I must go to my other task: I must go to watch at your father's bedside." The tone in which he uttered this convinced me he did not speak it in his earthly capacity. The lamp went out. I saw him no more, nor heard him more. He disappeared in the darkness, without the closing of a door, or the sound of a step.

Gracious

Gracious Heaven! what a sensation came over me when I felt myself alone after what I had heard and seen! I shrunk into my cloak. I wished sight, and hearing, and memory utterly extinct. I felt I had acquired a strange treasure. I felt that the visit and the communications I might probably receive were supernatural and marvellous; but I feared to look into my mind; I dreaded to think on them; they were all too wild and darkly shaped to be the companions of night and solitude. I wished to think deeply of what I had witnessed; but not till morning. I longed for a deep, heavy sleep, to ease my dizzy head, that throbbed, and whirled, and rung, till, grasping it with both hands, I tried to shut every avenue of thought and sensation. It was a dismal night. I heard the clock strike every hour. Morning broke; and when I saw, at length, the sun, bright and chearful, shining on my walls, I lay down to rest with

with a confidence, a satisfaction of mind,
that I believe I never shall again feel
going to rest at night.

Father Schemoli visited me, as usual,
in the day.   There was not a trace of
last night's business in his countenance.   I
shrunk when he entered, yet soon sur-
prized at his silence and unaltered look,
I spoke to him, spoke of last night, first
with questions of general import.   These
received no answer.   I became more
anxious ; I inquired, I demanded, I in-
treated in vain.   After staying the usual
time, he departed, without relaxing a
muscle, without uttering a sound, or in
dicating, by look or gesture, that he even
understood me.   He departed, leaving me
in that unpleasant state in which you begin to question the evidence of your own
senses, and doubt whether the objects of
your solicitude were not the shadows of
a dream.

The day passed on.   Evening came,
         I   with

with a train of sad and dusky thoughts. I could not exclude them. I ceased to attempt it. My mind had either sunk under the languor of a long and vain resistance, or had become familiarized to objects once so strange and repulsive to our nature. They seemed to me the proper furniture of my prison. I hung over them in gloomy listlessness, without shrinking, or repelling them as I first endeavoured. Of a mind in this state, no wonder the sleeping thoughts were as dark as the waking. Indeed, all my thoughts, at that gloomy time, floated between vision and consciousness. I have often started from a point where their pursuit has led me, and asked myself, Was it the dark object of a dream? That night, weary with the watching of the last, I threw myself on my narrow bed as soon as it was twilight. I had scarce closed my eyes, when I was invested with all those strange powers which

which sleep gives, beyond all powers of life.

I thought Michelo was still alive, and that he led me to the apartments of the west tower. They were decorated gaily and magnificently, and filled with crowds, who turned their eyes on me, as if something was expected from my arrival. I passed through them till I arrived at the chamber, that chamber whose ominous stains told me of dangers my curiosity or my fortitude defied. It was more magnificent than the rest. At the head of a sumptuous table sat my uncle and his wife, such as I had seen them in their portraits, gay, and young, and splendid. At a distance, they appeared to be smiling around them, and on each other; but as I drew near them, the smile was altered into a strange expression. It seemed an effort to conceal the sharpest agony. I came still nearer, and fear began to mingle with my feelings. As I

approached

approached, my uncle seized my hand, and drew me to him, then, withdrawing his gay vest, shewed me his breast pierced with daggers, and splashed with blood. I shuddered; but while I was yet gazing on him, he snatched one of the daggers from his side, and plunged it into that of his wife. She fell, dying, beside him; and, with one of those sudden changes, that in dreams excite no wonder, he suddenly became Father Schemoli, his head shorn, and his habit that of a monk, and chaunted the requiem over the corpse of his wife.   It was echoed by a thousand voices.   I looked around me; the company, so gay and festive, were changed into a train of monks, with tapers and crosses, and the apartment was a vault. As I gazed still, the lights grew blue and pale; slowly, but perceptibly, the body decayed away, and became a skeleton, wrapt in a bloody shroud.   The band of·

monks

monks faded away, as I looked on them, into a ghastly troop, with the aspects of the dead, but the features and movements of the living. Their eyes became hollow, their garments a blue discoloured skin; the hands that held their tapers, as yellow and as thin as they. Still I gazed, while they all around me, and standing on a single point of ground; I beheld them all go down, their forms deadening in the gloom, and the last sound of their requiem coming broken, and faint, and far from beneath. The whole scene was then changed, and I found myself wandering through rooms, spacious, but empty and dreary. From the floor, from the wainscot, from every corner, I heard my name repeated, in soft, but distinct accents, Annibal, Annibal. It came to me from every side. Pursuing it, but yet scarce knowing the direction, I followed it from room to room. At length, I was in one that had

an

an air of peculiar loneliness in it. The voice
ceased ; and there ran a hissing stillness
through the room, as if its object were
attained. I looked around me, expecting-
ly. On the centre of the room a sumptuous cloak was spread. I approached it,
conscious that this was the point and end
of my wanderings. I knew not why— I
raised, but dropt it again, shrinking ; for
a bloody corse lay beneath. I was retreating, but the garment began to move
and heave ; and the figure extending a
hand, seized mine—I could not withdraw
it—and drew me under that blood-drop-
ping covering by it. The floor sunk down
below us, and I found myself in a passage,
low, and long, and dark. The figure glided
on before me, beckoning me to follow.
Far onward I saw a dim, blue light. I
followed the mangled form. We came
into a place resembling a chapel. I again
saw my uncle standing beside an altar.
The tapers on it burned with that strange
light

light I had seen. There was a fearful contrast between the furniture of the chapel, which was gay and bridal, and the figure of the cavalier, and that of a lady who sat near the altar, wrapt in a shroud and cearments; the cavalier approached her, she rose, my uncle advanced, and began to read the marriage service. The cavalier held forward his bloody arm; the lady extended her hand—it was Ermiania. I said mentally, " Is this a marriage?" I rushed forward with a wild feeling of jealousy and fear. The lady saw me, she shrieked, she darted from the altar, and catching my hand, led me to my uncle. He gazed at me a moment, then clasping me in his arms, I beheld him again changed into father Schemoli. I shrunk from his embrace, twisting myself from him with motions of horror and reluctance.

I awoke with the struggle, and beheld the monk again seated opposite me; and watching

watching the time-piece, by the lamp that was not yet extinguished; with the full wakefulness of horror, I bent forward to see if my hour was yet come—it was past twelve. I felt a satisfaction at it, that even the presence of my visitor could not check. He spoke not, as on the former night; and his silence again bound me up. It was a strange and solemn form; we gazed on each other intently: I had no more power to withdraw my eyes from, than to speak to him. Whoever had beheld us, would have believed me bound by a spell, till his dark eye was turned to me, and his finger extended to dissolve it. The images of my dream were with me still, so strongly, that he scarce seemed to make a stronger impression on me by his real, than his visionary presence; he ceased to be an agent, but appeared come to be an interpreter. Again, as the hand of the time-piece pointed to one, he raised his eye, and.

and said, " Now I may speak." " What is it," said I, familiarized to his appearance, " What is it forbids you to speak till this season? You seem to have a strange freedom given you at this hour. I adjure you, to speak to me in the day, when our conference will be more natural, and like that of man; but you love to glide on me in darkness and sleep; to look on with strange eyes, to talk to me with the voices of sleep or of fancy." " That is, because in this form, my powers are limited; I cannot speak when I would, nor to whom. I am only permitted that at a certain hour, and to but one human being. This heavy vesture I am wrapped in, presses on me, and checks my movements; but tis but the weeds of a pilgrim-spirit, and enough has at times glimmered through it, to give token of its strange tenant." " What is it you speak of—what it that restrains and presses on you?" " This form

of

of seeming flesh and blood, that bears
about an imprisoned and penanced spirit."
Gracious heaven, how he looked at that
moment; so sad, so dim, so visionary.
My eye scarcely fixed his form, that seemed to mingle with the darkness that surrounded it. "Penanced, indeed," said I,
shuddering with partial belief, "if immured in such a form. But how wild,
how monstrous a fiction would your words
intimate. Gracious heaven, preserve my
reason while I look at you; save me from
credulity, that would deprive me of the
very use of my senses; that would make
me the victim of a horrid, and impossible
dream. What might I not be impelled
to do, if I could believe you? You
might make me a murderer, were I resigned to your influence. No—this midnight visiting, and the terrors with which
you would fill me, are but the beginning
of sorrows, my unnatural father threatens
me with. I see the malice of this persecution.

cution. Solitude and confinement, and
the privation of all that attends my rank
and time of life, have been employed,
and failed to subdue my mind; and now
he sends you, you, whom nature or habit has indeed made fit for a messenger
of horror; he sends you to depress and
terrify me; he causes voices to shriek in
the passage; and sends a face, like the visage of the damned, to stare at me, when
I start from my sleep. Gracious heaven," said I, rising, and stung with heat
and anguish of increasing fear, " how I
am beset; these are not his last resources;
he will persecute me to madness. I
shall shriek existence away in this den;
my eye-strings will burst at some horrible
sight; I shall die the death of fear, and
die it in solitude. Oh, turn your face
away; I see, I feel, a smile of mockery and
torment through all your silence. I know
it, I know you will be here to-morrow
night; I shall hear your shrieks rising
                                    through

through the darkness, and winds of night. Then you will stand beside me in some altered shape, or perhaps drag me from my sleep." I had worked myself to a frame, that felt and witnessed all it described. "Away," I cried, dashing myself on my bed, and hiding my head eagerly in my cloak, "away, I will shut mine eyes, and not look upon you." "If this was intended," said he calmly, "why did I not do it before, when the impression would have been more forcible from its being unlooked for? And why do I throw a veil over the visioned form of my nature, and confer with you, as man with man? If my purpose were to terrify, would I have acted thus?" "I know not; 'tis your office and habit to deal in mystery, to torment with perplexity; if it be not, why will you not explicitly declare your purpose, and begone. This chamber is dark enough without your presence.—Yet do not," starting up, and

grasping

grasping his hand, " do not to-night; to-morrow, speak to me to-morrow at noon, and I will listen to you." " To-morrow at noon I cannot; I shall be laid in my dark and bloody lair; I cannot walk in the light of noon, nor utter a voice that may be heard by man." " Your outward form," said I, " will be here." " It will be but my outward form," said he. " But why this necessity for night and solitude? Are you an owl, or a raven, that must haunt in ruins, and hoot by moonlight only." " I have a darker tale to tell than the owl that sits on the desolate ruin; than the raven that beats heavily at the window of the dying." " Then forbear to tell it, for I will not hear it, and leave me; the terrors of solitude, and my own thoughts are enough." " You did not think when you forced old Michelo to the West tower, to watch with you at the tomb, when you pursued me from haunt to haunt, and almost saw me at the task, which may not be

be seen." I was not then," said I, " confined in this prison ;" " and therefore I was
not permitted to speak to you." " Strange
being, who can at once lead on and repel;
who can so qualify fear with curiosity;
who just know when to strengthen while
you seem to remit all influence. I feel
I can resist no longer. You are possessed of every avenue to the human mind;
you can make me fear, and desire, and
retreat, and pause, and advance as you
will; even when I think I dread you
most, you can make an appeal to some
secret and cherished object of pursuit or
desire, that distracts me with curiosity,
that subdues me to concession and intreaty. I feel my heart, and mind, and
fate are at your disposal, or your sport.
You have been with me in solitude; you
have seen me, when no eye saw me; you
have over-heard my thoughts, when they
were not uttered. Go on, tell me what
you will; tell me what I am to do, or to

2   know

know—go on ; I fear, I feel I must believe
it all." " 'Tis twenty years since I was
what you are now, a mortal, with mortal
passions and habits. 'Tis twenty years
since my blood flowed, or my pulses beat
with life; when they did, their current
was keen and fiery; I lived the life of
sin and folly. Heaven and holy things
were far from my thoughts. The power
whom I forsook, forsook me : I was given
over to a reprobate mind. My life was
passed in a blaze of wickedness, and cut
off with an end of blood. I was dragged
to the grave by murderous and unhallowed
hands ; hands, like my own, on fire with
wickedness, and drunk with blood ; hands
that I am appointed to see every night
held up for pardon, and to tell they are
held up in vain. My body was thrust
into the hole where you found it, and
my soul——" " Where did it go ? I adjure you, stop not there ;—tell me, where
did your soul depart to ?" "I must not

tell, nor could you hear the secrets of the
world of shadows ; my taskers, who are
ever around me, would flash upon your
sight, and sweep me away before you, if
I told their employment. The bare sight
of them would shrivel you to dust, and
heap this massy tower in fragments over
your head ; you must not cross me with
these questions, nor interrupt me while
I speak ; my time is short, and my words
measured to me ; but of this be assured, no visions of moon-struck fancy ;
no paintings of the dying murderer ; no
imagings of religious horror have touched
upon the confines of the world of woe. After a term of years, (during which itwas a
remission of sufferance, to ride the night-
mares through the dark and sickly air ; to
hide me in the foldings of the sick man's
curtains, and slowly rise on his eye, when
his attendants withdrew, till he shricked
to them to return ; to wail and to beckon
from flood, and fell, and cavern, till the
wildered

wildered passenger, or wandering child
of despair, plunged after me, and with
dying eye saw who had waved them on
to do the loathed service of the foulest
of fiendish natures, the incubus, and the
vampire, and the goule; to bring them
from the various elements which have
swallowed them; their unutterable food,
our own corrupted remains: to see the
very worms conscious, and dropping from
the prey; to feel the pain of our own
flesh devoured with mortal sensation not
all extinguished, like the faint feelings of
pain in sleep, just vexing our dreams,
and warring on the outworks of sensation)—after a term of years thus passed,
one night, when the evil ones were lord-
ing it in the upper air, driven on by the
flaky forks of the lightning, the sharp-
bolted shot of the hail, and the hollo, and
shout, and laughter of the revelling host
of darkness, I shrunk into the recess of a
mountain, and called upon its riven and

rocky bowels to close upon me; but I was driven still onward; the sides of the mountain groaned under the fire-shod and hooky feet of my pursuers. I pressed on through the dark passages, through secrets of nature never seen by sun, clogged by the dews, parched with the airs, seared with the meteor fires of this dungeon of the fabric of the world; till through an aperture that would admit all the armies, I flew into a vast plain, in the centre of the mountain, where piles of smouldering and charmed rock, inscribed with forbidden names, repelled the escape even of a disembodied spirit. I believed this to be my final bourne, and almost thought with hope, that the last thunders would dash even this adamantine prison to dust; but I was deceived, yea, though a spirit unblessed, I was deceived by hope. This had been a vast plain, whereon, in elder time, stood a vast city, with all its inhabitants; they were idolatrous and

and wicked, and invoked the powers, and
studied the arts of the dark and nether
world.

Therefore, the supreme power had in
his wrath caused a vast body of volcanic
fire to rise out of the centre of the city,
which had consumed it, with all its inhabitants, in one night, while the stones,
and mineral masses, and solid fire spreading around, and arching over it, formed a
mountain around it, and hid its name, and
place, and memory from man for ever
and ever. It was now the favoured haunt
of unclean spirits; none others could
find their way to it, and live. There I
saw forms that must not be named, nor
how employed; I shrunk into a recess,
from the abhorred lights; but there I
found that my flight had been involuntary, that nothing was less meant than a
respite from pain, and that even the
sport of devils must have malignity.
In that recess, a volume of fire, fed with
                                    other

other substance than earthly fire, sent up
its long, flaky spires, of green, and purple, and white; around it, impressed on the
rock, and flashing out in its shifting light,
were the forms of men in solid sulphur,
or molten mineral, or those fused and
mingled bodies, the monstrous birth of
volcanic throes; they were a company
of sorcerers, that were met to do their
dark rites on the very night that they
were caught, and blasted by fires from
the nether world. They remained fixed
around a magic fire they had raised, each
in the very form and attitude in which
punishment overtook them, melted into
the walls of the vast temple of magic,
where they were assembled and which
was now a cavern in that inward region;
each still bore the frown, and the awe of
the potent hour in their smouldering
faces; each still was armed with sigil,
and teraph, and talisman. In the heart
of the fire, lay a human body, uncon-
                                    sumed

sumed for two thousand years; for they
had but partially raised it for some magic
purpose, when they were destroyed; and
till the spell was reversed, the body must
continue there for ever. But they were now
compelled by a stonger power than their
own, by the power of my companions,
to waken from that sleep of horrid existence, to renew the unfinished spell, and
to raise the corse that lay in the flames.
They obeyed, for they could not resist
the words of power; and they felt that
their crime was become their punishment. It was a sight of horror, even for
an unblessed soul to see them. Rent
from the smoking rocks, that they wished
might fall on them, and hide them; their
forms of metallic and rocky cinder, where
the human feature horribly struggled
through burnt and blackening masses,
discoloured with the calcined and dingy
hues of fire, purple, and red, and green:
their stony eyes rolling with strange
                                        life;

life; their sealed jaws rent open by sounds, that were like the rush of sub-terrene winds, moving around the fire, whose conscious flakes pointed and wound towards them. The spell was finished—the corse was released, and the living dead re-inclosed in their shrouds of adamant. Then words were uttered, and characters wrought, which no man could hear and live; and I, for further pe-nance, was compelled to enter the body to which the functions of life were re-stored; and to which I must be confined, till my term of sufferance was abridged by the interment of my bones, and the punishment of my mortal mur-derer." "Stop, stop," said I, vehemently, "I can listen no more.—My head is reel-ing—my eyes are flashing—while you continue to speak, while I look on you, my breath is lost.—Can man believe these things?" I repeated to myself, "can man believe these things? But, Oh," again I said

said internally, " can man invent the e
things?" " Yes," it continued, " these
are massive bones of the elder time;
this tawney skin was darkened by a sun
two thousand years older than that which
lit you yesterday. It was the body of an
inhabitant of that ancient city, that was
raised to be employed in the dark doings
of witchery, on the very night of its destruction. Oh, think what it is to be
again pent in sinful flesh, without the
power or desires of life; to look on the
world through the dim organs of death;
to see men, as shadows moving around me,
and to be a shadow amongst them; to feel
all the objects and agents of life striking
on my quenched perceptions, as faintly
as the images of sleep—but to be terribly awake to all that imagery, those motions that are hid from man—when I sit
among you, to see the forms, and hear
the voices I do; to converse with the dead,
and yet wander among the living; how can
I lose

I lose this dread sense of another state
of existence? It can be acquired by
no living being, but can never be lost by
the dead—if any dead are tasked like me.
I cannot tell you what words are whispered to me, nor what shapes are beside me
now."

Alternate bursts of enthusiasm and
fear were visiting my mind, like the alternate rush and ebb of an ocean-wave,
as he spoke. I had uttered my last words
under the influence of fear, and now,
I spoke alike involuntarily, under
the other impulse. " You can, you must
let me behold those froms; I must hear
those sounds. Are the secrets of another
world so near me, and cannot I lay hold
on them?" " You cannot; these things
man may not behold, and live." " I would
hazard life itself," said I, with frantic eagerness, " to look on them." " Mortal, per-
verse and fond, you would throw away
life to feed an unhallowed curiosity ; and
you listen, without emotion, to a spirit in
                                despair

despair, that cries to you for remission and rest from the pit where there is no water." " Me?—to me this appeal? Who cries to me ?—What must I do, or how am I involved? Oh! do not call on, do not come to me. I fear the snares of death are gathering about me, while I confer with you. Be satisfied; you have filled me with horrors; you have kindled in my mind a fire that can never be quenched.—Be satisfied, and depart. This is a wild hour, full of dark thoughts, and hauntings from the power of evil. Leave me. I have heard too much; I have thought too much." " No I cannot leave you; I must not leave you. Every night my visit must be repeated; every night my tale must be told perhaps by other voices than mine. Long was the name of my deliverer withheld. I was driven around the world for years, the sport of the elements, the outcast of man, unknown by, and unknow-

in

ing all, yet compelled every night to
visit the place where my bones decay,
unblest; and measure every night, with
groans that would thrill a spirit to hear,
the ground to the chapel, with my strange
load, rend up the earth with my own
hands, and place it in an unhallowed
grave, while the fiends, who watch the
lost souls in those vaults, with howl, and
charmed tapers, mocking the absent rite,
would cast it forth again, and bear it
with laugh and ban to that blood-
sprinkled hole where it cannot rest. It
was a weary way for me to wander every
night to that spot, though the sun had
set on me in the deserts of Africa. At
length, I was permitted to enter this
castle, in a character that procured me
exemption from the persecution of frequent notice, and of being compelled
to mingle much with human beings; yet,
secluded as I was, the domestics noticed,
feared, and watched me, and were punished

ed for their curiosity. Here I learned
who was to free me from my dark thrall.
Annibal di Montorio, it is you. You
must collect my unburied bones; you
must lay them in holy earth, with need-
ful and decent rite, with bell, and bless-
ing of holy men. Annibal di Montorio,
your task does not end here. From the
groaning ground, from the ground where
my murder was done, there comes a
voice, whose cry is, " Blood for blood."

"Stop, stop, before I run wild; I
must not hear these words, and deserve
to live : I know their terrible meaning:
I know whom they point to; but it is
impossible, it is unnatural, it is perdition ;
I must not listen to you, I dare not ; you
are indeed," (my thoughts sinking into
solemnity), " you are indeed, what you
say you are, an evil spirit. Such
things as you have told me, man could
not conceive, man could not relate. I
believe it all, and I believe you are a
tempting

tempting spirit, a spirit of lies; full of
horrible suggestions. Oh, Maria, my
brains wheel round; but, to think on
what you have darkly led me to!—Away
from me—avaunt, thou adversary! Whatever you are, you savour strongly of the
power that prompts you. A moment, and
I shall see you fly shrieking and defeated,
surrounded by hooting imps, goaded with
talon and fang. Oh, look not at me thus!
I pity you, by heaven and all its saints, I
pity, and will pray for you. All offices
of grace and love, mass, and prayer,
and pilgrimage shall be done for you;
your bones shall lay in holy earth, with
cross and relick, and holy water, and ce-
remonies to drive away the power that
has you in dark durance: all things that
may do peace to a parted soul, shall
be done for you; but further, name it
not, hint it not; I will not hear you
speak again. Do not look at me with
that dark, meaning eye; I know who he
is;

is; I know all—but some other hand—
Who made me an angel of vengence, to
ride air in the terror of my purpose
through the bowels of nature, through the
shriek of mankind, through the blood of
a father?"

Ippolito, if, from these broken sentences
of fear and aversion, you cannot discover
the meaning I ascribed to the words of
the phantom, I dare not tell it more
explicitly.   He understood me well.—
" You perceive my purpose, then; with
the purposes of destiny, it is the same
thing to be discovered and obeyed.   But
you are full of the flesh, and fleshly
fears.   You have not yet attained that
sad and lonely exemption from mortal
feeling, which is *marked on the brow* of
the agent of fate.   You have not stood
in the thick cloud of your purpose, from
which the lightnings and thunderings
issuing, terrify the congregation of mankind.   But we shall meet again."   " Never;
Oh!

Oh! never. By every holy name, if holy
name have power over you, I intreat
you to depart; haunt me no more; you
can drive me to despair, but never to
guilt. Begone, I adjure you, and command you. We must meet no more. I
know not to what the terrors of your
presence might drive me. Madness, or
worse than madness threatens me while I
look at you. Your words have sunk into
my soul. Nothing shall ever remove
them. Your appearance and your tale
can never be forgotten. There is no need
to repeat them. If you value the welfare and salvation of an immortal soul,
leave me, and never see me more."

He shook his head mournfully. The
motion continued so long, and was accompanied with a look so disconsolate,
that twice and thrice I rubbed my eyes,
and doubted that their weakness gave a
vibrating motion to what I saw. At
length he spoke. " My visits are involuntary.

2

tary. I was constrained to wander over the earth, till I found the being destined by Fate to give rest and atonement to my corse and spirit; and now that I have found you, your own shadow, your own limbs, your own consciousness, and heart, and soul, cannot be more intimate and ever-present companions to you, than I and my terrible tale shall be. I will visit you every night: I will hover round you all day: my whispers shall never leave your ears, nor my presence your fancy. Fly from me, plunge into other scenes and employments, change your country, your character, your habits—I will follow you through all space; I will live with you through all life; the eternal will has wedded me to you. Suspend the swelling of the sea, arrest the moon in her course, change all things beneath the throne of heaven, and then, despair of driving me from you. The powers of both worlds are alike armed against your

impious

impious opposition. Hell will not remit its torments, nor heaven reverse its decrees. I may haunt you in more terrible shape; I may speak to you in a voice that resembles the seething tides of the lake that burneth with fire and brimstone; your reason may desert you in the struggle, but I must pursue you till my body and soul are at peace. Then when the great blow is struck," (his eye rolled and his figure spread,) " and the thunder, the long with-held thunder of heaven, is smiting into dust these dark and blood-steeped towers—then, once, and for the last time, you shall see, in my original form, bestriding these blasted battlements, a giant-shape of fire, rending up the vaults where murder has slept for ages, and pouring out to day, the guilty secrets of a house, whose records of crimes and of disasters shall end in me."

I attempted

I attempted to interrupt him, or to forbear to listen to him, in vain. I might as well have interrupted the ravings of the Sybil, or arrested the storm of heaven. He rushed on the ear and soul with a flood of sound and thought, that left the hearer, gasping, bewildered, staring around to see had the voice issued from above, from beneath, were the walls around him in motion, or was the ground beneath him heaving and yawning with those terrible sounds. Till he had ceased, so suspended was my mind, I did not perceive I was in darkness. This circumstance, which I had determined to watch tenaciously, again escaped me in the confusion of my thoughts. I held up the glimmerings of my lamp. They shewed me his figure dimly retiring, but in what direction I could not discover, in the wide blackness of my vault. Quitting my lamp, and extending both arms, I felt around me, calling on
him

him till the echoes of my voice, so fancifully aggravated, and modified to a thousand wild tones, in those long passages, came fearfully back to my ear; and, with a sudden impulse, I drew in my arms, lest I should encounter his, or some other strange touch, freezing up my limbs with its chilling gripe.

When I retreated to my bed, I expected a terrible night; but I found that the energy of my feelings was a balance for their wild agitation. I was too much out of the sphere of human nature to be assailed by its fears. To every start and stirring of uneasy thought I felt myself replying with a power of resistance and careless defiance I had never felt before, and that now I wondered I felt. I slept heavily for the remainder of the night, undisturbed by dream or start of fear.

The next day, when I awoke, I looked around me with a new sensation. I spread out my hands, and said to myself, almost

most audibly, I am a new creature. I
rose, and strode across my room, with the
proud step of one who was elevated a-
bove the feelings and claims of nature.
I felt that I had held communion with the
inmate of another world, of that world,
so awful to our fears, so remote from
our conceptions.   I felt a shadowy dignity spreading around me.   A feeling of
pride, without the grovelling and precarious qualities of earthly pride, bore
me up.   I felt myself superior to kings,
and all the mighty ones of the earth.
What is their power? said I, internally;
It lasts for a few hours, and worms like
themselves tremble beneath it.   To secure it they consult with man, they arm
men, tremble for its preservation, and
are annihilated by its loss.   But the power
with which I am invested, extends to a
future and unending state.   Dependent
on me is the state of beings, whose substance is indissoluble, and whose duration
is

is eternal.   To solicit my aid the laws of
heaven are changed, and the veil of the
temple of eternity rent in twain.   I can
fix in passiveness, or bind down in torment, beings who could, if they were let
loose, scatter and ravish the system and elements in which I live ; and I can do this, by
powers beyond the most magnified powers
of my nature—powers peculiarly and ex-
clusively entrusted to me, and for a period beyond that of my own life, perhaps beyond that of mankind.

The ghastly character of these new
powers was lost in these contemplations,
or rather in that strong flow of renewed spirits with which every creature enters on another day, occupied by a peculiar train of thought, and illuminated
by a bright and morning sun.   When I did
look around, the few external objects the
circuit of my prison furnished, all became,
to my grasping and expanded frame of feeling, converted into fuel for them.   Their
impressions

impressions diversified my thoughts without diminishing them. I looked on the sun, or rather on the reflections that, chequered with the heavy casement work, fell on the thick arches of my windows. I looked on him as if I could have controled, and turned his beams backward. I thought with contempt of his task, employed in lighting myriads of half animated creatures to quit animal sleep for mental lethargy, a night of drowsiness for a day of vacancy; in calling up beings exactly the same, since he first dawned on earth, through exactly the same tasks, and to exactly the same repose.

And I thought of myself, set apart by the hand of heaven to work a secret and sublime purpose; to ope the hidden book of crimes, and read them to an appalled world; to gripe, like Sampson, the main props of the fabric of iniquity, and bear it to the ground, crushed under its huge and scattering ruin. I thought, that to the

the record of my life, the heart of man
would cling, by its most vital hopes and
fears, by its fond interest in life, and its
trembling solicitude of futurity; while
the histories of nations, and kingdoms,
and chiefs, the ephemeral bubbles of
time, mouldered away in their hands.   I
looked on the walls of my prison with a
contempt, a secret, invidious contempt.—
Yes, said I, ye may frown and lower;
ye may deepen your shadows, and make
your fastenings ten-fold more strong;
every wind of heaven may blow on you,
till your cement hardens into solid rock,
and your pile is as a pile of adamant.   But
before the arm of Him, who beckons me
to his strong bidding, ye, and all earthly obstructions, shall pass away like
smoke.   Ye may look grim on other prisoners; children of earth may languish
out their unmarked and valueless lives
here; they may look up, shuddering, to
your iron roof, and say, From hence is
no

no redemption ; but what are ye to me, whom the Power that leads, can bring from the bottom of the ocean ; can snatch from the crater of the volcano ; can bid the elements fall back ; yea, can make the very grave give up again, " because he hath need of me?"

I paused over these reflections. My mind was filled with a terrible courage, a daring elevation, a wild and gloomy sublimity. The sensation of fear was the ground of all my feelings ; but it was fear purified from all grossness of earth-ly mixture or infirmity. I was the as-sociate, not the prey of unearthly beings. I was no longer grasping at a shred of the falling mantle of the prophet ; but sailing up in his fiery chariot, careering through the extent of space, and bend-ing the forms of the elements to my pro-gress and my power. For hours I walk-ed up and down my prison, which was spacious and lofty, but whose limits seemed to drive back my breath—my velocity increasing, my frame mantling and throbbing, my mind soaring at every step, till the hour of my attendant's appearing was long elapsed.

This scarcely produced an impression on me. At length, I heard a step approach, and a key inserted in the door. My senses had been so quickened by the habit of intense observation on the trivial circumstances that exercised them, that I perceived at once, from the slow and irregular manner in which the key was turned, that it was not held by the usual hand. I had scarce time to notice this, when it burst open with an impetuous movement, as if my gaoler was incensed at the delay, and Filippo, half-sobbing, half-shouting, was at my feet. I never experienced, never will again experience perhaps, so strong a proof of the mutability of human feelings. In a moment all within and around me was changed. I was rejoiced

joiced to compound between the dark
and cloudy elevation of my mind, and
the warm, humble, sheltered feelings that
the sight of a human creature, my fellow
in the flesh, its infirmities, and affections,
and who appeared to have some kindness
towards me, excited. I rejoiced to descend
from the precipice of aerial existence, and
claim kindred with man. For some time
I permitted his emotions to flow on unrestrained. I was soothed and delighted by
feeling his warm tears and kisses raining on
my hands, my vesture, my knees, with rapid and impatient delight. I was only
moved to disturb him by the consideration, that we were perhaps observed, and
that the unequivocal marks of his regard might expose him to danger. I endeavoured to raise him. He understood
and answered my fears. There was no
one near us, he said ; no one dreamed of
watching or suspecting us ; all was trusted to him, thanks to the blessed saints,

and,

and, above all, his patron Filippo, that enabled him to deceive my father, and even that fiend-monk, as he called the confessor, with vehement bitterness.

I could not suppress my astonishment at his appearance and his information. I had believed myself shut out from all the world, from the approach or sympathy of man; least of all did I believe, that one exposed to the persecution which had immured me, should be permitted to visit me in freedom; but it was in vain to pour question on question. Filippo's eagerness and delight overbore and actually silenced me for the first half-hour, and scarcely even then could I obtain from him a coherent account of the means that had again brought us together.

"Oh! Signor," said he, "do you remember that last terrible night when you paused at the foot of the stairs, and threw open that dark door; and you entered it

it so pale, I thought I had beheld you
going into your tomb; but I had scarce
time to think of any thing, when I was
thrust back, as I attempted to follow them,
and the key turned on me in the passage.
I knew not what they intended. I feared
all things that were terrible. But there
was a heaviness over me, whether it was
the consequence of the sudden amaze
that had seized us, or the watching, or the
strange doings of the night, I know not,
but I sat down on the ground, and wrapped my head in my mantle, and continued
still, but not insensible; it was a strange
mood, Signor, now that I recal it. I felt
no fear; I uttered no complaint; yet I
believed I had not long to live. I listened
stupidly to steps approaching, though I
thought they were the steps of some appointed to dispatch me. But when I heard
them coming yet nearer, and felt that I
must raise my head, and look on what
was so near me, I uttered a loud cry,
though

though without any distinct notion of
pain or danger. It was the monk. He
raised me roughly by the arm, and bid
me follow him. Queen of heaven ! thro'
what places did he lead me ! What a prize
to the inquisition, or to a banditti, would
this castle be, with its passages and vaults,
and chambers in the solid wall, without
window or loop-hole, or a single avenue
of human comfort, and air that our lamp
could scarce burn in—air, like the breath-
ings of a vault ! I felt I should die, die
a certain and miserable death, if I were
left there, even without violence or hardship ; but I tried in vain to obtain from
the monk the slightest hint of what he
intended to do with me. Often I thought
I was as strong as he ; that there was no
one near to assist either of us ; that if I
even extinguished the light, and trusted
to the windings of those vaults for concealment or escape, it would be better than to
go on, like an ox to the slaughter. These
thoughts

thoughts often came to me, and often I
half-raised my eye to the dark face beside me, to see, was it assailable, was it
like the face of man that is liable to
weakness or danger. But Oh, Signor, I
drew it away again without hope. There
is nothing like man about him. I fear
no man. I could cling to life, and grapple
for it as keenly, if I knew my weapons and
my compeer, as any man in Italy; but
when I am near that monk I feel — Oh!
I know not how. The air that comes
from him is chill; his large dead eye
fixes me; the tones of his voice come
over me, like the roll of distant thunder
at night, when we half fear to listen, and
half to shut it out. Is he not a strange
being, Signor ?" said he, turning suddenly, and fixing his dark eyes, distended
with fear, on me. "He is indeed," said
I involuntarily; " but (after a pause)
proceed Filippo." " Do you believe him
to be indeed a man like ourselves?" he
continued,

continued, with increased eagerness, and
visage still lengthening. " I know not ;
I cannot tell ; I beseech thee to speak no
more of him ; go on with thy own narrative, but mention him as little as possible
in the course of it." " Well, Signor, I
passed four days in darkness and solitude ;
but how shall I proceed, if I am not permitted to mention the monk ? He was the
only person I thought of, the only person I saw, except you. Oh ! Signor, think
what it is to pass four days in total solitude, in total darkness, except when he
visited me with my scanty portion of
food ; and then, by the dim light he carried, I could partly see the vast and shapeless darkness of my vault. 'Twas strange,
Signor, but I saw it better in his absence.
When the light was brought into my
prison, a mist seemed to hang over every
object ; a kind of tremulous, blue damp-
ness spread all beyond the edges of that
pale lamp ; but no sooner was it removed,
                                        than

than all the dark nooks and corners, which
I had ver seen, came strong and clear before my eyes. It was in vain that I wrapt
my head tight ard tighter in my cloak; in
vain I said to myself, I am in the dark;
these things are not before me; I am in a
close, sheltered corner, where nothing is
approaching me, and from which nothing
is moving me—yet still—still would I
seem to myself wandering on, thrusting
myself down some steep, dark descent,
rooting in some gloomy nook, following
some strange light that glimmered and
flitted before me, till, all on a sudden, some
haggard face edging the dark corner, would
grin and chatter at me. Then I would feel
myself shrinking back to my straw, and
still it would pursue me, and still it would
seem to rustle through my cloak, and
peep at me in every fold; for still I seemed to see, though my eyes were closed,
and though I was in utter darkness."

Melancholy

Melancholy as this account was, I yet was delighted with human communication, and with an opportunity of comparing feelings different from my own, in a similar situation.

"Ah! Signor," said Filippo earnestly, " how happy are gentlemen of learning, learned Signors, that can search into their own minds, and recal their reading, and frame conversations, and have all they ever knew or loved with them in their captivity and loneliness, by force of mind. I thought I should never feel that deep and heavy solitude, if I could recollect something to think of, something that would take me out of that dark place, and set me among things and people that I once was happy with. Heaven help me! I knew nothing to drive that lonely feeling from my heart. All I could do, I did. I repeated all the prayers my uncle Michelo had taught me, whenever my my food was brought; for I had no other means of knowing the hour, and I tried to recollect, as well as I could, some verses of Ariosto, which I had heard a *recitator* at Naples pronounce. I found my memory marvelously improved by darkness and solitude; many lines I had long forgotten came fresh to my mind. I repeated them over and over again; nay, I even added some to them, very unlike the original indeed; but what would not a solitary prisoner resort to, and find interesting? Still there was a loneliness, an emptiness within me, a want of employment and of thought. I envied even the grim and silent being that came with my food. He had doors to lock, and passages to pass, and something to be employed in. And Oh! how I envied such as you, Signor, who have a power of filling up all solitude, of reading over your books, and conversing with your friends, though both are far from you."

When

When Filippo said this, I blushed involuntarily. I recollected how little of this
praise of felicity belonged to me; and I
felt how much it is in the power of circumstances to reduce minds to the same
level, to strip us of the trappings of lo-
cality, and shew what a kindred vein of
suffering and weakness runs through the
breast of us all, if the removal of outward
distinctions permits us to detect and to
trace its affinities.

"But proceed, Filippo, the period of
your total solitude was only four nights,
you told me." "Yes, Signor, it was on
the fourth evening, that the confessor,
after bringing my food, and waiting till I
had finished it, told me to follow him, and
prepare to quit the vault. He has so
absolute a manner with him, that all power
of inquiry or resistance dies within me
when he speaks. I followed him without a
word, and knew not, as he led me on, whether
it was to death or life. I began, however,
to

to mistrust that it was the former, when I perceived he was conducting me to your father's apartment. It was evening; but the tapers were already lit, for your father hates the darkness. When I entered the room he was standing. There was another figure there which I saw but dimly; for my eyes were weak, and my limbs reeled under me. Your father looked at me with astonishment. "Is this Filippo," said he, turning to the monk, "this spectre, this shadow, is it Filippo?" I was subdued to a childish weakness by my confinement. His voice sounded compassionately. What voice would not be delightful after a silence of four days? I attempted to supplicate. I believed him touched by the spectacle he had made me; but my voice failed me, and I stood, trembling and silent, before him. "Filippo," said he, "you see the consequences of disobedience; you feel that I have a power to punish, which it is vain for you to provoke

or

or to oppose. I know you to be not incapable of reflection, not of a vulgar mind, and therefore I deign to reason with you. If romantic boys and inquisitive menials are permitted to rove about, discovering, or inventing wonders, what family can repose in honour, what individual can rest in peace? I am not admitting that you can discover any thing that would tend but to your own confusion; but even the misfortunes of an illustrious family, if extensively known, involve a species of disgrace, from the prejudices of society; at least they are unfit for a domestic's tongue to sport with, and to scatter around."

All he said appeared candid and condescending; the voice of gentleness, of human feeling, was rare and delightful to me; I felt it convey shame and conviction to me; I inwardly condemned myself for curiosity and disobedience; I attempted to falter out an excuse—he interrupted

terrupted me. "It is enough," said he,
"I meant not to crush, but to correct you.
You have suffered enough; but as
long as the influence of your young master might expose you to repeated danger,
I should be to blame for your second offence, if I exposed you to it. Go hence,
therefore, and if gratitude can bind you,
you are bound to me. Marco here will
conduct you to the house where my Apu-
lian steward will call in a few days, to
bring you with him to my estates there;
he has my directions to settle you there
in a situation little inferior to his own,
where you may learn habits of regularity
and obedience. Do not oppress me with
your thanks—I—I do not wish to hear
them." I attempted to utter some inco-
herent sounds of gratitude; but he repelled me with impatience that confound-
ed me. "I will have no more of this—
I cannot bear it. Will you not take him
from me, father?" I forbore to speak.
"Set

" Set out immediately," said he, " night is
the best time: to-morrow will bring you
to your journey's end; and Marco will be
your guide." He retired, attended by his
confessor. "Come, fellow traveller," said
Marco, advancing, " shall we set out?
night is gathering fast."

I now saw him distinctly for the first
time; he was a strange, ferocious looking
fellow: I marvelled to see such a one in the
Count's apartment; among whose virtues,
condescension was never very distinguished; but every thing around me was marvellous, and the sight of Marco, as he was
called, was forgotten in the condescension of the Count, and the suddenness of
my own deliverance. I said I was ready
to attend him; but he saw me totter, and
look weak; he approached the table,
where stood a flagon of wine: " Come,"
said he, " this glass to your safe and
speedy journey; swallow it man, you will
have need of courage." I took the wine
from

from him, and looked on him as I took it,
with the vacant eye of weakness ; but the
look of his features rouzed me, weak as I
was ; it was a strange expression ; I do
not like to think of it, even now. We
went out immediately ; he took care I
should not be seen by any of the family.
We went to the stables. I felt myself inflamed by the wine I had swallowed, and
we rode off together in high spirits. In
a short time, however, my companion became silent and gloomy. I asked him a
thousand questions about my journey, its
object, and its termination ; I could get
no answer from him, but a short and general one—" Your journey is short and
easy ; to-morrow night will end it." Then
I spoke of the Count, and his condescension to me ; but I observed, that as I
spake on this subject, he became more
dark, and more restless ; then I began to
inquire how long he had been in the service
of the Count Montorio. " I have served the
                                    Count,"

Count," said he, "many years."   " Yet
I do not recollect seeing you before to-
night," said I.   " It is very possible ; I am
not always visible to the family, though
few, I believe, can boast of being more
constantly employed, or of having rendered more useful service to his Excel-
lenza."   "Secret ones, it should seem,"
said I, half jestingly.   "Very likely, but
not the less useful," said he, sternly.

We went on in silence, and lay that night
at a shed, in a vine-yard in the Cam-
pagna : those sheds, you know, in which the
watchers guard the grapes during the vintage, are constructed of straw, and branches,
and other slight materials—this was our
lodging ; I did not soon go to rest, for my
mind was tossed by the circumstances that
had preceded the journey ; and soon after
my companion lay down, I found all
thought of rest was vain. He talked to
himself with such loudness and vehemence, you would have believed that
armed

armed men were fighting in the hut, and
blood was spilt, and bodies were falling like withered leaves. Sometimes he
would cry out to wipe those daggers;
sometimes to hide those bloody garments; sometimes, " What, struggling
still! Press your knee firmly on his breast,
and gripe the skin of his throat! Aye,
that will do; now close his eyes, and
wipe that bloody foam off his mouth." Then
starting up, he would cry, "There, fellows, there, he has fled, he has escaped; fly
after him, pursue him; my lord the Count
will buy his blood with half his lands."

These were strange words; but I confess, that while I looked at the bright
and blessed moon, and caught the breeze
through my casement of leaves, so fresh
and cool after the damp heats of my
dungeon, I listened to them rather with
vacant curiosity, than fear. As I looked
on the clear heavens, I thought I saw the
very star, that when I used to be returning

ing through the woods to the castle, I
would see just rising over the battlements
of the West tower. It would glimmer
among them, Signor, just like a feeble taper at a casement; and when I saw it
rising over the dark hills of the vintage,
I thought of the castle, and of you.
Though my companion and my journey
were so strange, myriads would I have
given you were along with me, and I
determined as soon as I had reached Apu-
lia, to discover where you were, and to liberate you if possible."

"Filippo, I believe this is a gratuitous
addition to your narrative. In the sudden
joy of liberation, could you think of me?"
"Could I, Signor? Ah, you know not with
what keenness the mind, just escaped from
suffering, reverts to images that awaken
and contrast its former state. To think of
myself was to think of you; for to think
of myself, was to think of a lonely being,
a solitary being, a confined and pining
being;

being ; therefore I thought of you. All I
had so lately felt for myself was transferred
to you ; it was not sympathy, Signor, but
strong remembrance—remembrance of
the dungeon and the darkness, the dim
lamp, the meal that I scarcely saw, the
strange faces staring me out of sleep, and
the toads that I shook off as I awoke : all
this I thought of, and how then could I
forbear to think on you?

Early in the morning we set forward
again ; we rode through a wild, woody
country all day, only baiting to sleep in
the hollow of a chesnut during the heats of
noon. At the close of evening, we were in a
thick wood, the tracks were perplexed, and
appeared as if they were not much fre-
quented.   Marco often paused, and looked around him with uneasiness and distrust ; he often checked his mule, and
looked between the trees, and listened often, as the wind that now began to rise,
moaned among the branches, sometimes
                              resembling

resembling the sounds of a human voice.
It was to no purpose to ask questions; his
utter silence, and the gloom of the evening, were beginning to make me feel
strangely, when on a sudden, after muttering to himself for some time, he spurred his mule on violently; then turning
round, and bending his head low, he gal-
lopped on me so quick, that I had
scarce time to spring out of his way, and
ask what he meant. " It was a spring of
my mule," said he, " cursed jade," lashing
the animal, and falling behind me. " I
had better keep out of your way," said I,
crossing into another track. " Aye, aye,
you had better, if you can," he muttered.
Then darting forward, he disappeared
among a thick tuft of brushwood on the
right. I was startled for the first time, at
this motion, and followed him as fast as I
could—it was in vain; he had a better
knowledge of the wood, and its dark ways;
still I pursued him, though in a short time

I

I could not even hear the sound of his
mule's feet. But the wood opening suddenly to the right, I saw a large ruinous
building, that appeared like the remains
of a good dwelling, fitted up for the residence of a woodman ; there were no
offices about it, no appearances of any
country business being exercised by the
owner, it looked strangely dreary. Marco was at the door, dismounted, and talking to an ill looking man ; both advanced
when they saw me, with an appearance
of satisfaction. " This is your host," said
Marco, " this is Venanzio. You were
rarely frightened when I galloped away
and left you in the thicket—but I knew
you would follow the track ; few can miss
it, that have once set out in it."

" It was cursed foolish, however, to leave
him," said Venanzio discontentedly, " he
might have got away, and all pursuit of
him be vain. Come, young man, alight, you
will not be sorry of a good bed, and quiet
rest

rest after your ramble to-day." I alit, and followed him into a large, dreary room. A flagon of wine was on a large rustic table, around which sat one or two men, meanly dressed, with that peculiar staring wildness of face which great indigence, and remoteness of situation combine to give the inhabitants of a deserted country. They seemed undetermined whether or not to go away when we entered ; but Venanzio, with an air of command, bid them resume their seats. They sat down again, eying me surlily. There was a miserable old woman in the room, busied in a dark corner of it, who also looked at me from time to time, with a peculiar expression, of which I could not tell whether the meaning was hatred or fear.

We sat round the table, and drank; little was said ; and that little was broken and distant, full of allusions I could not understand; but which the rest seemed to consider as very significant. Marco,

2   drawing

drawing back his chair, measured me
with a slow and steady look, from head to
foot; and then nodding to Venanzio,
began twisting his fingers into a knot, and
drawing them afterwards with a straining
motion together; Venanzio only grasped
the hilt of his stiletto firmly, but both desisted suddenly, when they beheld me
looking at them.

There came a boding sickness over
me; I struggled with it, for I knew
not why I felt so. I attempted a conversation, for we had sunk to monosyl-
lables and silent looks. The name of
Venanzio I thought was familiar. " Certainly," said I to the host, " I have heard
your name before, though your namesake does not do it much credit." " Very
possibly you might," said he. " The
person to whom I allude," said I, " was
a famous assassin, in Messina; his atro-
cities were the most numerous and extraordinary I ever heard of." " Why do

you say *were*," said one of the fellows, " I
hear he is alive, and as wicked as ever."
" Oh, curse him," said another, " I could
forgive him any thing, but cheating his
comrades, as he did, when they had so
handsome a price for their work."

Venanzio looked surlily ; " Perhaps,"
said he, " he was ill paid himself." " You
seem to mistake me," said I, " the person
of whom I speak, was no mechanic ; he was
an assassin." " Well," said one of them,
" and don't you know, that such a one
must have assistants ; aye, and pay them
well too (darting an angry look across
the table), and must have work too—aye,
bloody work, tearing work ! ah, ah,
ah !" (cutting out large splinters of the
table with a clasp knife, and forcing a
horrid laugh). " But of this man," said
I, though I scarce knew how to proceed,
" I heard he baffled every pursuit of justice, and after numberless murders and
assassinations, being traced to the very
sca-

sea-shore, hid himself in the tackle of a
fishing vessel, and when the poor fisher-
man had begun to coast along the shore
by night, with a lamp at his stern (for that
is the mode of fishing there), Venanzio
started up, and compelled him to put out,
and stand for Naples ; and on their arrival,
immediately murdered his unfortunate
pilot, lest he should betray him ; and
interring him in the sand, changed his
name, and betook himself in disguise to
the woods—this I learnt was his last exploit." "No, no, this will not be his
last exploit, friend," said one of them,
" take my word for it." " You seem to
know him," said I. " Too well." " Have
you been a sufferer by him ?" " Incalcula-
ble," said he, shaking his head. " Do
you ever see him now ?" said I, pursuing
him with simple importunity. " As plain
as I see any one at this table," said he.
" And do you believe him to be alive
still ?" " As sure as our host there

is alive," said he.   "Come," said Venanzio, abruptly, "enough of my namesake;
perhaps, like many others, he is driven by
want to blood; without doubt, he re-
pents by this time being entangled with
ruffians, who suspect, and watch, and insult; but of whom he may one day get
rid, as he has done of other incumbrances."
Two of them began to growl in a lower
key at this, and the third, whose face was
peculiarly savage, said, "Aye, aye, few
men know how better to throw off incumbrances than Venanzio; his life belongs
to the hangman, his soul to Lucifer, and
his honour to the first man that will offer
him a dollar to cut his own father's
throat."

He ended this sentence with a burst of
wild sound, so unlike laughter, that it
chilled the blood; yet it evidently spoke
defiance and contemptuous hatred. "His
honour," said Venanzio, uneasily, "is un-
impaired; he never betrayed or threatened

ened his comrades." "No," said the other, eagerly, " he is content to use them so ill, that it is not in his power to threaten; and to rob them so unmercifully, that it is not worth his while to betray them." The others joined him in the conclusion of this sentence, with emphatic bitterness, yet with a kind of forced and savage derision ; their visages were inflamed, and their voices hoarse and broken.

Our host seemed to pause and bethink himself for a moment, then suddenly resting his arms on the table, and looking them stedfastly in the face, he said in a quick, decisive voice, " I'll tell you, comrades, one thing of this Venanzio, which shews he was a sensible, clear-headed knave :—there were two or three dogs, that he kept sometimes to bark, and sometimes to bite ; now and then he threw them a bone to pick, which they did not think was enough for their services.

They

They took particular care, whenever he had any *business to do*, to howl, and snarl, and disturb him; if a stranger came into their kennel, the whole set were in an uproar; all were raving to gnaw his bones, and lap his blood, before Venanzio had time to carve him, and give every one their share; whereat," (said he, stretching his brawny arm at full length on the table), " he one night ad-dressed them thus: 'Look'ye, ye blood hounds, if ever I hear ye again open your throats, by the holy cross, I'll stop them with cold iron. Don't ye know, with a curse to you, that I am the life of you, that my name only preserves you from the pursuit of justice, lodges you, feeds you, employs you; that if I am lost, ye are undone; that no one will employ such miscreants, but as spies, and then strangle them for their information. Where will ye go then, or what will ye do? Your chain is galling, and your food is bad; but what can such
mongrels

mongrels as you expect. No one would employ you, but to misuse and maltreat you; no one would keep you but to trample on you. Your only employment would be to fly at beggars, and mangle women and children; and, if ever you stole from your haunts, fire, and sword, and poison, and curses, would pursue you, and blast and scatter you, till the very crows and vultures would clap their wings in despair, as they flew over you. Do you not know this, dogs? Hounds of blood and hell, do you not know this, and will you dare to growl?"

His fury was terrible. He rose erect; he stamped; his hairs bristled; his eyes flashed; his voice was a roar; he smote the table with a violence that made the pannels start asunder. "I heard the dogs grew quite peaceable after that," said Marco. "He watched them still, for he knew they were but dogs," said Venanzio, with wrathful and venomous bitterness.

His

His speech was so sudden, so vehement, so voluble, that I listened with stupid astonishment; I tried in vain to follow the metaphor, for his passion had broke it; I knew not at whom the torrent was directed; it seemed to awe the souls of every one present; all that had heard him shuddered, and were silent.

But in the pause that followed, when the thunder of his voice died away, I began to comprehend, slowly and painfully, the meaning of all I saw. But the sting of agony was so piercing, so sudden, that I shook off the thought, as I would shake a reptile from my hand. It was too terrible to be believed—a gush of heat came over me, and then a deadly cold; my teeth chattered, though my cheeks were burning; cold, big drops of sweat stood on my forehead. I swallowed my glass eagerly, and then another, and still I was like one in a dream, who sees a hideous face, and tries to shut it out, but

but feels it spreading, and growing on
him, and staring at him from every side,
till it seems actually to get within his
eyes, and mount into his brain, and
madden him.   So I felt that thought;
still I resisted it, yet still it was in my
mind.

   " I am tired, I would be glad to see
my room," said I, rising, with that hopeless effort that looks for relief in the
mere act of motion.   " You shall *see it*,"
said Venanzio, rising.   " Ho! Bianca,
bring a light." The old woman brought
a light, which she held close to my
face as she passed me.   Her own resembled that of a sorceress.   Her earthy
skin, her sunk red eyes, her ragged hair,
with a peculiar look of glaring malignity,
blazed full on me as she passed.   My heart
sunk within me.   I followed Venanzio
up a flight of narrow, ruinous stairs.   He
opened a door to the left, and led me
into a room, like the rest, dark and wide.
The bed was in a remote corner of it.
                              Involuntarily,

Involuntarily, I glanced at the windows that were high, and well secured. They were the only part of the building that seemed in repair. " This is your room," said Venanzio, " I wish you quiet rest in it." I turned to him as he spoke, to read hope or fear in his face; but he held the light so high, that I saw only his dark head and brows as he bent over the bed.

" Stay," said I, as he was quitting the room, " I will go down and take another flagon with you." I was unwilling yet to be alone, though I had every thing to fear from these men. Yet still their presence gave me a kind of nameless refuge. I had a faint hope too, that I might have misinterpreted doubtful expressions or unpromising faces; and to the hope that flatters us with life, who would not cling as long as he can? Venanzio did not resist my going down. I was descending the stairs, when the old woman

woman called out to me, that I had left my cloak in the chamber. " Go you and fetch it for him," said Venanzio. Grasping at every omen that accident might give, I soon passed the old woman. who seemed to halt on purpose, and entered the room. I searched for my cloak all around it in vain. The old woman called out to me to examine a particular corner. I did so ; and by the lamp, that I still held, I perceived that corner was dyed in blood. My own seemed to flow back on my heart. Venanzio called loudly for the light. I tottered down stairs ; but he was gone. My eyes were dim, and when I reached the foot of the stairs, I no longer distinguished the passages ; they were dark and intricate. I wandered along without perceiving the direction I took, till I was startled by the peculiar dreariness and loneliness of the part of the building I had reached. The wind whistled after me with a boding cry

cry, and the ruinous casements rattled as if they were shaken by some forcible hand. I paused. The thought of escape came into my mind. All around me seemed deserted; and I felt, that if I could once get into the forest, I should have wings like a bird. I stepped on quick and lightly. The passage terminated in a low door at some distance. I approached it. It was open. But as I drew near, I distinguished voices within, the voices of Marco and Venanzio. I had rather have heard the hissing of a serpent. Oh! 'tis a most dark and soul-sinking feeling, when you know every human being near you, every one who could help or comfort, who could understand or unite with you, is armed with a mortal purpose again t you; and, secretly or forcibly, will, and must overcome you. Hopeless of escaping in any other direction that communicated with the more inhabited parts of the building, and

and anxious to gather what I could from
their conversation, I lingered at the door.
They spoke in that low, muttering tone,
that it is terrible to listen to; but my
hearing was so quickened by apprehension, that I did not lose a syllable.

" Where is he now?" said Marco. " He
is above, not half-pleased with his apartment.   " He will be less so, when he
finds it is to be the last he shall occu-
py; but why wait till he retires to rest?"
" I am afraid your retreats are suspected.
I have observed more travellers passing
near it than could have business in this
wild wood; and I wish to have no voice
or struggling till it is dark, and no traveller near.   Twas for that reason I blam-
ed your leaving him in the wood.   He
might have escaped; he might have taken a hint from that gloomy visage of
your's, and fled; for, after so many years
residence, a child might baffle me in the
windings of this wood; and then the first
                              intelligence

intelligence we should have got of him, would have been a stiletto in your heart for suffering him to escape." " How could I avoid it? By my soul, I was as much alarmed as you, your not meeting me at the place, owing to Nicolo's blunders. Besides I had almost forgotten the track. The fellow is almost as able as I am; and, I'll warrant, would have grappled fiercely for his life. Once I was in the mind to have put him out of pain. I found my mule full a-head, and galloped on him; and if I could have thrown him to the ground, I would have dispatched him with a few strokes of the stiletto; but he sprung on one side, and avoided me." " And did he continue to ride with you still?" "He did; he seems to have no suspicions, or Zeno and the rest would have alarmed him with their hints, and you with your fury in the chamber below. Ha! ha! ha! I could have laughed to hear him question so gravely,

a

a man, about his own existence, and telling him stories of himself. Or do you
think he was beginning to discover who
you were, and tried that method to cer-
tify himself."   " I know not. He appears simple and inapprehensive. Yet
just now, in the chamber, I thought I
saw a dark shade cross his countenance.
His cheek was white, and his lip shook.
But my eyes are none of the best.
Strange things sometimes seem to pass
before them ; that cursed old hag too—
but I may be mistaken. I thought she
left his cloak purposely in the corner
where the monk was murdered, that he
might take notice of the blood."   " Aye,
that was the business that incensed Zeno
and the rest."   " Aye," repeated Venanzio, angrily, " the rapacious dastards—
they think, if they cut the throat of an
unarmed peasant, or burn a hovel now
and then, they have a right to the same
rewards with men that have been employed

ed by the first nobility, that have made
princes keep them in humour and in pay,
that have dispeopled a whole country by
their mere name — the villains! because
I have been hunted to this dark den,
where I live in poverty and fear, and am
sunk to the cutting the throat of a wretched, single domestic—they think"——
"Hush, hush, was that the wind? it sounded like a human groan: what dreary
sounds come along these passages!" "Ha!
ha! why, your cheek is as pale as your
fellow traveller's. It would cure you of
these fancies to live as I do here, listening to the sounds that sweep through this
old building, and to others, of which I
dare not think whence they come." "In
the name of heaven, are you so beset?
Why, it were better to follow our business in the heart of a populous city, as
we did at Messina. There, we were only
posted in the corner of a street some dark
night, and when we had disposed of the
body

body quietly, in some vault, or ruinous building, we could resort to jollity, to some house of entertainment, and drink away the memory of the nights work, as soon as we washed the blood off our hands." "Aye, aye, but here, in the deserted haunts, in the dark forests, thoughts come to me that never came to me ·in Messina. I am not the man I was. 'Tis not that I repent. No. By the mass I am no flincher. If the fathers of the Inquisition were preaching to me, they would not get me so much as to mutter a pater noster, or to sign a cross, though often, often I do it unawares, through fear, and in the weakness of the moment. But yet I know not how I feel. Marco, you know I am no visionary. Will you believe me, when I tell you what I saw the other evening, as I sat in this chair, when the wind moaned through the chesnut trees, just as it does this evening?"

Marco

Marco changed his posture to listen to
the story. I moved away mechanically.
It was not that I had a distinct fear of
his presence. I believe had they both
rushed out on me, I could neither have
resisted nor deceived them. I could not
think a thought; but I staggered away, as
from an intuitive and mortal sensation of
dread at the sight or step of the murderers.
I know not how I got down the passage,
nor up stairs again; but I did so, and recollect leaving my lamp on the floor with
the same quiet regularity as if I should
ever have occasion for its light again; but
then all sensation appeared to leave me.
There was no doubt, nor shadow of hope;
no refuge in thought for me. I knew all,
and knew it all at once, and the worst at
once; I should never leave that apartment; a few moments were all I had to
live; death, sudden, unexpected death,
what a desolating thought! how it sweeps
the

the whole soul of man, with every resource of strength or hope, away. My eyes darted fire, visibly. I felt the sparks. My teeth chattered. Every pore was so wide, that I felt the cold, thick drops of sweat that every one sent forth. My hair rose, every hair sore with distinctness, and hissing on my head like a serpent. I gasped for breath. It was true and proper death that I thought was overtaking me. I tried to stir, but every limb was palsied. I tried to speak, and could only make a faint inward croak in my chest. The lamp, the ceiling, the floor, became tenfold and a hundred-fold in a minute; and then disappeared at once. I know not how long I remained in this state, but surely, whenever I die, I shall twice taste the bitterness of death. I recovered at once. I was so fully awake; so conscious of all I heard and knew, that I sprung on my feet lest they should enter and take advantage of my helpless posture. I
looked

looked and listened around me. All was still, save the wind, that was now becoming tempestuous, and whose hollow rush came along the passage of my chamber like the sound of garments and footsteps, and waved the tall trees, whose shadows crossed the casement, making strange motions to a fearful eye.

As I listened still, though hopeless of hearing a sound of comfort, I thought voices beneath the casement came scattering on the wind. They might be travellers in the forest; they might be those of whom Venanzio spoke. With the eagerness of sudden hope I climbed into the window-seat, and, holding by the bars, looked below. There was a dim moon, often hid by the clouds that were driven along the sky; nor was twilight wholly gone. Below, I could at first see nothing but the tuft of trees; but as I looked closer, I saw a man, whose cloak, ruffled by the wind, I had at first taken for a branch.

branch. He held something in his hand
which I could not distinguish. In a short
time he was joined by another, whose
head was bare. Their voices came up
distinct and clear. The latter was Venanzio.

"What are you doing here," said he,
"always loitering when work is to be
done." "I have not loitered," said the
other, sullenly; "look at this mattock,
and then look at the stubbed, tangled
roots of this pine. Do you call it loitering to have dug the grave in such
ground as this?" "It is not long enough,'
(stooping to measure it: Oh! I saw
every motion he made). "Lengthen it
yourself, then," said the other, throwing
down the mattock, "a man were better
work for the devil than you. Can I not
dig a grave now ? I was captain of as bold
a band as ever trooped at a signal, when
you were pitching up ducats in Messina
for a coward's blow, and a flight in the
2   dark.'"

dark." "Well, well, we need not quarrel; we both have seen better days and better work, than butchering a sorry lackey; and yet that fellow appears inclined to give us work too. He will require your bony arms, or Zeno's, to give him a firm gripe by the throat." "Will you not stab him, then?" "No, I'll have no more blood spilt; it stains the rooms, and gives strangers hints that it would be our wisdom to hide from them. You know how suddenly the pilgrims left us the other evening, of whom we thought ourselves sure. List, Nicolo, I'll have him strangled as soon as he is asleep. We will go and have another flagon in the room under him, and watch till he has lain down." "By my soul, I would rather meet a man armed with a dagger, and strive with him hand to hand, than strangle a sleeping man. I am not myself for a month after. The black and staring face, the set teeth, the forced-out eyes, are with me wherever I turn.

turn. Maria! do you remember the last
man that perished in that room?—still,
how he struggled, and gasped, and tore
out handfuls of Marco's hair in his
agonies! he was horridly strong; the
worse for him; there was no crushing
life out of him. He heaved as we laid
him on the ground; his eyes have never
been off me since; I see them in the
dark. Holy mother! they are glaring on
me from that pit—look—look—Venanzio." "Away you fool; and what if they
were? Can the eyes of the dead stab
you?" "They can, they can; take that
mattock; I would not look into that hole
again for the whole price of this night's
work." "Ha! ha! listen to the blast that
howls after you. Is that the dead man's
cry? Ha! ha!"

He pursued the scared ruffian with an
hideous laugh. I let go the bars in utter
agony and helplessness of soul, and fell
on the floor. I had heard my death determined.

mined. I had seen my own grave dug;
a sad sight, that few living men behold.
Before the lamp burnt out, before the
blast died away, before another hour, I
should be a corse, swoln, and stretched,
and stark. My mind ran with astonish-
ing swiftness through every circumstance
of the past days. Oh! how I cursed
your father's barbarity, for one offence,
so trivial and easy to be prevented for
the future, to send me to a distance, where
no cry could reach a human ear, to be
butchered by cannibals; to disarm me by
such promises and condescension; to keep
me immured till I was weak and pliant; to
leave me without the means of resistance
or escape. Oh! how I cursed my own
folly to trust him; not to profit by the
many hints my dark companion gave; to
go on like a sheep to the shambles. I
recalled every circumstance that had escaped them, hinting the past possibility
of my safety; I could have fled into the
wood;

wood; I could have struggled with Marco, " I was almost as able as he :" nay, yet—yet I might escape in the windings of the wood, if it were possible to reach it. All these thoughts, and a million more, came to me so clear, so keen, so stinging, that I was almost mad. Oh, the bitterness of feeling life lost by one moment's folly, and not to be recovered by the fullest stretch of thought and action after.

I seemed to myself to have thrust away my safety with both hands, and to have hunted and pursued away every chance of life, and run headlong into the snare that closed on me, and shut me round for ever. After a moment's sober and severe pain, I started into actual phrensy; I ran round the room, striking the walls, and grappling with the windows, and gnashing my teeth with the rage of madness. I am astonished they did not hear the uproar I made.   at length, I began to look round me more calmly; but

still with the fiery penetration, and glaring
eagerness of real insanity. I am convinced I was mad, yet one idea was still
so clearly present and powerful with me,
that I felt I was capable of exerting every
force of my soul and body, while it continued to stimulate me. There was no
furniture in the room ; nothing that could
present either a weapon of defence, or
means of escape. Despairing, but still
with forcible and unremitting intentness,
in the dusky walls and floor it was not
easy to discover any object; but poring
on the latter by the light of the lamp, I
discovered a pannel, with a ring in it ; it
resembled a trap-door. I had little doubt
of the use of such an instrument in such
a place, and as little hope, that I could
long lie hid in any place to which it might
conduct me ; yet still active from the restlessness of misery, I began to raise it, and
succeeded.

There was a dark cavity below, that I
judged

judged ran between the flooring of one
room, and the ceiling of that below, which
might possibly continue to some distance,
or be connected with other cavities and
passages. I got down, and scrambled to
some distance in it; it was filled up with
rubbish, which I struggled through, half
stifled with the dust; but I soon found
my passage obstructed; some soft substance was presented to my hand; slowly
and cautiously I withdrew it, and crawling backwards, brought it out with me;
the lamp was still on the floor, and by its
light, I perceived I held a heap of bloody
and decayed garments, pierced with more
holes than those of decay. As I gazed on
it, a wild blast shook the door, and raved
round the walls; the flame of the lamp
shivered, and blazed athwart and over-
blown.

I looked around in terrible expectation
of the wearer of the garments, that told
a dark story, appearing to witness the

discovery;

discovery ; strange shadows played on the walls, as the lamp burnt clear. After many bickerings, I replaced the garments, and again endeavoured to grop my way through the passage, in which I discovered a light, on my second attempt; I crept on, and found by the sound, as well as the light, that it came through the broken ceiling of the room below, where the whole group were assembled, and seen distinctly through many an aperture. I heard my name often repeated, and saw some motions horribly significant when it was repeated. The blast was now so loud, and howled so fiercely through the broken rafters, over which I leaned, that I could not distinguish any thing of their discourse, but my name ; nor perhaps, even that, had not my senses been quickened to that exquisite keenness, which the solicitude to overhear a conference about your own life, can alone produce.

In a short time, I began to think I might perhaps

perhaps make a better use of this passage,
than merely to overhear a conversation, of
which I already knew the probable purport but too well;—I crept on therefore
with breathless caution, and found, to my
inexpressible joy, that I had passed the
room where they were assembled. The
apertures were now more numerous, and
I conjectured I was near some ruinous,
and perhaps neglected part of the building, from which escape might—might be
possible; my obstructions grew fewer
too, and the passage itself wider and I
had no doubt of its being purposely constructed, and having therefore some certain outlet. As I crawled on, I again perceived a faint light beneath, supported
between two beams; I applied my eye
to the largest hole near me, and perceived
it proceeded from a dim lamp that burned
at some distance below; the light it gave
was so faint, that it was long before I
could distinguish it burned in a large desolate

solate room, in the corner of which lay
an obscure figure, stretched on a palle .
I gazed long before I could discover so
much, and it was not till the figure turned, that I had a view of the most wasted,
and ghastly form I ever beheld, covered
with rags that were steeped in blood.
As the wind howled round his comfortless
bed, I could distinctly hear his groans
mingling with it. For a moment I believed him to be some victim of the ruffian-
band—but why then should his life be
spared ? At all events, I perceived this
wretched object was in no condition either
to resist, or even to give an alarm to the rest :
the cries he uttered, were the weak tones of
one worn with pain ; if therefore, I could
let my self down into his room with safety, I had little doubt of escaping. His
apartment must be near the extremity of
the building, and I heard the casements
shake in the wind. I felt such a resolution
must be achieved in a moment; the murderers

ers were now drinking, the storm was high, and the sufferer incapable of opposition ; yet, not one of these circumstances might continue to favour me a moment longer.

I began to examine the largest aperture, through which, when sufficiently opened, I was to descend ; when I was checked by a loud noise from below—I desisted—a door opened, and one of those I had seen below entered with a lamp and some provisions, which he placed near the sick man, who appeared to decline them. The other spoke a few words of encouragement to him, from which I discovered, that the sufferer was one of the band who had been wounded in some late attempt, and who was now lingering under the festering tortures of his wounds without relief or hope, as they were apprehensive to procure assistance was to hazard discovery. After some careless consolation, he who brought the food was preparing to depart ; but the other, in the infirmity of

suffering

suffering, besought him to stay a few moments. "I cannot," said he, surlily, "I must be gone, we have business on our hands to-night. There is one lodged near you, who in half an hour must change his resting-place for a cold and bloody bed in the forest." (In half an hour! Who that has not heard his death denounced, and felt how dreadful it is to know and measure the approach of death can tell what I felt at these words?) "Oh, Saviolo," groaned the penitent villain, "talk not of those things to me; how can you mention them, and look on me stretched here, and think how soon the judgment of God may visit you for these things, as it has overtaken me." Saviolo replied only by a muttered oath at his lamp, which a blast of wind had almost extinguished. "Oh," continued the dying man, "if I could but have the benefit of some holy man; if I could but see a crucifix, and be taught one short prayer before

fore I go hence—dark and dreadful things
are on my conscience; no one knows
what I know; I have more thanthe petty
murders of an obscure villain to unfold;
I was engaged in a horrid conspiracy
against the peace and honour of a noble
youth; Oh, there were things once, that
would deceive the devil, to deceive and
ruin him, and I fear they have succeeded.
Again Saviolo cursed his lamp, which was
almost extinguished, and looking around
fastened his eyes on the ceiling, through
whose many holes the wind rushed in.
every direction.

I saw him eye it suspiciously, and I
drew back for a moment, terrified at the
delay which his observation occasioned,
for a half an hour's chance for life, who
would lose a moment? and till he left the
apartment, no attempt could be made.
He was again preparing to depart, when
the sick man shrieked to him to stay;
" Oh, stay," said he, " for the love of the

mother

mother of God, stay with me a moment, he is coming, I hear him in the wind."

" Who is coming," said Saviolo, stopping, and turning pale, as the light he bore glared on his strong visage.   " The wicked one, the wicked one ; he is with me every night; sometimes he stands beside me, and sometimes he rises through the floor before me ; Oh, he is ever—ever with me, and soon I must be with him."

" Peace, peace, you driveller, turn to the wall, and close your eyes, and try to rest ; and look, if you should hear any cries within half an hour don't come crawling from your bed as you did the last time, with those bloody swathes scaring us all before the work was well done."   " Oh, Saviolo, dear, good, blessed fellow, do not leave me for a moment—for one moment ; I see a hoof coming through the curtain."

Saviolo rushed out of the room with a curse, that shook it, and the conscience-smitten wretch shrunk under his rags.

Now

Now was the time; one was gone with precipitation, and the other would probably shrink from any thing he might see or hear moving near him. I had but half an hour to work for life. I began quietly, but swiftly to remove large flakes of plaster, which were so dry, that I found little difficulty in removing them, and the thin laths to which they were attached. In a short time I had displaced enough to admit an arm or leg: I was afraid of making too wide a breach, as the materials were so infirm, I feared they might sink under me, and supported myself on a beam while I loosened them. I tried to let myself down; the breach admitted me easily, and the beam supported me firmly. In the delirium of my joy, I was unable for a moment to proceed; I was obliged to wipe away the tears of joy, that prevented me from seeing my progress. I now measured the distance cautiously. I had at least twelve feet to fall, for the room was

lofty

lofty; such a fall, however, could neither
stun nor hurt me. I only dreaded the
noise might alarm the ruffians; this however, was not to be avoided. I determined
immediately on my descent to rush across
the room, and spring through the window,
or if possible to prevail on the wounded
man, who appeared averse from blood, to
inform me, in what direction I might
escape.

I now let myself down silently, but ex-
peditiously. The wounded man gave no
sign of notice; I neither heard him star
nor moan; I had sunk on the beams,
till only my elbows were supported, and
was endeavouring to detach those, and
let myself drop, when by some untoward
motion, a large heap of the rubbish I
had removed fell through the hole with
a loud noise, and part lit on the bed. The
frighted wretch screamed aloud, and
continued his cries so long, that though
my intention was to leap down, and implore

plore him to be silent, I heard steps approaching before I could execute it, or draw myself back, almost, into my hiding place.

Saviolo re-entered, as usual, with a curse in his mouth ; but I found the purport of his return, was not to sooth, but to threaten the sick man ; and with horror I heard him say, " Curse on your clamours, you will waken the man that is to be murdered, and give him a hint of where he is; and then we shall have a struggle, instead of finishing him as he lies." The terrified creature averred with earnest repetitions, that some one must be in the room, from the noise he had heard, and from the violence the roof appeared to have sustained. Saviolo appeared little inclined to believe him ; the noises he said were imaginary, and the roof had been shattered by the storm ; " For just over your head, there is a passage between the stories of the building, with the ex-

tent

tent of which none of us are acquainted,
and through which the wind rushes with
terrible fury; but at all events," he continued, " as they will not want me in this
business, I shall stay with you, and prevent you from crying out, till it is over;
they will have struggling enough with
him, there is no occasion to wake and put
him on his guard."

Oh, blessed virgin, and St. Philip, with
what agony I heard him cutting off my
last retreat, shutting up my last narrow
breathing hole of life. He would stay,
and it was impossible to descend; he was
a brawny, resolute fellow, a weaker man
struggling for life, might indeed have
overcame him, but I was unarmed; he
had a poniard, and pistols stuck in his
belt, and the very mode of my escape
would expose me, as in descending I
should probably fall. I lingered a few
moments in the mere vacancy of despair,
and then heard him tell the sick man,

that

Zeno was about to go up, and discover whether the stranger was asleep, and that if he were, he was to inform the person appointed to strangle him, who would dispatch him immediately.

At this terrible intelligence, I was almost ready to dash myself down, and trust to a desperate chance of safety, for every probable one had disappeared ; I was enclosed on every side, death actually stared me in the face.   The immediate danger, however, I felt an irresistible impulse to escape from.   If any of them should visit my room, and find it empty, he would quickly discover my retreat, and I should be butchered in that dusky hole without a struggle , back therefore, I crept, without a single hope to direct the motion ;   but with a blind resistance of inevitable evil, half smothered by the dust and rubbish, I scrambled through, crushing at every touch the eggs of the little domestic serpents, and displacing the nests of lizards

and

and toads, whose cold slime made me
shudder, as I crawled amongst them.

At length, I reached my own apartment, and as I raised myself out of the
trap-door, and caught the lamp that burned still beside it, I almost expected some
hand would push me back into the cavity.
The room was empty, and no one had been
there in my absence. After a moment's
debate, I rose, shut the trap-door,
placed the lamp on the table, and threw
myself on the bed, concerting with calm
desperation my last plan of deliverance.
I had scarce lain down, when I heard a
slow, heavy tread on the stairs; though
I had arranged something like a means of
escape, and though part of it was to admit
Zeno into the room without resistance,
as his intentions were not immediately
murderous; yet there is no telling the
agony with which I heard him approach—
certainly approach, nor the miserable
watchfulness with which I struggled to
distinguish

distinguish whether the steps were real,
or whether I was deceived by the wind,
whose force had made the ruinous stairs
creak all night—it *was* a step, the step of
the man who came to see was I prepared
for murder. He came up softly, and I
heard him pause at the door, and withdraw
the bolts slowly, like one who fears to disturb a sleeper; I heard him in the room,
I felt him approach the bed. I counterfeited deep sleep; as he came nearer, I
experienced a horrid sensation, like that
which accompanies the oppression of the
night-mare; it was the struggle of nature within me; my resolution was to
lie still, but nature moved within me to
struggle or to fly. He came close to me,
I heard him keeping in his breath; he bent
over me, holding his lamp almost close to
my face. I thought this might be a trial
whether my sleep was counterfeited; but I
dared not stir. I would have given the world
to have looked at him under my eye-lids
                                         at

at that moment; to have seen the expression of his face, whether there was compassion or any relenting in it; but I dared not. Yet at this moment, while I yet doubted but he was examining whether he could not do the deed himself, and that, in the next instant, I should feel his stiletto in me before I even saw it drawn. Even at that moment, will you believe me, Signor? an irresistible propensity to laughter spread itself over my face; over my face I say, for in my heart was nothing but despair; yet was it irresistible; my features relaxed into something that felt to me like the motion of laughter, but struggling with the perturbation of fear, and the paleness of expected death. It appeared so different to him, that muttering inwardly, " Poor wretch! he sleeps uneasily," he withdrew his lamp and quitted the room. I did not even dare to turn on my side, or unclose my eyes till he had shut the door.
I counted

I counted his steps down stairs, and then rose instantly. I had no refuge now but in myself. All that intervened between me and death was removed. The next visitor was to have my blood.

I hastened to the door, and secured it as well as I could. This was a means of delay, if not of defence. I then extinguished myl amp, and descended through the trap-door, and scrambled on to my former station, after drawing the trap-door after me as close as I could. As I crawled over the ceiling of their room, I ventured to peep downward. They were still sitting; but, as I looked, one of them prepared to rise; then I durst look no longer. I crawled onward, till I came over the room of the sick man. I looked downward. The sight was beyond the most sanguine calculations of my hope. The sick man was quiet; the lamp still burned; and Saviolo was asleep. There was not a moment to be lost. I let my-self

self down as quietly as I could through the hole in the ceiling till I hung only on the beam with my hands. After suspending myself for some time, till I felt my own weight, and was released from all obstructions, I commended myself to St. Philip, and let go my hold, and fell with less violence than could be imagined. The sleepers did not move. I looked around me for some time, without venturing to stir, to be assured of the reality of my descent, with so little noise or danger, and that the tranquillity about me was not counterfeited. All was still. I rose; and creeping with that caution, which none but such a situation can give or imagine, I began to explore the room. There was but one window; the lamp burned in the hearth, before which Saviolo was sleeping in a chair. Scarcely touching the ground, I proceeded to pass him. When I was opposite him I involuntarily stopped, and, with an impulse

I could

I could not resist, looked full at him. His eyes were wide open, and intently fixed on me. My terror did not conquer my reason. After a moment passed in the stupor of fear, I perceived he made no use of his observation; he neither spoke, nor offered to stop me. I ventured to look at him more closely, and I perceived, from the fixed and filmy glare of his eye, that he was still asleep. A moment's thought confirmed my confidence. I had often heard of people who slept thus, particularly those whose minds are gloomy or perturbed. I now withdrew myself quietly, and placed the lamp at some distance, lest its light should act too strongly on the exposed and dilated organs of sight. I glided across the room to the window. It was a large casement that appeared, from its structure, to be moveable; but with most distressful apprehension I perceived, that to reach it I must step across the pallet

to

of the sick man, nay, actually step on it. After what had happened, however, without disturbance or discovery, I had some hopes that a light step would be unfelt and unheard. I rose therefore on one foot, and, reaching across the bed, laid hold of the frame of the casement. A terrible blast that rushed against it that moment, almost made me fear it would be shattered in my hold. I released it for a moment, and looked round me with fear. I heard only the heavy breathing of Saviolo, and the groaning of the old and ruinated ceiling, as the wind swept over it. I felt these delays of fear would be endless; and, resting my knee on the frame-work, and holding it with both hands, drew my foot from the bed, when the sick man, with a faint cry, like that of weak surprise, extended one arm, and caught me by the ancle. In tha scene reason, life, seemed to forsake me. I neither felt nor thought; I neither

struggled

struggled nor spoke. I grasped the frame
with a force that shook it, and fixed my
hollow and bursting eyes on the hand
that held me. For my liberty, for my
life, again, I would not live over the two
moments that elapsed, before I perceived
that he had grasped me in the agonies of
pain, involuntary, unconscious, and yet
asleep; that he had laid hold on the first
thing that was next his hand, and held it
without being sensible of the act, or of
any relief from it. But this discovery
consoled me but little. He might hold
me till escape was impossible; and to liberate myself by a struggle, would be to
wake him. With anguish therefore, (such
as none but he who counts but a moment between him and death—death, aggravated by the near chance of safety,
and the certain increase of suffering, has
ever felt,) I awaited the dissolution of
his hold as my only hope of life. In
two moments, with the same suddenness

5   of

of motion, he released me, and, with some inarticulate moans of pain, turned to the other side. The instant he released me, I felt such a gush of heat through me, that I almost relinquished my hold of the casement from weakness. In a moment, however, I collected myself, and attempted to open the casement. This was done with difficulty; yet I dared not look behind me, lest I should see Saviolo's eye upon me. It *was* done however, and I looked out on the free air and the open woods. The night was now utterly dark, and the tempest terrible. I could hear the roar of the forest below; but knew not whether I should be in the forest on springing out of the window. For deliberation there was no time; nor could it teach me any thing. Around, above, and below me, were only tumult and darkness. I threw myself out of the window. I alighted, after a rapid descent, upon something solid. This gave way under

under me, and I felt myself falling again,
with more pain, and through more obstruction than before. At length I reached the ground, sore and bruised. Every
thing about me was soft and damp, otherwise, I am convinced, I must have broken
my limbs with my double fall. At a little
distance from me, I heard the growling
of a dog, and the rattling of a chain.
I did not dare to stir, nor even to examine
whether I was hurt or not, lest he should
betray me by his barking. In a moment,
however, I began to reflect, I had gained
but little beside bruises and danger, by
throwing myself out of the window. I
could be as easily discovered and murdered in a shed, which I believed my
present abode to be. I rose therefore
as quietly as possible, but sunk down
again from utter inability to stand. I
found I had either sprained or broken the
limb on which I alighted. Another thrill
of agony ran through me at this dis-

VOL. II.   K   covery,

covery, keener than the pain that followed my vain attempt to stand; but
however reluctant or perturbed, I was
obliged to sink down upon the damp
straw that was spread over the ground.
In a few moments, the moon broke thro
the clouds, and shining with strong light,
discovered every object around me. I
was in a large shed, rudely constructed of
mud and the branches of trees, and covered but partially with straw. I could not
see whether it was connected with the
principal building; but it was open every
where; yet I could not escape. The
roof was broken through where I had
fallen, and through the fracture I had a
view of other parts of the building, rude,
and ruinous, and dimly seen, from amid
dark clouds and masses of forest shade that
were spread around them. The anguish
of my mind would, I believe, have again
risen to madness, had it not been quali-
fied by a kind of stupid satisfaction at

5

the

the idea of being so far from the persons and weapons of the murderers, and a dream of impossible hope that I might be concealed by being where it was not probable any would search or suspect, from its nearness to the house. Thus pacified by contrary expectations, of which, nevertheless, the love of life rendered both probable, and compelled to reconcile myself to remaining where I was, since, to stir was impossible, I sunk down, but still kept my eyes fixed on the building, still listened eagerly for a sound. In a short time, I beheld a light moving slowly up a part of the building just opposite. It was so dim, and proceeded with such frequent pauses of mischief-meaning delay, that at once I conceived it was the person employed to murder me who was ascending to my room. I attempted to stand upon my feet; but the impulse was unable to contend with pain and infirmity. The light

K 2   stopped,

stopped, and disappeared for some time. In a moment after, the whole building echoed with cries of astonishment, and quick voices that called and answered each other, and lights darted and disappeared at every window in my sight. All this I interpreted aright. He had gone up to my room, found it empty, and was now alarming the rest to pursue and discover me. All this I was obliged to know, with a consciousness, that if any chance should direct them to where I was concealed, I was inevitably lost. After half an hour's intolerable suspense, during which every part of the building seemed to undergo a search, I distinctly heard them going out in another direction, apparently that by which I had entered the house, and which was opposite to the part of the building where the sick man lay. This was an intimation of safety to me; but still, how precarious was that safety! Any of them might take

1　　　　the

the direction where I was. A casual impulse, a motion unaccounted for, might bring one of them to my shed. Their voices, however, became more and more distant, and their whistles and hollows echoed from the remotest parts of the wood, as the wind bore them faintly to my ear. The hope of life revived within me, when I heard that devil, Saviolo, (who, it appeared, had been awakened by the uproar in the house, and joined with the rest in searching it for me,) bending from the window just over me, exclaim, " Here, here; this way; he must have escaped through this window; it is open, search for him here." I drew in my breath, and listened in despair. There was no answer; they were out of hearing. I heard him cursing their stupidity, and muttering something, as if he was about to descend himself. I tried to rise, and found, with the surprise of unspeakable joy, that my hurt had been trivial.

trivial. I was now able to stand and to walk, but feebly. Any degree of reco-vered capacity was matter of hope to me now, though I was still unable to make any considerable exertion for my safety. I crept towards the mastiff who was chain-ed near me, and whom I had some hope of making serviceable to me. He growl-ed fiercely at me; but as I drew nearer, to my utter astonishment, he stretched out his neck, and fawned on me with the utmost gentleness. I knew him almost as soon. He was a dog I had in Naples, who followed me every where, and fed from my hand; and though it was four years since I had lost him, he knew the first tones of my voice. Surely this was the providence of St. Filippo.

I had scarce time to slip off his chain, when a door opened near me, and, thro' the chinks of the shed, I saw Saviolo ap-proaching, holding up a lanthorn, and looking round suspiciously. His drawn
dagger

dagger was in his hand. He came up to
the shed slowly, but directly, and, entering it, saw me instantly; and, with a yell
of joy, rushed towards me.   I had formed my plan; and, urging the dog with
my voice and hands, the faithful animal
flew at him like a tyger, and, fastening
in his cloak, dragged him to the ground,
and held him there, as if waiting my
orders.   Saviolo, with a cry of horror,
and the visage of a fiend in pain, begged
his life with the most abject language of
fear and agony.   I told him I had no intention to destroy him; that I wished to
fly from destruction myself; but that my
safety required me to secure him, till I
could effect my escape.   I desired him,
therefore, to throw away his dagger and
his pistols.   " You will murder me if I
do," said the villain, with a horrible mixture of fear and malignity in his face;
for he had no thoughts but of treachery
and blood.   " I will not," said I, " nor
                                        would

I, for worlds, be a wretch with such murderous hands as you. Throw away your dagger and pistols, and you are safe: keep them another moment, and that dog shall tear you to fragments." He threw them to some distance. I took them up, and armed myself with them. He watched me with a fearful eye. He could not comprehend that any one could have another in his power without making a sanguinary use of it. I then compelled him to tell me where I should find the horses of the band; what direction they had taken; and whether they had left the house. I dared not ask him the way thro' the forest, as he would probably have pointed the way of danger. I now called off the dog, who released him in a moment, when the wretch, snatching a short knife from his breast, plunged it into my preserver's throat, who instantly expired. The vehemence of his motion was such, that I scarce perceived him turning on
me.

me. I closed with him, and, after an ob-
stinate struggle, wrested the knife from
him. I could scarce forbear burying it
in his heart when I got it. I struck him
to the ground in my rage, and when he
rose I bound him, with some ropes I
found in the shed, to a post in it, and left
him, grinding, and gnashing with his teeth,
and spitting at me, with the contortions
and fury of a demoniac.

I found the horses where he told me,
and immediately mounted one of them.
From the circumstance of their not being
employed by the band, I could only gather, that they believed me to be at no
considerable distance. They were therefore probably all around me; but if I
could get beyond the immediate region
of the house, I believed I should be safe.
I went out in the direction opposite to
theirs. I need not tell you of my wandering in the wood; how often I quitted
the track, and concealed myself in the

K 5   thicket,

thicket, which I quitted the next moment,
from the fear of what had impelled me
to seek it; how I dreaded to proceed,
and was yet unable to stop; how I listened in horror to the wind. and the hollow
whistle that ran through the wood, mixed with it; how I thought the whisper
of murder was in the underwood, as it
hissed in the breeze; and how often I
recoiled as the tossing branches of the
trees flung a sudden shadow across the
way. I got out of the wood, after all
my terror, safely, about the morning
dawn; but I was no sooner freed from
one danger, than the fear of another, as
urgent, smote me.

Whither could I go, or to whom? I
had escaped miraculously from your father's hands; but I knew they could reach
me in any part of Italy. Where could I
fly, that money could not purchase my
blood? He might list a whole army a-
gainst a single wretch; and, on a long
chase

chase, I knew St. Filippo himself could
be no match for him. I believe, Signor, you will think the result of this debate was actual madness. I pursued my
way eagerly to your father's castle.
determined to go directly to him, to
present myself before him. At a distance
from him I knew there was no safety; but
I felt that this strange confidence might
ensure my safety with him.

Without further danger or adventures,
I reached the castle that very evening.
The servants, who did not appear to
know the plan about me, admitted me
without surprise. I desired immediately
to see the Count. I was conducted to
him. He was alone when I entered; and
the tapers which were but just lit, burnt
on a table near him, so that he could
scarce distinguish me till I was close to
him. He then sprang almost off his chair,
and continued to stare at me, for some
moments, with a look of vacant horror.
During that time I could not speak. I
could

could not recover myself; the temerity
of my purpose appalled me in the moment of execution.

At length, I said in low and hurried
tones, " My Lord, you are surprised to
see me here. The villain with whom I
travelled had designs upon my life. I
discovered them, and escaped. Listen
to me, my Lord. You have suspicions
of your son Annibal; no living creature
but myself can verify them. Whatever
knowledge I possess will be lost to you
if I perish; and whatever may yet be
gained from your son, can be gained
only by me; for I possess his confidence,
and he believes me attached to his person. I can serve you more effectually
by my life than by my death. I can
serve you more effectually than any of
the villains employed to murder me.
Mark me, my Lord, my death may ruin
you; my life may serve you. If I were
this moment dragged from your presence,
or stabbed before it, a thousand tongues
                                            would

would tell it.   If I were even immured in
your dungeons, and poisoned, and buried
secretly there, my disappearance would
excite suspicion, and that suspicion would
persecute you to the end of your days,
and perhaps abridge them.   Let me live,
then.   I will be faithful from fear and
from gratitude.   No villain, hired by the
price of murder, can be so faithful as
he who serves for life—for life restored
and confirmed.   While at a distance from
you I might have saved myself by flight ;
but I fled hither, because I knew my
life was important to you, as well as to
myself."

Was not this a bold effort for life ?
I knew it was my only one.   I knew, besides, (and believe me, Signor, even in
that painful moment, I felt the force of
that consideration,) that my success might
be of the most material consequence to
you; that, if I was believed, I would
be admitted to you, might talk with,

plan

plan with, perhaps escape with you; that your sufferings would certainly be mitigated, perhaps your life preserved.

The effect produced on the Count was what my hopes had anticipated. He was overpowered by the suddenness of my appearance and language; and whatever attention the hurry of the moment allowed him, was impressed by what I said, by the promises of present discovery, and of future services. He waved me, however, to leave him. I urged him still for a promise of safety. He gave it on his honour; and I departed satisfied.

As I left the room, I could not but wonder at myself; my very existence seemed a prodigy to me, what no power of body or mind on their fullest stretch could have effected for me; one effect of lucky rashness produced for me, the pacification of an enemy, powerful and inexorable;

exorable; the escape from a danger that threatened me every hour of life, and in every part of the world. I mixed among the domestics, and wondered they did not feel the same surprise at my living appearance that *I* was conscious of, without reflecting, that of my disappearance they did not know the cause, nor would perhaps ever have known it.

In a short time, I was again summoned to the Count. I found father Schemoli with him, that sight of evil omen. The looks of both were fixed on me, as if they would search my soul; a moment after, they exchanged looks, that seemed to express I was too much in their power, to be an object of dread to them. I approached, and was instructed in what they expected from me. I did not understand till then, how my offers of service were understood; it was then evident that I was to be employed as a spy; that my having been honoured with your notice and

confidence,

confidence, was to be made a means of ex-
torting from you some knowledge, which
they did not describe very clearly, but of
which they seemed determined to get possession. My attachment to you made me
shudder at this proposal, till I recollected,
that to appear to enter into their measures, was the best way to defeat their
mischief; and that to betray my indignation and horror at them, would be only
to sacrifice my powers of serving you,
to an unseasonable display of my zeal.
I listened to them therefore in silence,
and by holding down my head in a posture of of deep attention, concealed the
changes that my countenance underwent.
I never knew so much of the iniquity of
the human mind; I could not believe so
much had existed in it, as I heard mani-
fested in the directions given me for ac-
quiring the knowledge of this secret they
believe you to possess. The object was
simple; but the means were crowded with
such

such superfluous, and complicated knave-
ry, the lessons of falsehood and deceit
ran from them with such facility, that
they seemed, compared with their usual
habits of speech, like foreigners, who are
suffered to speak their own language, and
who compensate by their sudden volubi-
lity, for long restraint and silence. They
seemed to speak a new and natural language. I promised strict obedience, and
affected to profit by their documents; and
at length was dismissed with an assurance,
that my fidelity was the only security of
my life; that on the discovery of the
slightest tendency to duplicity, my punishment would be what I could neither
conceive nor avoid. I was then given
these keys, with a direction to visit you,
and all plans of escape were banished by
the thought of seeing you; but I am permitted to be often with you, to attend you
in place of the confessor—nay, to pass hours
in your apartment. These are my instruc-
tions,

tions, and it will be strange, if with such advantages both for planning and executing, we should continue long in durance.

I was as willing as Filippo could be, to let the satisfaction of the present moment supersede all provision for the future. I dwelt with a pleasure I did not try to restrain, on his simplicity, his strong attachment, his miraculous escape ; and felt that whatever might be the success of any plans we might form, my mind, spent with unnatural force, would find relief in their discussion ; or even in the circumstances that made their discussion possible.

I collected myself, however, enough to remind Filippo, that the present juncture required the most dexterous conduct ; that it was not impossible, even the present indulgence was only a stratagem of deeper mischief; that it was necessary for him at all events to amuse my father by promises of success in his employment ;

ment; otherwise, his visits would be obstructed, and probably his life sacrificed
to their disappointment, or their suspicions; that he must frame his reports so
as to bear a due relation in point of time
to the execution of any measures we
might have adopted, so as neither to compel us to precipitate or delay them, but
just gain the proper time for their adjust-
ment. Above all, I charged him, with an
earnestness he did not understand, to observe the confessor, and repeat to me
every instance of his deportment he could
remark or remember. Our conference
extended to a late hour, and I was compelled to drive him away; for something
like hope began to flutter within me, and
I determined not to sacrifice its promises
to a casual indulgence.

He was hardly gone when I wished to
recal him. The terrors of the hour that
was approaching I shrunk from meeting alone. As my visitor threatened,
every

every night his appearance was becoming more terrible, and its expectation more insupportable to me. I dreaded in what this might terminate. He had darkly spoken of the possible subversion of my reason; I felt all the horrors of this prediction. There is no evil like the expected or approaching loss of reason; there is no infliction that cannot be tolerated in imagination; but that which sweeps all power of provision, resistance, or mitigation of any other. Even in the present state of my mind, this sensation was exquisitely painful, as it in a manner verified what, of all things I was most unwilling to believe true; viz. the agency and power of that singular being. I shuddered inwardly with reluctant conviction, with that irksome feeling, that cannot dispute the evidences; yet hates to admit the conclusion. One circumstance relative to his appearance, (which might in a great measure assist me to judge

judge of his supernatural pretensions), I
believed myself abled to discover still—
the mode of his entrance into my apartment. If, as it seemed, he was a being
that could glide through walls, and overcome material obstructions, I could resist
no longer the belief of whatever he might
disclose. If he required the assistance by
which human beings pass from one part
of space to another, I rejoiced in the
hope of discovering his imposture, and
obtaining a triumph over this wonderful
being, whose superiority to humanity,
mingled envy with my astonishment.
While I was occupied by these thoughts,
a strange drowsiness crept over me; I
resisted it at first, without an apprehension of its influence being so strong;
but in a short time, I felt all power of
thought gliding from my mind.

Half angry at so unseasonable a weakness, I rose, and began to walk about the
room; it was in vain. In a short time,
from

from utter incapacity of motion, I was obliged to throw myself on the bed, where a deep sleep fell on me. It did not continue long; I awoke I know not how. Before I was fully awake, I felt my eyes were in search of Father Schemoli; they discovered him, as usual, sitting by the table on which my lamp was burning still.

Without betraying any emotion, without uttering a single word, or interjection of fear, I continued to gaze on him, expecting something more than I had yet heard, to proceed from him; the idea of his supernatural power involuntarily mixing with my own thoughts, produced a full conviction in me, that he was acquainted with the real object and topic of Filippo's conference with me; and I awaited his declaration of it with as full reliance, as if he had been present at our conversation; but he spoke without allusion to that, or any subject, but the constant one of his visits.

visits. On that, he poured forth a flood of supernatural eloquence, which I no longer attempted to resist, or to interrupt. It was terrible to hear him—the admiration that follows impassioned oratory, was lost in more strange and awful feelings; there was evidently something of the power and evidence of another world about him. Delight was checked, yet heightened by terror; and attention was often suspended by the wonder, how man could hear him and live. The mind rose to the level of the speaker, I felt myself upborne and floating on the pinions of his voice over the confines of the invisible world, over the formless, and the void. I felt it with a wild and terrible joy—a joy that made me as strange to myself, as every thing around me was; a joy that from the very giddiness of its elevation, precluded me from measuring the height to which it had raised me—the remote point at which I stood from the common feelings and habits

of

of human nature. I know this was a
strange and wayward frame; I wonder at
myself; I can hardly describe or render it
probable; but I have heard of beings,
who, with unnatural strengh of feeling,
would hang on a bare and single point of
rock to see the ocean in a storm; would
rush out to cross the forky lightnings in
their dance, or howl to the storm as it
bent the forest, or shook the mountains
to their base. I have heard of such, but
scarce believed such a feeling could exist
in a human breast, till I listened to this
strange being, and listened with pleasure
as strange. But this night, whether encouraged by my silence, or whether in the
progressive fulfilment of his commission,
he spoke more openly of its object, he
dared to tell me I was doomed to be a
murderer. A murderer did I say? Compared to the crime, which he affirmed I
would perpetrate, that of murder might
be termed a benefaction, an honour to
society.

society. In language of horrid strength, without pause, or limit, or mitigation, again and again he affirmed it; nay, described its mode and circumstance, the process of preparation my mind would undergo, the gradual induration of my heart, and scaling up of my mind and conscience with that penetrating and emphatic minuteness, that proved an intimacy with the inmost heart and spirit of man, from which I shrunk in vain—in vain tried to shelter myself by arguing from the futility of his reasoning and descriptions, to the futility of his prediction.

But though I could not work myself into incredulity, I tried to work myself into rage; I endeavoured to awe or to repel him by my fury. I demanded how he dared to impute to me such crimes? Was I not a free agent? Had I not the power of choosing one mode of action, and declining another? To the perpetration of such horrors as he predicted, no-

thing

thing but insanity could drive me, and insanity would relieve me from the burthen
of consciousness, as well as the guilt of vo-
lition. I charged him in my turn, successively, with being an impostor, a maniac, and lastly, an evil spirit, embodied
and empowered to work my eternal woe,
and confirm his own by his infernal triumph.   I abjured all further commerce
with him ; I heaped him with reproach and
malediction.   I stopped my ears, I closed
my eyes against him ; only my voice
was free, and with that I cursed, and bid
him begone. When the bellowings of
my rage had ceased, and the echoes of my
prison were still, he burst into a laugh;
my blood curdled to hear him, and when
I raised my eyes to him, he was gone.

The impression he left with me was
stronger than any preceding night ; but
it was more tolerable ; the sense of oppression or persecution wakens us to rage
and to resistance. There was something so
determined

determined and tenacious in these nightly hauntings, so persevering and obtrusive in his mention of the subject I had abjured and refused to listen to, that I felt it like a challenge to my powers of resistance, and I met it with my full strength of mind. There now appeared to be an obvious and definite ground whereon we were to contend; a trial of powers common to both; his, of importunate persecution, and mine, of unremitted opposition. I pleased myself in collecting the forces of my mind, and ascertaining the ground and point of our conflict. I resolved if I must yield, not to yield without a vigorous struggle. I forgot, that by all this I only confirmed the identity of my torment; only gave it form and substance, instead of endeavouring to dissipate it as the vision of solitude, as the dream that floated on the heavy vapours of my dungeon.

L 2   They

They must repose great confidence in Filippo. They have this day permitted him to bring me materials for writing. These were indeed welcome, like others. I trifled with my indulgence for the first hour. I scrawled the paper over with strange figures; but when I examined them, I was struck with the number of instruments of death and punishment I had described among them : how strong a tincture my mind communicates to trivial and indifferent things!

Filippo tells me, they continue to importune him with questions about me, and the knowledge he had obtained from me. " I have told them," said he, " a plausible story about your former visits to the tower, and about the communications you are daily making to me. But I take care not to make any extravagant or momentous representations, lest they should expect some verification of them,

from

from your movements or sentiments, which it would be impossible to give. In the mean time, their suspicions are eluded, and time is obtained, which is all we require."

It is obvious to you, that in his narrative and conversations, I have always *translated Filippo's language.* The vulgar often express themselves with force, particularly in descriptions; but they are insufferably tedious, and abound in repetitions. Nor, since I retained the substance of his narrative, was it necessary for me to retail his idioms and vulgarisms.

He sits by me, and talks of plans for our escape—talks merely—for even his sanguine disposition cannot trace a vestige of rational hope in any he has yet proposed. The castle is too well guarded; filled with domestics all day, and every passage locked at night. He believes it to be full of subterranean passages and secret

secret recesses; but even if we reached them, we might perish in them by fatigue and hunger.

I have now begun my journal; and, within these three days, wrote the preceding account. You must henceforth only expect it in fragments.

Filippo often looks at me with unspeakable solicitude. He confesses to me, I am so altered, so reduced, and haggard in look, and abstracted in manner, that he cannot believe such a change to be produced merely by my confinement. He importunes me with an earnestness I often find it difficult to resist, but must not yield to. He would either think me a maniac, or a being leagued with, and under the power of some evil spirit. The very name of Father Schemoli (of whom he has notions justly terrible) would inspire with terror, and perhaps even his attachment might not be proof

against

against the aversion which the idea of our intercourse might produce.

"Signor," said he, "there was a man in a village where I was born, who believed himself haunted by the evil one, and that the object of the temptation was to make him commit murder. He told this in confidence to some one who pressed to know the occasion of his constant melancholy; and he told it to another, and in a short time every one shrunk away from the poor wretch, as if he had been a real murderer. No one would meet him alone; no one would pass near his house at night; no one would sit near him; for whether they believed him really beset, as he described, or only visionary, it inspired them with a dread and a suspicion, that made every one shun him as some evil thing. After lingering some time in utter solitude, he at length disappeared, and

and strange things were whispered about his departure.

" Some months after that, however, we heard of an extraordinary murder committed at Venice. The murderer had had no enmity to the person he killed, nor even any knowledge of him. He had inquired his situation in life; and, on learning that he had no relations who would suffer by his loss; that his character was good; and he had come that moment from receiving absolution—he exclaimed, ' That is my man,' and immediately stabbed him. He then surrendered himself to justice; said he was perfectly sensible of his crime, and desired no mercy; but had taken care that his offence should be attended with as little injury as possible, either to society, or to the sufferer.

" When we inquired the name of this extraordinary man, we learned he was the very

very individual who had left our village.
Now Signor, you must forgive me ; but no
human being ever looked as that man' did
but you. You have exactly his dark, fixed
eye, and that peculiar contraction of the
forehead, and hollowness of the cheek.
I saw him the morning before he disappeared. He was tracing some lines in a
bed of withered leaves, over which he
bent ; and, as you hung over your paper
just now, drawing those melancholy lines,
you were the picture of him. Do, Signor,
tell me, for the love of grace, what it is
thus presses on your mind. It is something
else than your confinement, I know. When
I speak of that you are quite easy and
resigned, and listen to all I can say with
composure ; but if I mention night, or
solitude, or the confessor to you, your
countenance changes, that I scarce know it."

You may conceive with what pain I
heard him. The sympathy the unfortunate subject of his story had met with,

L 5   taught

taught me what I was to expect from a
similar disclosure. I silenced him as soon
as I could ; but, as he left the room, he
murmured something about father Schemoli. Is my persecution written on my
forehead ? Can the very menials read that
I am tempted to murder ? If so, 'twere
almost better committed ; there would be
less suspicion, and less of " fear which
hath torment."

His visits are unremitting, and his persecutions increasing in force and frequency. He now names the object of it
directly, proposes means, and, withou
remitting his mysterious character and
language, discusses them with a familiarity
that chills my blood.

What shall I do ? I am strongly beset ;
I am sore pressed and straitened. Would
to heaven I could make my escape from
this durance. Even if he has the power
of pursuing me, may not that power be
diminished or increased by the circumstances

stances of time or place ? He hinted that
himself.   He talked of his power being
limited to a certain hour and spot.   If
I could but fly from him ; if I was to
hear the terrible voice no more ; to lay
my harrassed head where *one* night would
be unbroken by these visits of horror.
He has no longer the power of feeding
curiosity, or of fascinating imagination.
My only sensation at his presence is un-
mixed aversion, mortal repugnance and
fear.   It is not to be wondered at.   No
human mind can longer endure the pitch
mine has been strained to lately.   It must
relieve itself by insanity, or by a deep
and motionless stagnation of its powers.
The objects that have occupied me are not
the natural topics of human meditation ;
the mind can only bear to see them re-
motely, and partially, and transiently ; it
cannot confer with, and be habitually conversant with them, without changing its
properties, nay, its very nature.   The dis-

L   tant

tant cloud, whose skirts are indented with lightnings, and whose departing thunders roll their last burden on the winds, we can bear to follow with the eye, and feel our hearts quelled and elated with the fluctuations of grateful horror; but who could bear to live for ever in the rage and darkness of the tempest; to sport with the lightnings that quivered around him, and grasp at the bolt that rushed to blast him. My mind is utterly changed. I shrink from these things, and would fly back to life for shelter, if I could. I feel a kind of indignation at the perversion of my powers. Why should I be shut up in this house of horrors, to deal with spirits and damned things, and the secrets of the infernal world, while there are so many paths open to honour and pleasure, the varieties of human intercourse, and the enjoyment of life? I struggle to regain the point I have quitted; to feel my-self

self a man, and amongst men again; to
" confer with flesh and blood."

What are these bodings that oppress
me? Must I never return to life, never
be myself again? 'Tis but the involuntary
recollection of his words. I cannot dismiss, but I will not believe them. He tells
me, my first stirrings of curiosity, my
conferences with Michelo, my visits to
the tower and to the tomb, were a series
of acts which I could neither produce
nor forbear, which belonged to that great
chain of agency that bound me to him,
and him to me indissolubly—a chain
which I could neither forge nor break;
of which one link could neither be added nor detached by the power of all
nature. I will not believe this ; yet how
consistent is it with the process of my
feelings! how suddenly did I rush into
the pursuit, without any preparation of
mind, or of circumstance !   This was not
natural nor right; nor did I feel any surprise

prise at the greatness or suddenness of the transition from quietness and indifferency, · to the rage of sudden zeal, the impetuosity of resistless activity. This was not natural either. How do I heap up arguments to my own confusion ! How do I set out resolved to disbelieve an assurance, yet employ myself only in collecting proofs of it, and observing the repugnance I pretended to confirm ! Curse on the impulse, whether fated or voluntary, that first led me to the pursuit. What motive summoned me to it ? My conscience was clear and my rest quiet. Who made me an inquisitor of the secrets of blood, a searcher of the souls of men? What had I to do with it ? No voice called on me ; no hand beckoned to me; I was warned neither by dream nor vision ; my officiousness was wilful ; my obstinacy was incorrigible. What if I had heard these dark reports, had I a right to investigate them ? If a pit opens at

my

my feet, am I to plunge into it to examine
the cause? Could I not have walked over
the unsafe and suspected ground I was
led to, with the quiet fear, the shrinking caution with which a child passes over
the place of graves? Whatever secrets
may be around and beneath him he cares
not, so he may get safely through them.
He treads lightly, lest he should break
their tremendous sleep; he will scarce
breathe, least it should sound like a call
to them; he will scarce name the divine
name in the stiled prayer of fear, lest
it should have some unknown power in
that place of awe.

Oh that I had thus glided past this
pursuit! The fatal affectation of supernatural dignity; the conscious pride of the
agent of Heaven; the chosen instrument
of Him, (to be the dust of whose feet is
above all earthly power); this, this undid
me. It is a sensation rarely felt; the
modes of life seldom admit it; the heart

f

of man has scarce room for it.; but it is of surpassing and magnificent power. Would I could exchange it for the most timid humility, for the most servile ignorance, for the most impotent superstition that ever depressed the human breast. Such are safe from danger by the excess of fear, instead of being, as I am, mated and leagued with these horrors, blended in unhallowed intimacy with what it is frightful and unlawful for human nature to know. Would I were the gossip-crone, who, shivering over her single faggot, crosses herself to hear such things named, and trembles to see her dim and single light burn blue, while the tale goes round; or the child that seems to sleep at her feet, lest he should be sent to rest before it is finished, and imagination fill it up too well when he is alone, and in darkness—would I were one of those. Their fear, their ignorance is their security. Heaven never selects such instruments for

its

its higher purposes.   They may eat their
humble bread, and drink their water in
peace, while the servant of heaven, who
tarries on his way, is torn by a lion.
They may remain, like their own rustic
hills, covered with useful verdure, and
content with quiet beauty, while those,
whose deep roots extend to the world
beneath, whose feet have supplanted the
foundations of the earth, are impregnated
with fire and destruction, blast all the
region around them, and are rent and
ruined by their own explosion.   Why
did I assume this fatal responsibility?
What were the crimes of others to me?
The whole world might have laboured
with some prodigious discovery; yet I
might have passed my life in it, unsoli-
citous and unconscious of it.   These
things do not come in quest of us; 'tis
our fatal curiosity that removes the natural barrier of separation.   The earth on
which I trod might have quaked and
groaned

groaned with untold secrets; every breeze might have brought to my ears the cry of an unappeased spirit; the tapers that burned before me might have been tipt with blue; the very dogs might have crouched and shivered with a consciousness of invisible presence; I might have set every step upon an untimely grave, and slept every night in a chamber stained with secret blood, so I had known nothing of it, my sleep would have been quiet, and my mind undisturbed. I would have passed through life as calmly as the sea-boy sleeping in the shrouds, while the spirits of the storm are mustering and hurtling in the blast that lulls him to rest. A search into the secrets of crimes we have not been privy to, is like an acquired faculty of seeing spectres. Before its attainment, all was safety and innocence; after, solitude becomes uneasy, and darkness terrible. The **consciousness of guilt** is as bad as the commission.

commission. He who obtains the knowledge of another's crimes, shares their burthen and their torment; he is either summoned to expiate them, and forced from the quietness of life, and the natural current of human action, to a line of daring and desperate adventure, which he pursues without sympathy, and without reward; (for the feelings, attached to that state, are too uncommon for participation, and its termination is not his own exaltation, but the punishment of others) or he sinks into the partaker of another's crimes, by forbearing to disclose them. He suffers more than the real agent; his painful consciousness is the same, his dread of detection the same, and his sense of the injuries of the sufferer, and the consequences of discovery are greater; for he fears to be found wicked, only from the love of wickedness, without the motives of enmity, or the temptations of reward.   To a

personal

personal action, if brave and daring, nay, if egregiously flagitious, the wonder of mankind involuntarily attaches some degree of honour; but the gratuitous villain, who was not guilty, not because he *dared*, but because he *feared*, is deservedly heaped with the contempt and maledictions of all. To such an alternative has my fatal curiosity reduced me ; an alternative, aggravated by circumstances of peculiar horror to me. Whatever be the object disclosed to you, Ippolito, can it be so terrible as that which my hints have told ? Do you understand me ? Involuntarily I hope not ; yet you should understand me, to estimate the struggles of my mind aright. A month past, I would have believed my heart contaminated by the casual visitation of that thought which is now its constant inmate. I dread lest it should lose its salutary horror of which this habitual contemplation must divest it. And what shall I do ? What

What security shall I have then? A villain in theory, is half a villain in action. Habit is as strong a security for our virtues as principle ; to a mind beset as mine, perhaps stronger : 'tis impossible for the purest mind to dwell long on villanous and murderous thoughts, even as indifferent and neutral, without feeling their pollution not only infecting its frame, but partially influencing the actions ; impulses of malignity, of mischief, of revenge, will be felt unchecked, and unrepented. I feel it myself—I feel the fiend growing strong within me. What, oh what will become of me, Ippolito ? I can hardly breathe, I can scarce hold my pen ; these are the last lines it shall ever trace ; you will never behold them, they will be buried with their writer. I shall not outlive this night. Filippo is weeping beside me—I cannot describe circumstances ; the shock of death is too forcible for my mind. I know not what to think,

think, or almost where I am; but I feel what I must shortly be.

About an hour ago, Filippo rushed in with horror in his face. He fell at my feet, and gasping and speechless looked up in my face. When he could speak, it was only in broken tones and howlings of despair, to tell me I was " to die." " I had but a few hours to live." I listened with the incredulity of amazement. The mind cannot readily admit the thought of death —of death so near and so sudden. At length, his agony excited my fear. I then spoke unheeded in my turn, for he was unable to hear, or almost to speak. With difficulty and many interruptions, at last, he told me, " He had of late, observed my father and his confessor often engaged in conferences from which *he* was excluded; that his suspicions were awakened, as hitherto he had been a principal agent in their consultations; that this evening, owing to my father's abstraction,

tion, he had succeeded in concealing himself in a part of the room, as the confessor
entered.   It was a dangerous experiment,
but he felt such a peculiar, boding sensation on his entrance, that he could not resist making it.

"They conversed in whispers at first,"
said he "and with such long intervals,
that I could collect nothing ; at length,
the Count, as if many things had been
proposed, and none had satisfied him,
throwing himself back in his chair, said
aloud, "I know not how to dispose of
this incumbrance."   "An incumbrance,"
said the monk, " is only another name for
something we want resolution to be freed
from."   "I do not want resolution," said
the Count, "but I know not what means
to employ."   "He who does not want resolution, could not hesitate to employ *any*
means," observed the confessor.   "But
my own son, father," said the Count.
"His crime is therefore aggravated by disobedience,"

obedience," said the monk. "But in my own castle," said the Count. "You can therefore be more secret and secure," replied the monk. "But another—another—another"—said the Count in a piteous tone, and as if unable to force himself to finish the sentence—"Another is rendered necessary by those that have preceded; the first movement is voluntary, all that follow are consequential and inevitable," urged the tempter. "By my soul," said the Count, apparently answering his own thoughts, "I am neither safe nor secret within these walls, witness"—he stopped suddenly. "Our success depends as much on the choice, as on the use of means," said the monk. "When we employ violent passions as our agents, their explosion will often extend to ourselves; but there are still and unsuspected means." "Do you know of such means, holy father," interrupted the Count. "I do," said the monk. "And are you acquainted with

with one who would apply them," asked
your father, in a lower tone. " I am," said
the confessor. There was then a long silence; the children of satan appeared to
understand each other without speech. I
could have rushed out, and pierced their
false hearts with my own hand.

The Count seemed to force himself to
break the silence, and said in a hurried
manner, " Good father, it is needless to
observe to you, that this must be done
so, so—as neither to excite suspicion nor
disturbance. You have of course witnessed
many proofs of the efficacy and expedition
of what you propose." " I heard many
proofs," said the monk, evasively. " But,"
continued your father with increased eagerness of tone and gesture, though almost whispering, " they are such as
leave you in no doubt of its certainty "
" Would you have me doubt my senses ?"
said the monk, impatiently. " Pardon
me, father," said the Count, " you did

not mention any thing of seeing a proof
of its operation." "But is not hearing
one of the senses," said the confessor, re-
collecting himself. It struck me, Signor.
when I heard them conferring thus, that
leagued as they both were in wickedness,
each of them felt a wish to be possessed of
some knowledge of the other's previous iniquity, that might supply an influence
over him at some future period. To such
a motive I attributed your father's anxiety to draw an ocular confession of the
power of these means (which I suppose
to be poison) from the monk; for though
the guilt of either could scarce be deve-
loped without implicating that of the other,
yet the fears of wickedness are perpetu-
ally impelli g to provisional caution, and
security for the subordination of its as-
sociates. The monk rose to depart, "You
mu t no go in anger, father," said the
Count. " ardon me, ' mean to set about
it in cold *blood*,' said the monk, in a peculiar

culiar accent. "Go then, but send my attendants to me quickly—quickly, father, and throw open all the doors as you go, that I may hear the sound of your steps till I see *them* approaching. I cannot be alone a moment—I am a miserable man!" This last direction was fortunate for me, for I glided out from behind the hangings through the open door, and reached your apartment in a moment.

Having told his tale, he again fell at my feet, and wept. It had been more merciful to have let me die without this intelligence; for die I must. The poison will probably be conveyed in food, undistinguished by any peculiar taste; its operation will probably be like the approach of sleep; I should no thave tasted the bitterness of death; the interval of expectation and agony. He has suggested a thousand plans for escape or resistance; they are wild; it is not a single enemy, or a single

M 2   emergency

emergency I have to contend against; they have me utterly in their power, these walls must bound my struggles. If I resisted violence, they might leave me to perish by famine; this is horrible. Oh, for a single weapon to grasp in mine hour of need. There is none; death comes on like the night, shutting up all creation in darkness, hopeless and impenetrable——I have driven Filippo from me—driven him almost by force; his clamours disturbed me. I would think if I could; my mind is wonderous heavy and beclouded. I am stunned and blasted by this stroke. Death, death—What is death? Men talk of it all their lives; and the wise will talk well and smoothly of it; but who hath understood it? Who has seen it approach so near, and measured it with their full power of mental vision, described and embodied its just dimensions, and said to it, Now I know all thou canst be, or bring to me. No, it is impossible; if speech could

could be obtained in the last agonies, we might know something of it; if they could even make signs to signify the gradual obscuration of sense, and exclusion of the world and its objects; if they could intimate at what moment they let go their hold of the life of sense, and feel the dawn of their new perceptions   No, I was born to die—I have seen many that died; yet I know nothing of death.   Great and invisible being, whose name is to be uttered by silence, where am I going? all conjectures of reason, all illuminations of faith fail me now.   I could talk of these things like others, and believed my notions of them clear and authentic; but now all around me is tenfold darkness. A mountain rises between the regions of life and futurity; through it, or above it no power can obtain for living man a a glimpse or a passage; clouds are seated on its top, and its centre is mantled over by darkness.   I sit at its feet, and look

upward

upward in vain; I tremble in ignorance,
I gasp in expectancy. Whither am I
going, or to whom! How many fears of
flesh are compassing me round! How
much am I a mortal even at this solemn
hour! The dread of pain, though it is
the last I shall suffer, the throbbings of
curiosity, though I shall never be sensible
of their gratification, are I think more
strong within me, than all other feelings.
The mode and circumstance of death are
more terrible to me, than the act itself;
of that, I have no conception; but of the
possible pain and agony of the struggle,
I have too, too clear an idea—Will it first
affect my intellect, or my senses? Shall
I feel my mind obscured and declining,
or mine eyes growing dim, my pulses
fluttering, my hearing mixed and dizzy?
Oh, what will be the first symptoms, that
the pilgrim is setting out on her journey;
the first faint beat of the march, that calls
the coward to the last great conflict; and
when

when I try to " go forth, and shake myself as at other times," to scatter these
faint assaults of infirmity; to feel, to
know that no power can arrest or subdue them; that, feeble as they seem, they
are the beginnings of that wondrous process, that in a few moments will change
my body into dust, and shut out my spirit
to wander in a state new and unknown;
f which, the conception can only com-
mence with the existence?

I will wrap up my head, and think no
more—it will not be. Shall I suffer much
pain? Will my struggles be long? How do
we know but the approach of death is plea-
surable? None have returned to tell us;
perhaps our fears are all that invest it with
pain. Oh, no, no, the aspect of the dead
bears no expression of pleasure; the pointed nostril, the grim and rigid mouth, the
distended and bursting eye, the hair
bristling and erect, like resistance—these
are not the features of one who is at ease.

No,

No, death is every way horrible. I have heard, too, that the young and those in health are more susceptible of severe pain, and longer struggles, than the weak and aged. They cling to life with terrible force, and repeated blows, and hard butchering violence must rend them asunder. Yes—death is every way horrible to me! Almighty powers, can this be possible? Have two hours elapsed since I was told I must die? It appears that I have heard it but now. Oh, who can think life long who knows he must die? Who can slumber over the hours, whose lapse lead to futurity? How fast, how fast, even to the eye, the hand of this time-piece travels—even while I write it changes its place! If it were arrested for an hour, what injury would the world sustain for an hour?—It might stop for a day, for a year without mankind being sensible of it; and, if it should, its termination would only find me, as now, lapt in in terrible conjecture! To prepare for what is indefinite, no time would be sufficient—all around me is wondrous, as if I had but just begun to live. This little instrument, can its minute workings lead to an effect so stupendous? Can the progress of that small line precipitate an immortal spirit into futurity? I have heard of the current of the stream before; but now my eyes see it, I have felt its force, and measured its rapidity; nothing may turn it back or withstand it. A few moments more, and—was that a step? It was a step; I hear it—they come! I must die! Gracious heaven, is there no help, no respite? Oh, for the swords that are playing by the sides of the idlers of the world this moment! Oh, that I were in a forest, and could rend the branches from the trees for my defence! Can I not tear out the beams or stones of these giant-walls to cast at them? By heaven, I will not hold out my throat to them. I

M 5

will

will fight for life, and that terribly. I will make a weapon of something; or they shall feel that the naked hand of despair can scatter firebrands, and arrows, and death."

Here the manuscript ended, and Cyprian, when he had finished it, looked with wonder at Annibal to behold him yet alive. Its termination had indicated death, aggravated by hopeless resistance. Annibal pursued the narrative verbally.

I wrote those last lines with many intervals of fear and of meditation. It was long after midnight, that I heard a step approaching. After a struggle, which neither my power nor voice can describe, I started up, and stood fixed opposite the entrance; my only instrument was a massive chair, which in my frantic strength I wielded like a wand. I am convinced I would have crushed to death, the being against whom I lifted it. The step came nearer. I set my teeth close, and rose

on my feet, and my sinews felt like iron
The door was unlocked, and before I
could raise my arm, Filippo rushed in.
There was no time for inquiry or explanation; he was gasping for breath, and only
beckoned me to follow; that motion
calmed me in a moment. I seemed to
understand intuitively it was a sign of
safety and freedom.

I caught up the lamp, and followed
him. On quitting the room, I was about
to turn down the passage, but he graspt
my arm, and though still unable to utter
more than interjections, gave me to understand we must take another direction.
He passed before with quick, but steady
steps. I held the lamp low, lest our
speed should extinguish it; for the passage into which we had entered, appeared
longer and loftier than the other, and the
air, though damp and still, was strong in
its current. I was amazed at the apparent
incaution of Filippo's movements; for

he

he walked as he would at noon day; but
at the end of the passage, he suddenly stopped, and taking the lamp from me and
shrouding it with his cloak, stepped forward with breathless and shivering slowness, motioning me to do likewise. I did
so; but in the room we entered, I could
discover no reason for this sudden caution; it was spacious and desolate, and
as the half veiled light threw a partial and
thwarting gleam upon it, I could only
see masses of dusky obscurity. As we
drew near the opposite door, Filippo con-
tracted his steps with increasing fear, and
I now threw round me a glance of serious
inquiry. I discovered then with difficulty, a dark heap in the corner we were approaching; it was too dim and shapeless
to suggest any cause for the caution he
betrayed; yet-his eye as he drew nearer
it, rolled in horror, and his steps almost
falter e. I leant over him to view it
more closely, and in that moment I
thought

thought I beheld it move. Filippo murmured something between a groan and an exclamation of affright, and darted forward so quickly, that I found myself alone and in darkness, almost before I perceived he was gone. I followed him, but know not why I shuddered as I passed that strange dark heap. Just as I reached the door, it moved again ; I heard it distinctly rustle in the darkness. I sprung past it with the quickness of real fear. My perceptions were entirely changed ; but a moment past, and I dreaded nothing but the terrible monk and his poison ; but the sudden and causeless appearance of Filippo, the dim light that led me, this still and fantastic gliding through passages of unbreathing desolation, and the last strange object I had beheld, combined with the confusion and horror of my recent feelings, had rendered me as susceptible of momentary and local impressions, as if I had no other, no personal concern

concern ; as if I was not flying for life—
for life hardly held and hourly threatened. Still, under the influence of what
I imagined I beheld. I eagerly questioned
Filippo, whom I had now overtaken, and
who had renewed his swiftness. "That
chamber," said he, incoherently "ask
not—hurry on; your life depends on a
moment—he is quiet."

I obeyed him in silence ; we crossed other
chambers and wound through other passages I had never beheld before, or knew this
vast fabric contained ; but as I passed, I
could not help glancing a thought of horror
upon the numberless victims of the guilt
or cruelty of its former possessors, so far
from the knowledge or sympathy of their
fellow creatures, though under the same
roof, and within the same walls; that it
was perhaps unknown to their nearest re-
latives where they existed, or what they
suffered ; that the groans they uttered,
might form a part of the respiration of a
friend

4

friend or a brother, without conveying
to them, that the lips from which they
issued were so near. We now appeared
to have traversed that wing of the castle. We had entered a large hall whose
doors had a loftier moulding than any
we had passed, and which seemed from
the bolder and simpler character of its
structure, to be near the extremity of the
building, and probably to communicate
with the court of the castle.

Here Filippo paused, and uncovering
the lamp, began eagerly to examine the
doors : at several he shook his head with
the impatience of disappointment. I
followed him mechanically ; at length,
he darted towards one, that lay deep in
the shade, and vehemently applied to it
a key, which he snatched from his bosom.
By the delay, and the imperfect sound
that followed the application, I knew its
success too well ; the sound struck upon
my heart. Filippo the next moment
withdrew

withdrew the key, and disappeared down
a dark arch, which I had not seen before,
bearing the lamp with him. I remained
in utter darkness. My mind had been
weakened by trials and sufferings both
real and fantastic. The moment he was
gone I became the victim of visionary
terror. I recollected his sudden appearance, almost impossible to be effected by
human means; his strange swiftness and
silence, his look so wild and unnatural,
his few words. so ominous, his disappearance without noise or preparation; I recollected the strange warnings given
to those who were near their dissolution,
by those who had already undergone it;
I recollected how probable it was Filippo had exposed himself to danger, even
mortal, by his zeal for me; I recollected
with horror, the mysterious heap in that
dark chamber, at which he had seemed to
pause with portentous shudderings; its
dimensions and shape were like those
of

of a corse. I felt it impossible to nurse
these horrible imaginings long ; they were
invading my last half-rallied remains of
reason ; there was a more probable cause
for his desertion; but my habitual reliance on him long resisted that.

I looked around me, to see if any hope
remained from my own exertions; the
clouds of a heavy night, appearing at
the high and pillared windows, excluded
every gleam of light, and prevented me
from conjecturing, even in what part of
the building I was.

As I gazed around, a faint noise came
to my ear. I listened, it was the mixt
sound of a voice that whispered, and steps
that hesitated. I stood motionless be-
twixt hope and fear. " Hush," said a
voice at some distance ; willing to believe
it Filippo's, I answered in the the same accent. " Is it you," said the voice more
articulately, " I have been in search of
you." As the last words were uttered,
        I perceived

I perceived the voice to be that of my father!

I neither exclaimed nor moved, I was stiffened and speechless; to have felt a stiletto in my breast, had been almost a relief to me at that moment. The steps drew nearer; the blood which appeared to have deserted my frame, now rushed back with a sudden and feverous glow; strange and accursed thoughts were with me. We were in the dark; I remembered the visitation of the spectre monk; I remembered words never heard by man, but me—never to be heard. My eyes grew dim; a blaze of purple light quivered through the hall, yet I could see nothing by its glare. My limbs tottered under me; but the influence whose terror would have betrayed me, abated. The steps were evidently receding; and as they retired, I thought I heard curses hissing along the walls. I remained gasping for breath. The air of the hall grew cool again, and though the darkness was not diminished, its shades, I thought, were less dense and oppressive.

On a sudden, I felt myself grasped with violence. I struggled to free myself. I heard the voice of Filippo. I believed him treacherous, and all the mystery was solved. " Wretch," said I, grasping him in my turn, "you have betrayed me." " What madness is this?" he whispered in low but vehement tones, " for the holy Virgin's sake, follow me ; but speak not." " You lead me to death," said I ; yet I followed him without resistance.

I now found we were in complete darkness. After descending a few steps, we stopped. I was urgent in my whispered inquiries ; but obtained no answer. I became impatient of fear and expectation, and almost remonstrated aloud, when I heard a noise near me, like the opening of a door ; and, in the next moment,

Filippo

Filippo led me into the court of the castle.

It was the air, the free, open air, the blessed air of heaven. I breathed it in freedom; it was no dream of transitory freedom. I opened my bosom to it; I extended my arms, as if it were tangible and material. I was delirious with sudden and incontrolable joy.

When my senses returned, I found we were in a ruinous enclosure, surrounded by buildings I had not remembered to have seen before; but which, from their appearance, I judged to belong to the servants of the castle. In one or two of the turrets, that were grotesquely perched here and there on the blank and giant walls, I still saw lights twinkling. Filippo, stooping to the ground, raised up the lamp, which he had dexterously hid behind the fragment of a fallen battlement; and we crossed the court in silence, with steps often obstructed by the ruins that

were

were scattered over it. We glided thro'
other arches, whose darkness was partially
broken by our half-hid light ; and at
length reached a low door, which opened
on the rampart. Here still greater caution was necessary. This has been long
in a ruinous state; our steps were confined to a narrow ledge of rocky path,
and our only hold of support was the
projections and weedy tufts of the dismantled wall.

At length the glare of the lamp flashed upward on a rude and ruined arch,
which appeared once to have been connected with the remains of a draw-
bridge. We crept under it, and, clinging to its rugged and indented sides,
which the bickering gleams of the lamp
carved into fantastic shapings, descended to the moat, which the fragments that
had fallen from above, had almost filled
up beneath the arch. We crossed it ;
descended

descended the mound; and reached the wood in safety.

I now heaped thanks, inquiries, and applauses, in the same breath, on Filippo, who was too busy crossing himself and praying to his patron to heed me.

At length, as we lay behind a tuft of chesnut trees, for he would not permit us as yet to proceed, I procured from him the intelligence of the means.

" When you drove me from you, Signor," said he, " and seemed determined to die, I left you with a resolution to do something desperate. I was resolved you should not perish unaided. This was necessary for my own safety, as well as yours. I could not imagine they would spare *me*, who was permitted to live, only as a means to betray you, when it was no longer necessary to employ that means. I went back to the

Count's

Count's apartment ; I found him preparing to quit it, in order to join the family in the hall, where they usually sup.

" I could not observe any change either in his looks or his language. He suffered my attendance, as usual, without notice. I followed to the hall, and mixed with the other domestics. On this night I observed the confessor had joined the family. Through the air of deep abstraction he always wears, it was impossible to discover his thoughts, or whether the frame of his mind was habitual or peculiar.

" As he approached, where the family were not yet seated, I observed him bring forward, as usual, a small vial of lemon juice, which he mixes with water, and which constitutes his only beverage, and place it beside his cover. I was near him. The motion of his arm shewed me another small vial in his vest

vest. I grew deadly sick as I beheld it. I had no doubt I saw the instrument of your death. As he turned round he displaced his girdle and rosary. He observed it and began to adjust them. In order to do so, he found it necessary to place the other vial on the table, to which his back was turned. This was the critical moment. The vial of lemon-juice was on the right; the other on the left. With the quickness and silence of thought I changed their places. He turned round; put up the first vial into his vest; and emptied the latter into a glass of water that stood beside his cover.

" When I had done this, I reflected that I had only gained time; that it must be soon discovered that the monk was poisoned, and that you had only swallowed lemon-juice. If, therefore, I could not devise some means of escape in the interval which I had gained, I felt it

was

was unavailing, except so far as to punish
an intentional murderer; but the success
and promptitude of my first movement
suggested a flattering omen, which I accepted, not unreadily.

" In the mean time the family assembled.   The Count and his confessor
whispered often. With unspeakable delight I saw the latter employ the vase
that stood beside him.   Towards the conclusion of the meal, the Count desiring
the chamberlain to be summoned, spoke
some words to him in a low voice, on
which the latter detached a rusty key
from his girdle, and gave it to the confessor, who lodged it in his vest. I understood every motion.   It seemed, that
for some reason, probably that of concealing the corse, the monk had found
it necessary to procure the key from the
chamberlain. I had glanced on the size
and shape of the key, and though it was

nothing remarkable, I guessed from the former, and from the apparent intention with which it was procured, that it belonged to some external door of the castle, to which, if we could procure access, our safety was assured. I therefore resolved to watch the monk silently. I concluded, from the conversation that I repeated to you, that the poison was of a rapid and quiet operation. I doubted not that the monk would soon feel its effects, and if I could be near him at the moment, and secure the keys, all was well.

" The family now separated. The monk retired. I watched him at a cautious distance, and saw him enter his apartment—to that terrible apartment, even at noon-day, I know not what force could have compelled me ; but now, at night, alone, and in darkness, save the dim and solitary lamp that burned in the

passage'

passage, I knelt at the door, and watched every sound within. It was now past midnight, when I heard him advancing abruptly to the door, as if a sudden thought had smote him. I retired with speed. He came out. I saw him first bend forward from the door; and, holding his lamp high, look far into the passage. Not a sound breathed along it. He advanced; and I thought I heard him sigh. He then went rapidly forward, so rapidly, that I was alone in the passage. His steps, however, were a sufficient direction for me in the deep stillness of the night. He took a direction to your apartment. Every moment now I expected to see him falter, or to hear him groan, as I glided after him on tip-toe, led by the taper that streamed distantly on the darkness.

"He proceeded, however, without hesitation, till he entered a large hall, not immediately near your apartment. It

was

was empty, and far from any inhabited part of the castle. I almost shuddered to follow him so far; but the thought of you inspired me. I paused in the passage which led to the hall. When he entered it, I heard him groan audibly. He stood a few moments in the centre of the room, and then advancing to a picture at the opposite end, held his taper close to it. He gazed long; and, as he turned away, the light fell full on his countenance. I never had beheld it before so singularly impressed. There was a look of human agony in it I never before had seen, or believed him capable of feeling. He then laid the taper down on a marble slab, and sat down, with his arms folded, beside it.

" I eyed him intently. There was neither change in his countenance, nor weakness in his motions. I grew sick with fear. He was not like a man that had swallowed poison. I doubted, and I trembled.

trembled. I recollected all I had heard of him, and some things I had seen. I condemned my own temerity in supposing him assailable by the modes of human destruction. He was evidently incapable of being injured by them; and if he were not, what must befal *me*?

" While these thoughts beset me, I will confess to you, I was only with-held from flying away, and relinquishing the whole in despair, by the thought, that if he were indeed a being not of this world, all distance of space would be ineffectual to protect me from him. While I yet debated and trembled, he rose suddenly, as if from an impulse of pain. I leaned forward, breathless with fresh hope. At that distance, I could not observe any change in his features; but, as I gazed, methought a yellower tinge mixed with the paleness of his visage. In the next moment all doubt was removed. He gasped, he shivered, and he fell.

" I now

" I now came forward with confidence.
I approached him. His eyes were glazed
and reverted. He was evidently in the
agonies of death.   I did not wait for
the mere decencies of humanity. I searched his vest. I found the keys. I hastened back to your apartment, unable to
speak or to explain. I hurried you to
the hall where the corse lay ; for I knew,
by his pausing there, it must be in the
direction of some outward passage or
door. I followed the track, partly from
conjecture, and partly from memory;
for I had traversed that part of the castle
before, and succeeded in my pursuit.

" And now, Signor, adieu to dungeons,
and poison, and monks. We are safe on
the outside of those grim walls ; and if
ever we enter them again, St. Filippo
will have a good right to disregard our
prayers for deliverance."

Such was Filippo's narrative, to which
I listened with wonder and thankfulness.
                                    I readily

I readily admitted the interposition of divine power for our safety; yet it was not without horror that I thought of the monk and his sudden and terrible fate. A degree of involuntary incredulity mixed, and still mixes itself with my feelings on that subject. He appears to me a being above the vicissitudes of humanity—a being who does not, in a mortal sense, exist, and who, therefore, cannot, in a mortal sense, perish.

The impression recei ed in the chamber of my confinement at Muralto, nothing has yet effaced. I mentioned to Filippo the voice I had heard in the hall, when he left me so abruptly. This he ascribed to fancy; and perhaps that was its only cause. His own hasty departure was owing to the sudden recollection of a door in an adjacent passage, which he wished to attempt without agitating me by probable disappointment.

I now inquired why we did not proceed;

ceed; and was told, that the man who brought ice to the castle, and who travelled at night to avoid the heat, was probably on the way which we were to take, and that it were better to avoid being seen till we reached Naples.

While we lingered in the wood, I raised my eyes, not without awe, to the castle, whose huge and massive blackness strongly charactered itself, even amid the gloom of night, and the dusky confusion of the forest and mountains. Far to the left, I saw the ruined chapel, that spot which awoke so many terrible recollections. It stood in shapeless darkness. As I gazed on it, I almost expected to see that mysterious light wandering along its walls, and gleaming on the dark tufts of wood and shrubs that invest it. As I still looked in vague expectation, a light indeed appeared, which I watched, not without emotion; but discovered it to be but a star, (the only one that twinkled

twinkled through the darkness of the night,) just appearing beneath the arch of the shattered window.

At this moment, steps passed near us, which Filippo affirmed to be those of the person we waited for; and we pursued another direction with our utmost expedition. When we had penetrated about a mile into the forest, a bell from the castle sounded in the air above; and, on turning, I saw distinctly a light, that, pale at first, as if seen through a casement, grew suddenly brighter, and poured a broad glare on the darkness of the upper wood. I believed this to be only an indication, that the person who had passed us, was admitted, by some one at the castle, from whose taper proceeded the light we had beheld; but Filippo, under more serious apprehensions of pursuit, persuaded me to hide in an intricate part of the forest, as it

N 5　　　　　　　was

was impossible we could reach Naples
before our pursuers would overtake us.
Subdued, but not convinced, I consented to conceal myself in a pit, the mouth
of which was mantled over with tangled
and briery shrubs. The event was only
a day wasted in watching, solicitude,
and famine. No step passed near us;
no sound or signal of pursuit was heard
in the forest. Towards evening we quitted our retreat, and reached Naples in
safety, which, since I perceive there is
no immediate persecution excited against
me, I shall quit with some hope of safety.

I distrust this calm, however; it is unnatural; but while it continues, I may
take advantage of its influence, to escape
from danger that is only meditated and
distant.

I shall leave Naples to-morrow.
'Do you then hold your intention of
going

going to France?" " I do; but first I
shall go to Capua. There is an uncle of
my mother's, a wealthy ecclesiastic, from
whom I expect assistance and protection,
as he has long been on terms of enmity
with my father. The present contents
of my purse would scarce convey me to
France; and it is necessary for an adven-
turer to conciliate credit by his appearance, as my peculiar circumstances exclude other recommendation. Poor Ippolito! would he were with me; but
the tumult of my own feelings and situation has not allowed me to waste
much sympathy on him. When you
write, Cyprian, tell of my unhappy circumstances; but do not mention my disappointment on discovering his absence;
for that would only aggravate his own."
" And the inquiry, begun and terminated
under circumstances so extraordinary, do
you intend to pursue it no more?" said
Cyprian, timidly. " Name it not; the

2   sound

sound is hateful and terrible to me. I abjure the idea of spectres, mysteries, and disclosures. I will fly from ruins and the gloom of antiquity, as I would from the mouth of hell, if it yawned at my feet. I will chuse the airiest structures for my abode, the lightest topics for my conversation. My companions shall be those whom levity can easily procure, and folly can amuse. The being who indulges in the dreams of vision, and courts, whether with intentions pure or foul, the communion of the forbidden world, makes himself a mark for the imposition of mankind, and the malignity of infernal ones. He is a fit and willing subject for the machinations of hell; he is given over to them by the power he has offended by seeking them. I am convinced that Satan is permitted a greater latitude of temptation, and fierceness, and frequency of assault, on such a being. The pursuit must tend to sub-

1   vert

vert his reason and deprave. his heart.
No, no; whatever I have witnessed or
been engaged in, whether it be true or
false, whether it be solemn or futile, I
here renounce it.   Let them find another
agent for their purposes of horror; let
them harden, by familiarity of temptation, and assimilate to their own demon-
natures, by frequency of communication,
the alien and apostate soul, that seeks
their secrets or their presence.   I shall
heal and sooth my distempered mind by
images of softness and beauty; by the
agencies of humanity, and the enjoyments
of nature and life."

As he spake, he drew forth the picture
he always bore in his bosom; kissed it,
and gazed on it with complacency.   Cyprian, who saw it too, with strong emotion, begged to look on it more intently; and, while he held it in his hand, his
tears streamed fast upon it.

   " Do you know that picture, then ?"
                                        said

said Annibal in amaze: How is it pos—ible you should know it?" "Ask me not; it is impossible I should tell; yes, I know it too well." "What mystery hangs over this picture? All that see it seem to know it; yet none will communicate their knowledge." "There is a mystery, and it is inscrutable." "Does the original of this picture, then, live? Do you know her? Tell me but her name: I will not ask by what means you obtained the knowledge of her, nor will I endeavour to solve the mystery of resemblance between one so long dead, and one who lives; of resemblance without possibility of connection." "The original of this picture lives, but not to you. If you love her, seek not to disturb her quiet or your own, by a search, of which the success is hopeless. She never can be your's." "This is beyond all comprehension; the influence pursues me still; my whole

whole life is to be overshadowed by mystery."

After a night of fruitless inquiry and exclamation, Annibal took leave of Cyprian ; and, accompanied by Filippo, set out for Capua.

CHAP.

CHAP. XVII.

———

These men, or are they men, or are they devils,
With whom I met at night ?—they've fasten'd on me
Fell thoughts which, though I spurn them,
Haunt me still.

MISS BAILIE'S RAYNER.

In the mean time, Ippolito, without any
object but that of flying what was inevitable, had quitted Naples with a single
attendant, and no other preparation for a
journey, than an utter indifference to its
vicissitudes or hardships.   On the first
evening, without having pursued con-
sciously,

sciously, any direction, he found himself on the banks of the Lake of Celano. It was now the close of autumn, and as the wind swept over the dim waters of the Lake, and the mists moved in fantastic wreaths over the remote and rocky shores, sometimes giving the forms of ancient structure to the cliffs and headlands, and sometimes shapings still wilder to the scattered fishermen's huts, and villas on their points; Ippolito mechanically looked around for some place to which he might retire for the night, without the hope of repose.

"These winding roads," said the attendant, " Signor, are so wild and lonely; the nearest town to which we can resort, is that of Celano, a good mile further." Ippolito, too weary of spirit to communicate with his servant, silently took the direction pointed out to him towards the town of Celano, which they reached at the close of evening.

They

They entered a wretched inn, to the many defects and inconveniences of which Ippolito was insensible, since he procured in it, the only luxury he could enjoy—a solitary chamber, against the very casement of which the waves of the lake were beating.

Here for the first time he thought on what direction he would pursue. Many were suggested, and many rejected, till Ippolito, wondering at his own fastidiousness, began to examine into its reasons, and discovered, with a sensation nearly amounting to horror, that there was spread over his mind a sense of invisible and universal persecution, which impelled his thoughts in their flight from place to place, with the same velocity that its actual influence would have chased his steps. When this conviction struck him, in utterable anguish he started from his chair, and paused for a moment between the impulse of fright, and the torpor of despair.

despair. That this influence should have
attained this absolute dominion in his mind,
and asserted that dominion in the very moment when the change of place had
flattered him with partial victory, was not
to be borne. His distraction almost applied to the stupendous frame of the Psalmist,
when he exclaimed, " Whither shall I go
from thy presence?" Of the latter clause
he felt the truth too forcibly, " If I go
down to *Hell*, thou art there also." As he
stalked about the room, some persons
in the next spoke so loudly, that he was
compelled to hear them without any effort of attention.   As he listened to the
voices, he recollected the speakers were
a party of vine-dressers and labourers, who
were returning to their native territory—
the Abruzzo, from the neighbourhood of
Naples, whither they had been allured
during the summer, by the hope of higher
wages.   They were now drinking in the
adjacent room with the landlord.   " it is

a s range

a strange business," said one, addressing the host, whose name was Borio, " nor do I like speaking of it much. I never liked to have Satan's name often in my mouth; for, *Christo benedetto*, one is so apt to think of him, when one is alone. When I have to cross the mountain near our village by night, or to watch the grapes in the hut alone, I never listen to stories such as those in the day; I always fill my mind with store of good hymns; but when there is a good number of us together, as we are now, I feel that I have as much courage as another. And so, comrades, as I was saying, they talked of nothing else all over Naples. Some said that the cavalier had devoted himself, body and soul, to Satan; and that he met him every night in some place underground, *where* no one could discover; that his servants never could trace him further than the portico of the palace; and that some who attempted to follow him, were all invested in in a glare of blue fire, and their torches were dashed out of their hands by a hoof of red-hot iron.

Others said, that it was not the young cavalier's fault, but his great-grandfather's, who had sold all his posterity to the old serpent, for a great heap of treasure he gave him; but that the purchase was not to be claimed till this generation, and that it was forfeit at the time of the last carnival; when the fiend appeared to the unfortunate youth, habited like a minstrel, and playing on a harp, whose strings were the guts of necromancers. 'Your time is come, you must away!' and that all the grove where he glided along, has been blasted and bare ever since."

"Now by what I have heard," said the host, " the fiend has more Christian bowels, an uses the Cavalier like a man of honour, for I hear he has given him permission to wander over Italy for a year and a day; and if he can get a priest to

give

give him absolution, he quits his claim on him for ever." " Ha, ha," exclaimed another, in a tone of superior wisdom, " do you, friend, take the devil to be such a fool ? no, no, rely on it, if he quits him on the simple score of witchcraft, he will stick his claws fast in him on an action of bond and compact. It is marvellous, neighbours, how simple ye are ; why it is just in the world below us as it is here ; witchcraft is like contracting a debt, but a compact is like a bond—if once Satan is able to produce it in open court against the defendant, the inquisition itself must acknowledge it ; nay," (exalting his voice with his argument), " his holiness the pope himself must sign as a competent witness."

All seemed struck by the force of this argument, and a pause of general meditation ensued, till one of the party, whose voice was that of an old man, said with an apparent diffidence of his own sentiments,

ments, " Now were I to give an opinion,
it would be that the Cavalier was neither
devoted to Satan by himself nor his an-
cestors. Ah, neighbours, did you see
what a goodly and noble youth he is to look
at, ye never could believe he dealt with
any thing evil—no, no, as long as I remember, or as long as my father could
remember, the Montorio were a great,
proud, wicked family ; they did deeds of
mischief enough among themselves, without the aid of Satan ; they were always
threatened with discoveries ; and dying
assassins, employed by them, confessed
terrible things, it was said.   Now perhaps
something of this kind is about to be
disclosed, and the Cavalier's noble heart
is breaking to think of it, and he cannot
bear to stay in Naples any longer, to witness the ruin of his family."

At this mild construction of Ippolito's
flight, every one uttered a murmur of
disapprobation. The love of the marvellous

lous is too jealous for its gratifications, and too irritable for its credit, to yield to incredulity so easily. And the former speaker, elated by his success, was anxious to preserve the popularity it had acquired him. " Old man," said he, " you are much mistaken; if the Cavalier be permitted to traverse Italy, rely upon it, 'tis for the purpose of bringing others to his master's service, in order to escape better himself; for that is the way Satan always deludes those poor wretches. He promises reward and honour to those who are zealous in his service ; and when they have seduced souls without number, and finally lost their own, then he rewards them after his own manner, which any one knows that has once seen the great picture near the shrine of St. Antonio, at the Church del Miroli, near Naples.

There, all the degrees and kinds of punishment that ever were invented are exercising upon the hosts of ruined spirits;

spirits; one would think the devils had been all in the Inquisition, they are so clever at it; you could swear you smelt brimstone, and felt a heat like that of a furnace, breathed over you from it; but only to tell you of one group in it, there are three figures——"

Here Ippolito heard the clustering sound of his hearers drawing more closely around him, his misery became suddenly intolerable, and he groaned aloud. Terrified at the sound, they all desisted to speak or to listen, and without venturing to comment on the cause of the disturbance, the last speaker said in a voice of fear, " I believe we had better cease to speak on this subject, unless some ecclesiastic was in the house with us." " There is a convent of Dominicans near these walls," said the host, who was anxious for the conclusion. " How near," said the other, whose desire of exciting wonder was contending with fear. " You may hear the ves-

per bell from this," said the host, evasively
" But how near, friend Borio, tell me
precisely how near?" " 'Tis a long
mile," said the host, reluctantly. The
speaker declined to finish his story on
this security. " The devil's in it," said
the host in his disappointment, " if the
toll of that bell, and the chaunt of the
monks at vespers, are not sufficient to
frighten the devil, if he were in this
room."

His companions reproved him for pro-
faneness, and the host, to retrieve the
credit of his sanctimony, said, " Whatever
be the cavalier's intentions in this journey,
I would not be the host to receive him
for the wealth of the Vatican. I warrant,
the smell of sulphur never would quit the
room he lay in ; and if I received a single
coin from him, I should expect it to turn
into a burning coal in my hand." " You
had better be on your guard, friend Borio," said another, in the mere wanton-
ness

ness of wisdom, "I hear he was seen to take this direction." " By the holy saints, there came a cavalier to my house this evening."

There was now a general commotion of fear, followed by a whispering consultation. Ippolito's first impulse was to quit the inn, but he recollected that would only confirm their suspicions, and perhaps make his further progress difficult. Another expedient occurred, but his proud heart long struggled with the necessity of deceit. At this moment he heard his servant passing under the window; he called him, and without specifying his reasons, desired that he would on no account, mention his name or rank in the house, nor during any future part of the journey, which he must be in readiness to pursue as soon as possible. The man, proud of a charge that resembled an approach to confidence, readily promised to observe it; and that his fidelity might

not

not want the merit of resisted temptation, immediately repaired to the room
where the vine-dressers were seated with
the host.

They had just resolved to send for him,
in order to discover whether his master
was the Count Montorio, and now received
him with the overcharged welcome, that
suspicion gives to hide her own purposes.
" Pray friend," said the host, after they
had drank some time, " what is the cavalier, your master's name?" "His name—
his name"—said the man, who in the de-
termination to conceal the real, had forgot to provide himself with a fictitious
one. " Aye, his name," continued the
host, " I suppose you have lived with him
but a short time?" " I have lived with
the Signor several years," said the man,
in his eagerness to prove he was not un-
prepared for every question, and to retrieve the ground his embarrassment had
lost. " You have lived with him several

ral years, and yet do not know his name; that is strange indeed, stranger than any thing I have yet heard?" "Why what have you heard of the Signor?" said the man, glad to become the inquisitor in his turn. "I have heard he sometimes walks at night," said the other, significantly. "To be sure he does, and so do all the cavaliers in Naples," said the man triumphantly. "Aye; but do you know where he goes?" said the host, lowering his voice. "No; nor does any one else," said the man, betraying a material part of his intelligence, in his solicitude to prove that no one was wiser than himself. "You never attend him on those occasions?" pursued the host. "Santa Maria, no," said the man shuddering. "What would you take, and accompany him in one of his nightly wanderings?" said the host, pursuing his victory. "Not the wealth of Loretto," said the man, who recollected the terrible stories he

had

had heard of his master at Naples, and
who had answered his own thoughts, rather than the questions addressed to him.
" Then it is all true," said the old man.
". Holy saints ! what a pity !" " What is a
pity ?" said the lackey, roused from his
abstraction by the exclamation. " What
you have just confessed about your master !" said the host. " I confess ?" said the
man ; " I would not confess if I was torn
with pincers; I confessed nothing." "Nay;
it was not much either," said one of
the men, a shrewd fellow; you only
acknowledged your master was one of
the Montorio family." " I will be torn
in ten thousand pieces first," said the man,
with increased vehemence ; " you are a
horrid and atrocious villain to say I acknowledged it : I never did, and never
will." " Come, come," said his wily op-
ponent; " you need not be in a fury;
perhaps I mistook you; but you must
confess, that if he is not one of the family

mily he is remarkably like them." "To be sure," said the man, again sacrificing his cause to his power of answering a partial objection, " to be sure ; there is a strong *family*-likeness among them all."

Here a general cry of triumph arose, which drowned even the angry exclamations of the servant; and Ippolito, distracted by the consequences of his folly, and the superstition of the rest, silently quitted the chamber, remounted his horse, and pursuing the first track he discovered, with all the speed that darkness and weariness permitted, was many miles from Celano, before the party had resolved whether to summon the Dominican brethren to their aid, or to send express to the Inquisition at Naples.

The hardships of his wanderings, rather than his journey, were lost in more painful subjects of meditation. The secret of his soul was known—that deep and

and eternal secret, that he believed buried in the bowels of the earth. It was known; and the tumult of his thoughts forbid the conjecture by what means it was known, or how its further diffusion might be prevented.

The only sensation that prevailed in his mind, was a confusion undefined, and unappeasable, that could neither trace the forms of danger, nor discover what way of flight from it was to be pursued. He trembled, though he scarce recollected what was past; he deprecated, though he knew not what was to come; he fled without an object in flight; and he increased his speed, as the motives of fear became more and more obscure to his mind. The darkness and remoteness from human resort or notice, in which the transactions at Naples had passed, had utterly excluded all suspicion that they were known, or could be known to any individual but himself,

himself. And such was the abstraction and intentness of mind with which he was engaged in them, that had such a suspicion occurred, it could not have suspended the pursuit a moment. Along with the circumstance itself, all consequences, remote or obvious, were equal strangers to his mind. When, therefore, the fact itself, with all the consequences that the suspicions of ignorance, and the rage of superstition could attach to it, rushed on his mind, unforeseen and unweighed, without a power of preparation or resistance, he staggered under the shock; it blasted and astounded him. For a moment, visionary and remote fears were banished by substantial and imminent terrors. The anguish of terror that cannot name its object, and of guilt that cannot ascertain its danger, gathered over his mind. A sensation of rare and excruciating influence; the sensation of all our measures being antici-

pated;

pated; our progress measured aud ruined; the exact reach of our boundary calculated and shadowed out; the inmost recesses of our mind violated and laid waste; and Omniscience engaged on the side of our enemies to destroy us, overcame him. No murderer, at whose feet a sudden whirlwind would dash the witness of his guilt before unsuspecting thousands; no traveller, at whose naked breast the lightnings are aiming, before a cloud has been seen to gather in the heaven, ever gazed around them, so transfixed and appalled.

His immediate impulse was flight. He urged his horse to his utmost speed; and still all speed sunk under the velocity of his thoughts. His mind was rather irritated than appeased by the tumult of motion. An imaginary line seemed to run beside him, which he could neither measure nor out-run. His speed left nothing but space behind; and his

his progress seemed nothing but an approach to mischief.

Towards morning he found himself in a part of the country, whose wildness and savageness insensibly poured quiet and confidence on his mind. It was man he dreaded; and here there was no trace of man. Rocks and waters, whose wreathed and fantastic undulations, almost resembled the clouds that hovered round them, melting their hues and shapes into their own unsubstantial forms of misty lightness, presented a range of scenery, more meet for the haunt of an aerial genius than a mortal inhabitant.

Far to the left, as the fuller tints of morning deepened and defined the shadowy characters of the mountain landscape, Ippolito descried a dim cluster of cottages, perched in the hollow of two hills, whose antic and spiry pinnacles seemed to have been cleft for its reception. The opposite features of its

wild

wild and sheltered situation presenting
a contrast that divided the feelings between awe and pleasure. To the inhabitants of a place so sequestered, Ippolito believed he might safely apply for
food and refuge.

Thither therefore he directed his course,
and found, that whatever wonder he excited, was occasioned by the appearance
of a stranger in so remote a region.
Here he reposed for some days, like a bird
that, chased and wounded, regains her
nest amongst inaccessible rocks, and
spreads her torn plumage to the winds
of freedom. He was excited to personal exertion to render existence tolerable.
Here were no artificial resources, no expedients to disguise the waste of time,
and renew the spirit of enjoyment. He
was impelled to vigorous bodily exercise,
at first to exhaust the throbbings of
inward pain, and afterwards to gratify
a newly-acquired sense of pleasure. An

1 ·   extraordinary

extraordinary vigour of frame, which the voluptuous indolence of Naples had enervated, was renewed by his mountain habits; and the change was in some time extended to his mind. He was at first soothed by the dash of the cataract, the hum of the winds in the mountain caverns, the masses of rock, bold, abrupt, and detached, that often assumed the port of some ancient Gothic structure; their marked and storied ascents and towery summits, shaping out the fantastic forms of its architecture; and the beams of the setting sun, reflected from a surface, resplendent with hues of verdure and stains of marble, aptly portraying the illuminated windows, glorious with the colours of blazonry.

By these he was at first soothed, and weaned from painful remembrance; but in a short time, he visited them with positive pleasure, not for the sake of what

what they took away, but of what they gave.

It is impossible for a mind, not conscious of great crimes, to be conversant with nature, without feeling her balmy and potent influence. The quiet magic of loneliness, the deep calm of unbreathing things, the gentle agitations of inanimate motion, poured themselves into the very recesses of his soul, and healed them.

At first, when he rushed into these solitudes, he mentally resolved to devote himself to the contemplation of his situation, and of some bold, gigantic effort by which he resolved to free himself from his thraldom; but as weariness and distraction were the only result of his deliberation, he suffered it gradually to steal from his mind, and balanced between the reproaches of indolence, and the refreshment of tranquillity.

He

He was amused in his solitude by some papers of Cyprian's, which, in the hurry of his departure from Naples, he had unintentionally taken along with him. They related to that mysterious story which he had left unfinished. Ippolito had almost forgot, that the object of it had been attached to him. The other extraordinary circumstances of the narrative, strange and remote as they were, Cyprian's enthusiasm had thrown a shade of incredulity over; and Ippolito read it as a representation of events that had never existed.

In the papers he now read, the author's mind appeared weary of the ordinary modes of language, and progress of narrative. She had selected different periods, as eras in her melancholy history, and written a few lines on each in the language of poetry.

They were monotonously melancholy. It was a passion apparently unbroken

by

by an interval of tranquillity, unillumin-
ed by a single ray of hope. She had
loved as none had ever loved, and suffered as few had suffered. Nor would
Ippolito have understood the reason or
possibility of such despair, had he not
recollected to have heard from Cyprian,
that the unfortunate female had been a
nun; that she had not seen the object that fascinated her, till she was under irrevocable engagements; and that
though her " love, stronger than death,"
had survived in these posthumous lamen-
tations, it had not the power to make
her transgress the barrier of religion, by
a disclosure of it while she lived. The
first appeared to have been written when
passion had lingered long enough to know
it was hopeless; when the first clouds of
melancholy began to gather over her feelings—it was written on a second accidental
view of the object of her affections.

Once

Once more I caught thy form—'twas but a mo-
                ment—
A moment! passion lives an age in moments.
Feeling can trace the boundless range of being,
Each maze of fancy, each abyss of thought.
Joy's rose-twined bowers, and memory's pictured cells
Recal the past, anticipate the future,
Exhaust all forms of life, and dreams of vision
Within a moment's lapse.

  So Mecca's seer, as the wild legend tells,
On the supernal wing of vision soared;
Explored the star-strewn paths of Paradise,
Drank the rich gale, that laps her pearly gates,
And swept the circle of the seven-fold heaven
Ere mortals marked a moment's flight below.
So bright, the while I caught thy passing form;
So brief, or ere I lost it.

  Chance, 'tis thy checkered influence to dispense
The hour that gives him to my visible eyes—
The hour that memory treasures; but I boast
Beyond thy sport or spleen, one solace yet,
One last, one dear, one sad—Oh, 'tis when eve
Dispreads her dew-wove veil, when no rude eye
Marks my wan cheek, slow step, and start abrupt
(Pale passion's guide, the weeds of fancy's thrall),
To wander and to muse unmarked, unknown,
To trace the thought, no breast has e're conceived,

                                        To

To heave the sigh, no ear has ever drank,
And *thine* must, never—*thine* of *all* must, never—
Oh, 'tis to wish impossibilites!

   Yet start to think them real, 'tis to trace
My sad tale in these sands, while aimless hope
Points the approaching in th' imagined hour ;
Wooes to the storied spot thy wandering eye,
And all's disclosed'.   Oh, then I fly! deface,
Disperse them quick, lest one surviving trace
Should tell the tale, I'd—give a world thou knew'st.
'Tis oft to pour the secret yet untold
In lines like these, of love's despair that hopes,
Then rend the fragments, give them to the winds,
Tremble, lest one be wafted to thine hand,
While dreams th' extinctless hope, " Perhaps it may."
Oh, 'tis to waste my life in prayers to see thee,
And when thy distant form re-lumes my view
To hide me, and to fly ; then, when thou'rt past,
To kiss the light-pressed path, th' imagined spot
Thy shade has crossed and hallowed—oft my soul
Sunk in voluptuous vacancy, resigns
Herself to float down fancy's fairy stream,
(Unconscious and unheeding of its lapse).
Oh, then, how bright the dream ; its magic tints
Paint passion possible, and nature kind.
Thee, thee, I see, I hear, I touch—hark, hark—
The vesper-bell—it tells me of despair.

Of the next, whatever the execution might be, the subject was perhaps the most interesting that could occur in poetry : it purported to represent a mind deeply sunk in passion, yet alive to a feeling the most painful and hostile to passion that can exist ; a conviction of the unworthiness of its object.   The struggles of reluctant conviction, and the anguish of involuntary fondness, were portrayed as in a narrative ; but Ippolito easily discovered the sentiments and situation of the unfortunate nun.

—————————He died—living he died.
Living, but dead to her, whose ceaseless toil
To win him from the weary paths of sin,
Long with vain essay strove ; but when she found
That on a mind so weak, no lofty precept
To virtue's lore, wrought with incitement high,
That on a soil so light, instruction's seed
Fell fruitless ; like the exiled Hagar of yore,
(Who wandering in the wilds of Beer-Sheba,
Saw the last morsel of her pittance spent,

                                        Saw

Saw its last drop scarce wet her babe's parched lip,
And seeing, said, with hopeless anguish bowed—
Let me not see him die!—and went far off
And wept) : so went she to a spot remote,
And wept—ceaseless and silent wept ; no gleam
Of tremulous light played on her evening hour,
No sheeny phantoms of the tints of morn
Wove to her eye the painted visions of joy,
Or struck their airy harps far heard.   Her life
Was lone, her purpose strange, but never brake.
She reared an antic structure, wild and simple,
Like some lone eremite's tomb, and called it *his.*
She watched beside his tomb, in patience, pale,
With sunk and tearless eye, and lips that moved
In inward prayer for him, whom she deemed dead
To all worth living for.   She hung that tomb
With garlands, fancy-wrought, and dim of hue ;
They were as wild as mountain-spirits' song,
They mocked all rule, and scorned all art—and yet
 No child of feeling true, might see that wreath,
Nor wake their waning colours with a tear.

   Far other employ she *hoped* for them—with these
She would have strewn his path, or wreathed his brow,
Or decked the polished hours of virtuous life.

   But little did he reck of virtuous life,
Or aught but the loose flow of dance, and song,
And roar of midnight revel—sad she heard,

                                        And

And still she sat in pale and pined constancy;
Yet not without impulse of natural sorrow,
(Strong throes of anguish, cleaving still to life),
She thought on her last hopes, her withered heart,
Her youth departed, and her mind decayed.

  Yet still she loved—yea, still loved hopeless on.
Infatuate passion desperate, still lit
Her hollow eye, still warmed her fevered lip—
The memory of her first love, like rich music
Sung in her witched ear.   She was condemned
T' outlive the object, but the passion—never

The author appeared to have had a knowledge of the unhappy life of the person she was attached to, deeper than was necessary to furnish the garniture of poetical sorrow. She appeared intimately to feel, and to deplore with the mingled zeal of religion and love, the evil habits that had overspread and abused a noble heart. Such were the feelings intended to be portrayed in the following lines :

                  I.

I

That tempting fruit, how ripe it hangs,
    How rich it grows on high;
And there I reach my helpless hands,
    There fix my straining eye.

II.

Oh, not for me, those gay tints rich
    Its mellow cheek adorn;
Ah, not for me, its odours fine
    Vie with spring's bud-wreath'd morn

III.

Oh, but to taste those nectar'd sweets,
    That I a bird might be;
Oh, that I were the common air
    Uncheck'd that blows on thee.

IV.

How o'er thy ripe cheek's glowing down,
    Would I my soft tale sing;
How faint amid the sweets I fann'd,
    With rapture-dancing wing.

V.

How would I chase each reptile rude,
    That saps thy wasted bloom?
How would my whispering pennons play,
    To wake thine hid perfume.

                                   VI.

VI.

Enough for me the joy, to view
　　Thy purer beauties glow,
Bid unrestrained those odours rise,
　　Whose sweets I ne'er must know.

In these lines Ippolito discovered an attempt made to express a strange and complicated feeling, that often occurs in real love, when existing under a desparity of circumstances—'tis that feeling which arises from a mixt sensation of moral debasement, and worldly rank and splendour; of which the effect is partly to awe by magnificence, and partly to interest by compassion

The unfortunate vestal seemed to be betrayed by the very feelings on which she depended for her defence; she was evidently fascinated by the rank, the spirit, and the excesses of the man she loved, as well as by the qualities by which love is more properly excited; she was daz-

2　　　　　　zled

zled by the glare of the very vices she affected to deprecate; she was struck with involuntary admiration of splendid disso-luteness, and tumultuous grandeur—yet often the sentiments of these lines spoke merely the sighs of desire, such as are poured out in the involuntary excess of the mind, and without a reference either to hope or to despair.

Such were the following:

I.

I wish I were a vernal breeze,
    To breathe upon that cheek of down;
Then I might breathe without a fear,
    Then I might sigh without a frown.

II.

I wish I were a burnished fly,
    To sport in thine eye's sunny sheen;
There wing my raptured hour unheard,
    There dazzled droop, and die unseen.

III.

I wish I were a blushing flower
    Within thy breast one hour to reign;

The

Then I might live without a crime;
Then I might die without a pain.

Sometimes amid this blaze of luxuriant fondness, a sudden cloud of remorse and horror would intervene, as in these lines.

I.

Oh, come to my arms, whose faltering clasp
  Is still folding thy phantom in air!
Oh, visit mine eye, whose fancy-wrought spell
  Is still raising thy form in its sphere!

II.

Oh, let my languid head sink on thy breast,
  Other refuge or rest it has none!
Oh, let my full heart once heave upon thine,
  And its throbs, and its tumults are done!

III.

And I'll lose, while my swimming eye floats on thy
    form,
  All thought, but the thought, it is *thine*;
And I'll quench in the nectar that bathes thy red
    lip,
  The fever that's burning in mine.

IV.

And lapt in the dream, I'll forget that a voice
    Would recal, that a fear would reprove—
Till I start as the lightning is lanced at my head,
    And wonder there's guilt in our love.

With these alternate struggles of passion that could not stifle conscience, and
of principle too weak to contend with passion, many others were filled. One arrested Ippolito s attention, from having the
following sentence in prose, prefixed to
it : " The disguise I have assumed, supplies me with many an hour of weak indulgence. Sometimes I pass almost close
to him, catch the sounds of his voice, linger at night near his dwelling, drops of
slow poison each—but how fatal-sweet!
Last night, I touched the very railing on
which I saw him lean but an hour before,
as he descended the steps—touched it!
Ildefonsa reproached me; but I have resisted other reproaches than her's—Why
should I yield to human monitions, what

I

I have refused to those of my own heart,
and of heaven ?"

I.

'Tis vain—'tis vain my lips to move,
　'Tis vain my arms to sever ;
Thou hast my everlasting love,
　And thou shalt have it ever.

II.

Oh, why to tempt my doubted faith,
　Those dread recitals borrow ?
Know, trifler, they who dare to live,
　Dread not to die of sorrow !

III.

Why tell the pangs of vows unheard,
　The woe of hopes undone ?
To weep was all my vows e'er woo'd,
　To weep was all they won.

IV.

I asked to view thy heaven-lit eye,
　Till these weak eyes were blasted ;
I asked to view that bliss-bathed lip,
　Till mine with wishing wasted.

V.

No soft reward of blameless love
　E'er sooth'd mine unheard wooing;

For

For oh!—a glance was phrensy's fire,
　　A touch had been undoing.

VI.

Not mine to love with florid art,
　　I wove no poet-willow;
My inward tears prey'd on my heart,
　　My hush'd sighs scorch'd my pillow.

VII.

No cherish'd hope of rich return
　　E'er sooth'd with promised pleasure:
Love rifled all my native store,
　　But gave no added treasure.

VIII.

The tear that seeks the shade to fall,
　　The sigh that silence breathes;
And this fond moment's wilder woe,
　　Are all that love bequeaths.

IX.

Chill emblem of my iron fate,
　　Yet guiltless, I may grasp thee;
Woo thy cold kiss without a blush,
　　And wildly, fondly clasp thee.

X.

Then take, oh take this feverous kiss
　　To meet his lip vain burning;

And

And take, oh take this smothered sigh,
   That woos no fond returning.

XI.

And crush, oh crush this harass'd breast,
   No more to wild hope waking,
And take (oh, would it were the last)
   Throbs of a heart that's breaking.

XII.

I'd rather breathe these hopeless sighs
   Than vows of sanctioned duty ;
I'd rather leave this lost kiss here,
   Than press the lip of beauty.

XIII.

But oh, the bitter—bitter thought
   That thus it must be, ever
To woo thy shade, to watch thy step,
   But nearer—never, never!

XIV.

To feel my lips unbidden form
   What they must never say ;
To feel my eyes in gazing fix'd,
   In gazing waste away.

XV.

Of vision'd days, and restless nights,
   A weary length to roll,

                               With

With passion on my fever'd lip,
    And anguish in my soul.

XVI.

Yet some relief to weep and vow,
    What time can frustrate—never,
Thou hast my everlasting love,
    And thou shalt have it ever.

Ippolito had perused these lines, stretched on the mossy roots of an ash in a wild
dell; when he had finished the last, he
perceived that the evening had already
gathered round him. He rose, and re-
mounting his horse, which was fastened to
an adjacent tree, rode homeward to the
hamlet.

He lingered in the way, for the images
of sadness, had combined with the hues
of evening to pour a voluptuous melancholy over his soul. Within a furlong
of the hamlet, he entered a woody defile,
where the branches of the tall, thick trees
meeting above, excluded light even at
noon-day, and now deepened the gloom
of

of gathering night.   Across the high banks and matted wood-path of this dell, the roots of the trees branched into a thousand antic ridges and curvings; while above, the foliage, so thick and bowery, scarce admitted the wind to whisper through its leaves, or the birds to find their way to the nests, that seemed woven into a verdurous wall.   Ippolito paused as he entered it to mark the rich gleam of western light its opposite extremity admitted.   At that moment a face appearing beside him audibly pronounced, " Why do you linger here ? your fate may be forgotten, but will not be long unfulfilled."   It seemed to pass him as it spoke, and was lost in the gloom of the wood.

It was the voice, the face of the stranger; in darkness, in midnight he would have known it.   He lost not a moment in thought; the very force of his fear gave him speed like a whirlwind; calling, commanding, adjuring him to

stay

stay or to return, he plunged into the wood, and while he could trace his shadow in thought, or the vestige of motion, or sound that followed him, he pursued it with a speed that seemed to make all human flight unavailing. It was in vain; in an hour he was many miles from the dell in the wood, but had not obtained a a glimpse of him he pursued. His feelings were too tempestuous to weigh circumstances, or pause over doubts; he had but one object— to discover if this dreaded being could really pervade all space, and overtake all flight. If he had in vain called on the mountains to cover him, and hid himself where even the jealous rage of superstition had failed to discover him. He paused on a rising ground, to catch the last remains of the light, as they faded over the wide prospect before him. He saw at a distance what he at first believed to be a young tree, whose branches were tossed by the wind; but

his

his eye, sharpened by fear was not long deceived—it was a human figure, tall and dark, that moved onward with amazing swiftness, and whose outspread and streaming garments were flung to the wind, like the foliage of a tree.   Again he called, again he hastened forward, but his voice was only echoed by winds and woods, and his speed only led him to wilder haunts, and remoter distance.

He rode all night with unabated eagerness of pursuit, and towards morning, first felt his confidence decline on seeing before him a town, from whose numerous avenues, roads branched in every direction. But though not successful, he yielded to the weariness of the noble animal that bore him, and entering the first inn he saw, summoned the camariere, and inquired, had a person of the stranger's appearance, which he described shuddering at his own precision, passed through the town. The man listened to him with

a look

a look, which Ippolito thought might be
owing to the stern earnestness of his
own; but replied without hesitation,
there had not. Ippolito then dismissed
him, and wearied by the wanderings of the
night, sunk into a perturbed and broken
sleep.

When he awoke, he perceived he had
devoted more hours to repose, than his
time admitted; the day was far spent, and
he called impatiently for his horse. No
plan of pursuit was suggested to him, but
he determined to follow the open track
of country through the principal towns,
and inquire for the stranger as he passed
through each.

As he quitted the inn, a servant appeared with his horse; a rustic was leaning
carelessly against a post of the shed from
which he had been just led. Ippolito
observed as he sprung into his seat, that
the servant eyed him intently, and inquired the reason. " You are very like
a cavalier I have seen in Naples, Signor,"
said

said the man. "And what of this cavalier?" said Ippolito, pausing. "Nothing, Signor, but that I should not like much to see him in this house—I do not think I should ever sleep in it again." "Has the cavalier the power of banishing sleep from the houses he visits?" "It is said, he never sleeps himself, Signor; he has other employments at night." "What may those be?" said Ippolito. "Pardon me, Signor, I dare not speak of him or them." He crossed himself with signs of strong fear. "But I would wish you to be more circumstantial," said Ippolito, who readily comprehended whom he meant, and who wished to know the probable extent of his danger, and become familiar with its terrors. "I should wish to know him, should it be my chance to encounter him.' "You will easily know him by yourself, Signor," said the man retiring, "he is just your stature and figure."

This comparison suggested another idea

to

to Ippolito—the stranger and he were
exactly of the same stature ; he pressed
his inquiries on the man, adding, " It is
of importance to me to be acquainted
with the description of this person. I
am in pursuit of one myself, whom perhaps it may assist me to discover." " The
person of whom you are in quest," said the
peasant, who had not before spoken, " is
already gone before you, Signor ; he is
by this time at Bellano." Amazed at this
intelligence so abruptly given, yet unwilling to expend time in inquiring how
it was obtained, Ippolito hastily asked the
distance and direction of Bellano. The
peasant informed him, and Ippolito was
hasting away, when a suspicion of this
strange intelligence crossed his mind,
and he waved his hand to the peasant to
approach him. The man lingered with a
reluctant air. Ippolito again signified
his wish to speak with him, and the man
advanced slowly and irresolutely. " From
whom

whom had you this intelligence ?" said
Ippolito. " I do not know, Signor."
" How—not know? Is it possible you
could converse with a human being, and
not know to whom you spoke?" "I know
not, if he were a human being," said the
man. " What is it you say, what manner of man was he that spoke with you ? "
" Why do you ask ? I pray to the virgin
I may never see either of you again—you
know him well enough, I dare say he is
beside you now, though no Christian eye
can see him." What insolence is this; or
is it phrensy rather ? Slave, do you know
to whom you speak?" said Ippolito.
" Slave," repeated the man, with strong
resentment, " 'tis you are a slave, and to
the worst of masters ; I would not change
with you, though this shed is my only
dwelling, were you on a throne of gold.
Poor, wretched, deluded creature, your
grandeur is lent on hard conditions, and
for a miserable moment of time ! I see
even

even now melancholy appearing through those noble, beautiful features you have assumed. I wonder all those gold trappings do not blaze up in rows of sulphur, while I talk to you. But I have discharged my conscience. I dare not say farewell to you; but I trust to see you soon in the dungeons of the Inquisition, and that is the best wish a good Catholic can give you."

Ippolito, overpowered by the impassioned tones in which the man poured out his horror and aversion, and by his fears of more general and serious persecutions, retreated without remonstrance, and hastily took the road to Bellano. He understood too well the suspicious hints of the groom, and the open rage of the peasant.

There is no country in the world where pursuits, such as Ippolito's, are observed with more jealousy, or abhorred with a more " perfect hatred," than in Italy.

Ippolito

Ippolito saw all the horrors of his fate, and cursed his visionary imprudence too late. The innocence of his intentions, and his exemption even from the transgressions to which it might be supposed to lead, it was useless to avow to himself; and who else would believe him? To have sought the secrets of the other world, as a diversity of levity; and to be conversant in them, without sacrificing our spiritual welfare, was what could not be easily, nor indeed probably believed. But all excuse or vindication was too late. Suspicion haunted his footsteps; the relentless vigilance of superstition had an eye on him for evil, and not for good. Once excited, her persecution was inexorable, and her rancour mortal.

His dark and secret trials were known; and, instead of exciting compassion, and ensuring shelter and protection, they had only awakened hatred and fear. It was

little

little consolation to him to reflect, that
the conversations he had heard had passed among the rustics of obscure vil-
lages. The rage of the vulgar is more
deadly and indiscriminating, less liable to be pacified by representations,
less assailable by any medium of rational
vindication, and more apt to vent itself
in sanguinary violence, than that of the
higher orders. Besides, the knowledge
that had reached them must have been
first diffused through every other rank in
society.

A dreadful feeling of abandonment
and proscription began to overshadow
his soul. The rudeness of the scene—
rocks and waters seen in a cloudy twilight — fed the dark tumult of his
thoughts. As his consciousness of the
hatred of mankind increased, a sense of
hatred to mankind increased along with
it. He wished, in the wildness of the
hour, for some banditti, or mountaineer

to

to cross his path, or rush from the hollow of the rocks upon him ; his tall dark figure, and waving sabre, like the pines which bowed their branches almost to his saddle-bow, as he passed them. He wished for some object of enmity, some struggle of violence, to exhaust the eager beatings of his fury ; to quench that aversion to mankind which he felt their persecution had already kindled in his heart.

Impatient of solitude, he contended with nature and the elements ; he spurred his horse to passes that seemed inaccessible ; he delighted to gallop up precipices, to ford streams, and to wind along the giddy and pointed ridge of rock, where the heron and the crane were first startled by the foot of man ; he pushed right against the blast when it blew with vehemence ; and held on his path where, for a mile, the foam of every

returning

returning wave of a lake beat against his horse's mane.

It was now the close of evening, when he descried Bellano. A few scattered huts, interspersed with larger buildings now in ruins, overspread the view to some distance. From what this desolation proceeded Ippolito could not discover. The soil was fertile, though neglected; but in the houses and their inmates, there was an appearance of staring wildness, and of squalid dejection, such as he had never yet beheld. He looked around in vain for an inn, or any place where he might either procure repose for the night, or information on the object of his journey.

As he passed slowly through the narrow streets for the first time, he imagined that the eye of all he saw was fixed on him; that his name and fortunes were legible on his brow. Whatever knowledge

ledge of him had been betrayed before, was communicated in hints and
whispers; was avowed with timidity, and
murmured round till it was lost in the
fears of the speakers. But now he seemed to feel that a general spirit of inquisition had fastened on him; that every
one either pursued him with suspicion,
or shrunk from him in terror.

Wearied, dismayed, and disappointed,
he struck into the skirts of the town.
They were now dark and lonely. He
flung the reins on the neck of his horse,
and loitered on without object. At this
moment, the figure of the stranger visibly passed him. He paused a moment;
and then, throwing himself off his horse,
adjured him, with the most earnest and
solemn supplications, to appear, and inform him, in audible words, why he was
thus pursued and persecuted. Not a
sound followed his adjurations; not a
step crossed him.

After

After following an imaginary track for some time, he found his progress checked by a rising ground, on which stood a large edifice, dimly seen in the evening light. Its buildings, spreading over an extent of ground, presented a range of shadow, heavy, sombrous, and solitary. It bore no mark of habitation; no smoke ascended from the roof; no step echoed round the walls. Ippolito gazed on it irresolutely; yet with a strong impulse to enter it. It was certainly the point of termination to the direction he had pursued; and the direction was what the stranger, if he moved on earth, had probably taken.

At a little distance, he saw a peasant approaching, who seemed, like himself, to linger near the building. There was a promising confidence and simplicity in his manner. Ippolito thought it best to preface his inquiries with some vague observations on the desolation around them.

them.   " Yes, Signor," said the peasant,
" something has happened to the place :
I think it looks as if it were cursed."
" But what has been the cause of the
indigence and loneliness I see prevailing
here, not only among these ruins, but
among the inhabitants of the village ?"
" They are wretched and oppressed, Signor. A strange suspicion hangs over this
place. There is a horrible tale told of
it. I do not like to relate the circumstances, I have heard them related so dif-
ferently ; but since they happened, the
inhabitants of this place, which was then
flourishing, have been scattered and de-
solated."   " What are those circumstances
so strange, that could depopulate a country, and leave such marks of ruin behind
them ?" said Ippolito, glad of the relief of
local curiosity.   " They relate," said the
peasant, " to a murder committed, or
supposed to be committed, on a man who
was entrusted with some affair of ex-
                              traordinary

traordinary import. The murderer was
never discovered, nor his motives for the
action even conjectured ; and however the
circumstances are told by a hundred
mouths, the wise seem to imply, none
of them in fact ever transpired." "But
is it possible no steps were ever taken to
trace this mysterious affair?" "I know
not, Signor. There was a great, powerful, wicked family, said to be concern-
ed in it. They had influence to crus
all inquiry. No one that contended with
that house ever prospered. They do not
want power for outward means, nor vil-
lainy for secret ones. So, whoever op-
poses them fares like the inhabitants of
Bellano." "Was the whole village then
implicated in this strange transaction?"
"They were punished as if they had
been, Signor. Good night, Signor. I do not
like lingering near the spot at this hour.
This is the very house in which the deed
was done."

The

The peasant retired. Ippolito surveyed the structure. He saw it was safe,
from solitude and fear. In the village,
wild and deserted as it seemed, he dreaded discovery; he dreaded the unknown
effects of the stranger's machinations.
Weary of persecution, and impatient for
gloomy quiet, he thought with pleasure
of plunging into the recesses of a solitude, from which even superstition, that
haunted him in every other retreat, would
recoil with shuddering.

Again he surveyed the building, and,
ascending the rising ground, traversed
the dismantled wall that enclosed it. It
was spacious and ruinous. The dark
lines of the building were strongly defined on the deep blue of a clear au-
tumnal sky, in which the stars, faintly
emerging, tipt here and there a battlement, or a turret with silver. He found
the principal doors fastened; and, as he
examined the wall more closely, to discover
5

cover some means of admission, he thought
a figure started and disappeared in the same
moment, from behind a projecting angle
of the building. He pursued eagerly, but
vainly. Yet as he turned away, something like a sound issuing from the in-
terior of the building, struck on his ear.
He listened; all was still. He now renewed his search, and soon discovered a low
door, which required but little force to
open, and which admitted him into a
passage, lofty, and dimly lit. It conducted him to the principal hall, from which
doors and passages branched in every
direction. All were alike dark and deserted. No foot seemed to have trod
there for many years; and their long
perspectives led the eye to a shadowy
depth it feared to penetrate.

As Ippolito gazed around him, a shadow, faint and undefined, passed along the
other extremity of the hall. He would
have looked on it as one of the imaginary

nary shapes that seem to people the
shades of obscurity; but the next moment he heard a sound too distinct to
be the production of fantasy, that seemed to die away in distance.

He sprang forward, and found himself
at the foot of a spacious staircase, over
whose broken steps the darkness made it
difficult to proceed. As he ascended
them, he loudly and repeatedly called on
the person whom he imagined he had
seen, assured him he had nothing to
apprehend from violence or malignity;
that he was himself a lonely traveller,
who was willing to unite with him for
mutual security in that solitary mansion,
and to whom it would therefore be more
prudent to disclose himself. No answer
was returned to his remonstrances; and
he was checked in their repetition by the
loud clapping of a door in a remote part
of the building. That this dreary place had
inhabitants, he had now no doubt. Who

they might be, or what was their purpose,
he resolved to examine, with a boldness
which was the offspring of desperation.
He was delighted with a summons that
seemed equal to the powers of his mind,
and did not threaten to taint him with
guilt, or blast him with infamy. The
stranger was not here to demand from
him the energy of a hero, and then
predict to him the fate of a villain. The
event of this adventure might perhaps
exercise his imagination or task his courage, but could scarcely affect his peace,
his principles, or his character.

He had now ascended the stairs, and
paused for some moments in a gallery
which seemed to communicate with several
chambers; from one of them a light appeared to issue at intervals. He entered it,
and was surprised to see some embers of
a wood fire, dimly burning on the hearth.
From their blaze, which rose fitfu'ly and
expired, as the wind hissed through the dismantled

mantled casements, waving the feeble
fire, he discovered an apartment like
the rest, spacious and dreary. Not a vestige of furniture, or any circumstance
but that of the fire, indicated the presence
of a human being in the building; his eye
wandered over walls, ceiling, and floor;
not an object struck them, but the damp,
misty obscurity of decay. The room was
chill, he approached the fire; the blaze
became more strong, and by its increasing
light, he discovered in the wall opposite
him, a narrow grating; the dusky bars
gleamed in the fire-light, and, as he continued to look on them, a human countenance appeared distinctly on the other
side. Ippolito started; he advanced to
the grating; the face disappeared, and a
piteous cry issued from within. Ippolito now earnestly demanded who was
concealed in the apartment, threatening,
with serious anger, to punish any one he
might discover, unless they avowed them-
Q 2 selves,

selves, and the causes of their concealment.

The grating was then thrown open, and the servant by whom Ippolito had been so imprudently betrayed at Celano, threw himself at his feet. "Oh, Signor," said he, after a long and unintelligible vindication of himself, "why did you leave me at Celano?" "Why did you compel me to do so by your folly, in exposing my name?" said Ippolito. "It was not my fault, Signor—it was not my fault; I never travelled with a wizard before, and I could not know." "A wizard, idiot! you will drive me mad." "Illustrious Signor, I kiss your feet, be not angry with me in this dreadful, solitary place! alas, I have suffered enough for it since; those devils at Celano were near tearing me to pieces, and when I escaped from them, I lost my way returning to Naples, and after wandering about in this wild country, dreading to make inquires, lest I should

should be discovered and sent to the Inquisition, I crawled in here to-night, to
sleep in one of these waste rooms, and
pursue my journey to morrow, and little
thought I should have the ill luck (good
fortune I mean), to behold you again."
" But why," said Ippolito, " did you fly
from me on the stairs, you surely must
have heard my voice, and when have its
tones denounced danger to you?"   " I
did not fly," said the man, " I was not on
the stairs." " 'Tis but now I pursued some
one to this very apartment," said Ippolito.
" By all the holy saints, I have not quitted
the room since I entered the building,"
said the man. " This is most strange," said
Ippolito, musing, " I am pursued by a
power that seems to possess more than human resources—resistance is vain; I am
spent in this struggle. But how was it
possible you should conceal yourself, if
you did not fly from me?"   " The door
by which you entered, Signor, is under
                                    the

the windows of this room, and when I saw
you, I concealed myself, and have not
quitted this room since you entered the
door below." "And why did you conceal yourself?" said Ippolito, " to me,
in the same circumstances, the sight of
you or of any human being would have
been most welcome." The man hesitated.
" Why did you conceal yourself," repeated Ippolito, " you knew me, and
knew that from me you had nothing to
fear." " I knew you indeed," said the
man, shuddering, "and therefore I hid
myself. Ah, Signor, it is well known for
what a purpose you seek these solitary
places, and whom you are accustomed to
meet in them; I thought the roof shook
over my head as you came under it.
He crossed himself with the strongest
marks of fear. " Mother of God," exclaimed Ippolito in agony, " is it possible? Am I so utterly lost? Do my own
species tremble at my own approach?
Hear

Hear me, my good fellow; you who have
lived with me, who have known me, who have
been lavishly nurtured with every indulgence a generous master could afford, can
you believe the horrid tales that are told of
me? I attest the blessed name I have just
mentioned, and every saint in heaven, that I
am as innocent as you are.   I have entered
into no compact with the enemy of souls;
I am no dealer in witchery; I am a crossed
and care-haunted man; a restless and unhappy spirit is within me; it has driven
me from my home, and instead of being
soothed and healed by the compassion of
mankind, it is aggravated and maddened
by the brutal rage of ignorance, till existence has become loathsome to me."

In the ardour of his appeal, Ippolito
had laid his hand on the man's shoulder;
the man recoiled from his touch. Ippolito felt it in every nerve, and was again
about to expostulate with him, when a
strange hollow sound seemed to issue
from

from a distance, and approach the room. "I will believe it, I do believe it all," said the man eagerly, "but say no more now Signor, this is no time or place for such subjects." "Can this place have other inhabitants," said Ippolito, pausing from his remonstrance to follow the sound. "Surely it has," said the man. "Have you seen or heard any thing since you entered it, any shape or sound like this?" "I have indeed, Signor; just before you entered, the shadow of a dark figure passed the door, and I am convinced I afterwards heard heavy steps on the stairs; but in these old mansions, the wind makes such strange noises, that unless one's eyes assure them——"

Here the man's face underwent a convulsion of terror, and flying on Ippolito, he held him with the strong grasp of fear. "What have you seen," said Ippolito, supporting him, "or what is it you fear?" "A hand beckoned to me from that grating," said the

the man, in inward and struggling tones.
" 'Tis this bickering blaze deceives you,"
said Ippolito, stirring the embers with his
sword, and looking at the grating; " the
light it flings on these mouldy walls is so
pale and fitful." " No, no, Signor, I
know this place, and its history well; I
marvel that its inhabitants have taken so
little note of our intrusion yet; but they
will not long neglect us." " You know
this place is inhabited—and by whom?"
said Ippolito. " By the spirits of a murderer, and its punishers," said the man,
rolling his eyes fearfully around him.
" Why do you pause with so many starts
of fear," said Ippolito, " speak plainly
and fully what you have heard of this
place, and of the cause of its desertion."
" You know them perhaps, better than I
do, Signor," said the man. " How is it
possible I should know them, it is scarce
an hour since I entered these walls?"
" Because they relate to your family."

" To

" To my family ?" said Ippolito, as recollection faintly wandered over his mind ; then added in an evasive tone, " there are many circumstances relating to my family, of which I am ignorant." " Do you wish to hear what is told of this mansion, Signor," said the man, pursuing the subject. " If your courage is sufficiently recovered to relate it," said Ippolito, wishing to suggest an excuse to him. The man proceeded in his narrative.

"It is some years back, Signor, since this was an inn, and as the town was flourishing, and in good repute, I suppose the inn was so likewise. It so happened that this inn was full of company on a night, and they were all employed speaking of some strange mysterious business that was about to be disclosed shortly, that they said would involve one of the *first families in Naples* ; I know not whether it was a monk, or an assassin that was to make the discovery ; but, whatever it was, the import
port

port of it was expected to be most singular and terrible. So, as the guests were all conversing, and each giving his conjectures and reasons, a person was ushered in, accompanied by a guard of soldiers, not as a prisoner, but in order to defend him on his journey; he spoke but little, and seemed dejected and terrified, like a man labouring under a great secret.

It was immediately whispered about the house, that this was the person who was to make the discovery, and many inquiries, and hints of advances were made, to learn what it might be; but the stranger was so distant, that, one by one the guests all dropped off to their own rooms, and left him to go to his about midnight. So he did—but never was seen to return from it, Signor; no trace of him was the next morning to be seen, nor ever since.

The house was examined, the guests were
detained,

detained, the host and his family committed to prison, from whence they never
emerged. Then the fury of the law
fastened on the town; the wretched inhabitants were sent, some to the Gallies,
and some to the Inquisition, but no intelligence of the stranger was ever procured; but ever since that night, this
place has been visited with strange appearances. Tenant after tenant quitted
the house; and at length it was deserted, and left to decay, as you see. The
very last inhabitant told me, that as he
was sitting one dark evening about the
close of antumn, it might have been in
this very room"——"Hark! hark!" said
Ippolito and his servant to each other at
the same moment.

A pause, deep and breathless, followed.
"Did you hear a noise?" said Ippolito,
in a suppressed tone. "I did, Signor;
it resembled, methought"——"And I see
a shape," said Ippolito, springing forward;
"it

" it glided past the door that moment ; I saw it with these eyes; I saw its shadow flitting along the gallery."

He was rushing out. " Holy saints !" cried the man, clinging round him, " you will not follow it." " Away, dastard !" said Ippolito, snatching a brand from the fire to excite a stronger light. " I shall die if I remain here alone," said the man. " Then follow me," said Ippolito, who had already reached the stairs. He looked around. All was dark and stilly. The flaring and uneven light of the brand quivered in strange reflections on the walls. As he still looked down the gallery, the shadows at the farther end seemed to embody themselves, and pourtray something like the ill-defined outlines of a human shape. He held up the light, and it vanished with visible motion. Ippolito impetuously pursued. The passage terminated at the foot of a narrow and spiral staircase. As he ascended

cended it, the echoes of another step
were heard distinctly above; and something like the brush of a vestment, floating between the shattered ballustrade, almost extinguished the light.

Encouraged, not repelled, Ippolito
sprung upward with greater velocity, and
soon reached the top of the staircase.
A figure, strongly visible, but still obscure, now appeared at some distance;
and, waving to him with shadowy gesture, disappeared to the left without a
sound.

At this moment, the last blaze of the
brand quivered and expired. Ippolito
stood lapped in uncertainty. A step
from below approached. It was the servant, who, binding two of the faggots
together, advanced with a stronger light.
" Come, quickly," said Ippolito; " it disappeared here—here to the left." The
man followed him, aghast and reluctant;
but dreading solitude more than even the
apparition

apparition they were pursuing, they entered a room, the only one to the left. The figure he beheld appeared to have vanished through the walls. Ippolito examined the wainscot and the casements; the latter commanded a view so extensive, that he discovered the room was situated in one of the turrets of the building. All was silence and desolation still.

" By what mysterious agency," said Ippolito, " does this form hover over space, without being confined by it?" A sound, like the fall of some ponderous body—a sound that seemed to shake the walls, and sink into the depths of the earth, roused him from his musing. The concussion was so violent, that it flung open a low door in the wainscot, which had hitherto escaped his notice.

Ippolito approached it. Within, he beheld an apartment, the extent of which was lost in shades, that were, for a moment,

ment, dispersed by a pale blue light tha
fluttered over them, and then disappeared.

Ippolito, taking the light from his
servant, whose countenance spoke the
very despair of fear, entered the room.
" This," said he, as he waved the light
above his head, that slowly broke through
a gloom of frowning and peculiar blackness, " this should be the very seat of
those marvellous operations. There is a
depth of shadow, a majesty of night and
horror here — here I pause — that wandering shape rested here — here he will
either return, or appear no more." " What
is that dark mass in that corner?" said
the servant, who had crept after him.
Ippolito approached the spot he pointed to, and discovered the remains of
an antique bed. " Make haste, Signor,
and quit this apartment, the brand is
almost extinguished," said the servant.
" You must go down and relight it ; I
                                    shall

shall not quit this spot to-night," answered Ippolito. " Go down—by myself! blessed Virgin! no; not for the Pope in person," said the man. " Did you not come up by yourself?" " Aye, but, Signor, I was coming to you, I heard your steps, and thought of you the whole way. But to go to an empty room, to feel every step I am getting further from you, and at length to venture into the very hold and haunt of other things than myself! no, Signor, not if I were to get a Cardinal's hat for it." " We must then remain in the dark till morning. I shall on no account quit this spot." " Then, Signor, I shall throw myself at your feet, and wrap my head in my cloak; and, for the love of grace, speak no more till you tell me that morning has dawned, and that you have seen nothing all night." " I subscribe to one of the conditions; the other, perhaps, it will not be in my power to observe."

The

The man threw himself at Ippolito's feet, who, glad of an opportunity of silent meditation, leant against the wall, fixing his eye on the dying flashes of the brand, which he had placed in the hearth. Its broad glare danced on the ceiling, transforming the characters of damp and decay into forms as fantastic as the lines of magic, and now, shrunk into a point, scarce shewed the rude and blackened stones on which it was consuming. In the veering light, Ippolito once thought he saw a form in a remote part of the chamber; but the next moment it expired, leaving a thousand imagined shapes to darkness.

At this moment, the servant, half-raising himself, whispered, " Signor, I hear a person breathing near me." " You hear *my* respiration probably," said Ippolito. " No, Signor, no; it is the breath of one who breathes with difficulty, as if he were trying to sup-

press

press it—there—there—it passed me
now—blessed saints, how near! Signor,
if I live, I felt the rushing of a garment
past me that moment." "Hush," said
Ippolito; "you will not let me distinguish if any one is in motion near us."
They both paused some time. Not a
sound was heard. "I am stifled holding in my breath," said the man. "You
may draw it in peace," said Ippolito;
no one seems inclined to molest us; and
if there should, against visionary assail-
ants I have innocence, and against corporeal ones, a sword."

He spake the latter sentence aloud; for
the objects he had witnessed were such
as human power could easily produce;
and he endeavoured to resist his strong
propensity to search for supernatural
powers in every object above ordinary
life. In a short time, the servant forgot
his fears in sleep; and Ippolito, exhausted by recent fatigue, slumbered, as he
leant

leant against the wainscot. The visions of his sleep were like the spirits whose agitation had produced them, wild and perturbed.

He dreamt he was kneeling at the altar of a church, which was illuminated for a midnight mass. Around or near him, he saw no one either to partake or administer the right. At length, a figure advanced from the recesses of the altar, and approached him; at the same moment, he perceived his father and brother kneeling beside. A deep stillness spread over him as he gazed around; he experienced that sensation so common in sleep—the consciousness of some mystery we are unable to penetrate; but of which we silently expect the developement. The figure distributed the consecrated element. His father, on swallowing it, shrieked "poison," in a tone of horror, and fell back expiring. At that moment, the figure, throwing off his monkish weeds, discovered

discovered the person of the stranger, arrayed in a voluptuous and martial habit.

He gazed with a fixed eye of horrid triumph, on the contorsions of the dying man, bent over him to catch his groans; and, as his dim eyes wandered in agony, presented himself in every point to their view, exclaiming, " Behold." The vision suddenly changed its scene and circumstances—Ippolito found himself in a vaulted passage, lit by a few sepulchral lamps; Annibal was beside him, and the stranger bearing a torch, and in the habit of a funereal mourner, stalked before them.

As Ippolito slowly seemed to recover his powers of observation, he perceived he was in a part of the castle of Muralto, he remembered to have traversed before. The stranger, waving them to follow, entered an apartment hung with the insignia of death; he remembered it well—it was the last of the chambers that communicated

cated with the tower so long shut up. In the centre of the room, stood a bier, covered with a pall: the stranger withdrew it, and pointed to Annibal and Ippolito, the corse of their father beneath. Ippolito, retaining his natural impetuosity in sleep, snatched the torch from the stranger, and held it over the countenance of the dead; they were fixed in a kind of visionary sleep. As he still gazed, the lips began to move; and at length uttered some words of extraordinary import, which Ippolito vainly tried to recollect when he awoke. As he still gazed, the body extended one hand to him, and another to Annibal, seized on both, and drawing them under the pall, lapt them in total darkness. He shuddered and awoke.

The light had long expired; it was succeeded by moonlight, dimly breaking through the discoloured windows, and figuring the floor with the rude imagery of their casement work.

He

He looked around him to dissipate the forms that still flitted before his eyes; on a part of the floor, where the light fell strongly, he observed a dark spot he had not beheld before, whose shadows by their depth seemed to fall within the floor. He approached it, and perceived a chasm of which he could not discover the depth. He examined it with his sword, and found there was a descent by steps within; he tried to follow them, but found their depth extended beyond his utmost reach. Here he paused for a moment, but his resolution was soon taken to descend and explore it.

There appeared to be something designed to tempt and to baffle him in the circumstances he had witnessed, that tempted his courage as strongly as his imagination; they were circumstances beside, such as human power and contrivance could easily produce, and such as human fortitude could easily cope with. The

2   jealousy

jealousy of imposition operated more powerfully on his high-toned mind, than even his appetency for the marvellous; and of the latter too, there was a lurking impulse that expedited his resolution.

His servant still slept, and Ippolito wished not to disturb him, as he would be equally clamorous at either alternative of accompanying him into the vault, or of remaining in solitude; his sleep would probably continue till the morning, and at morning he might depart in peace. He therefore commended himself to all the saints, and began to descend the steps. They were winding and irregular. He soon lost the faint reflections of moonlight, and for a few moments advanced in total darkness. He paused, for to advance in darkness, was to encounter superfluous danger, when a flash of sudden light from below played on the dank, black walls, and shewed him the rugged steps winding downward to a depth it was

giddy

giddy to think of. The paleness and flitting disappearance of the light, indicated the distance from which it issued; but as Ippolito, encouraged by this dubious omen, eagerly proceeded, frequent flashes of a stronger light convinced him it was stationary, and that he was approaching it. He advanced; the light increased; it seemed the faint gleam of a lamp struggling with darkness. In a few moments he perceived it glimmering at a determinate distance, and sending up long streams of abrupt light on the upper darkness. A few steps more brought him to a level; he entered a vaulted passage low and black, hoary and chill with damps; at the entrance of it a lamp burnt feebly. He disengaged it from the wall with difficulty, (it was iron, of coarse and ancient structure), and proceeded with it slowly, extending his sword before him. In the deep blackness of the perspective, no object near or remote could be descried ; the air seemed almost materially thick and dark. A dim atmosphere of bluish light spread round the edges of the flame Ippolito carried, which shivered almost tó dissolution, though he advanced with the most cautious slowness, dreading lest its extinction should leave him wandering for ever in darkness, or its motion should kindle the foul and pent-up vapours to a flame of which the explosion would be fatal. As he glided onwards a sound, he paused to distinguish, came to his ear. He listened—it was a human groan ; it was repeated ; it was like the expression of mental anguish, more than of bodily ; it seemed to issue from an immense distance. Ippolito called aloud in accents of encouragement ; the sounds ceased. As he turned in the direction from which they had proceeded, his foot struck against something which he stooped to examine ; it was a rosary and crucifix

fix of wood, they were corroded by damp,
but their shape was yet distinguishable.

As he examined it with that disposition
which desires to look for proof in casual
things, another light twinkled like a star
in the passage beyond him, and a figure
dimly defined, appeared and vanished with
the swiftness of a shadow. Ippolito with
alternate cries of menace and intreaty,
adjured it to pause, or to approach. It
hovered for a moment on the remote edge
of darkness, as if doubtful whether to
obey him or not; but as he hastened forward to urge his importunity, it disappeared. Its motion was so evidently human, that Ippolito felt inspirited with a
hope of success as he pursued it, till his
progress was suddenly entangled by
something that lay on the ground. Impatiently he endeavoured to remove it
with his hand—it was a heap of dusky and
decayed garments, of which the shape
was indistinguishable. As he threw it from

him

him, the clank of a human bone rung against the vault.

He was now irresistibly checked, and holding down his lamp, tried to discover whether any memorials of horror were near him that might be avoided in his progress. Shuddering, he perceived the remains of a human skeleton scattered to some distance around him; the skull had dropped from the garment that was entangled round his steps. As he gazed around unwilling to linger, and unable to depart, the lamp darted a bright and tapering flame upward, and then sinking down, quivered as if about to expire.

For a moment he believed the fluctuation of the light was owing to an influence connected with the object before him; but on looking upward, he discovered an aperture of which his eye could not measure the height, in the roof of the vault, through which the air rushing had almost extinguished the lamp. Comparing this
circumstance

circumstance with the spectacle before
him, he immediately conjectured that the
unfortunate person had been precipitated
through the chasm, and dashed piecemeal
by the fall, as the bones were scattered at
various distances.

All thought of further pursuit was for a
moment repelled; and in the interval, as
Ippolito was withdrawing his eyes with the
slowness of fascination from the object
before him, the other light appeared approaching from a distance. Through the
thick vapours of the vault, Ippolito could
scarcely discover that it was supported by
any visible hand; but as it approached,
he perceived it was the stranger who bore
it! He had no time to collect his facul-
ties; the stranger was already beside him.
They viewed each other for some time
without speaking a word, while the lights
they held reflected to each, the visage of the other as pale and fixed as that
of the dead. At length, " Wherefore are
                                       you

you here?" said the stranger. Wherefore am I here?" repeated Ippolito. "Is that a question? What other shelter have you left me? Where can I fly without persecution and danger? I have been torn from life, and from society, from the objects and occupations that are congenial to my age, my spirit, and my fortunes. I have been banished the presence and the sympathy of my own species; I hear nothing around me but the hiss of suspicion, or the mutterings of hatred. You have written a character of horror on my brow, that my own menials read and fly from. You have poured a poisonous atmosphere around me, that blasts and withers the feelings of every human being that approaches it. In the whirlwind of your pestilent progress you have rent me from my own soil and station, and flung me on a bare and isolated precipice, where I stand the sport of every storm, shivering at my own desolation. You have done

done this, and dare you ask me why I
follow you even here? Why I pursue
you to the very verge of being, to ask
you for myself?" "You do well," said
the stranger, " to harbour amid such
scenes as these, to such your fate is about
to lead you; and you are right to habi-
tuate yourself to them; you are in your
proper abode. Child of despair, I greet you
well. Do you see these walls? Such shall
soon be enclosing you; what the object
at your feet is now, such you shall shortly
be." "Away with this horrible jargon,"
cried Ippolito, " I will be duped by it
no more. I have grovelled under you, till
I am weary of suffering and submission.
These struggles are not of despair, but resistance; I have fled, not to shun, but to pursue. Mysterious and inscrutable tormentor, I have too long been your vassal;
your power was illusive and imaginary—it
was borrowed from *my* weakness; my visionary folly arrayed you in the attri-
butes

butes of imagined terror, but it can strip
and mock you for its sport. *My triumph*
shall have its turn now. I will change in
a moment the parts my abject folly as-
signed us; you shall fly, and I will become
the pursuer now. Yes—I will haunt
you as you have haunted me. I will proclaim you to the vulgar—to children I will
proclaim you; your shadowy movements,
your mysterious dignity shall be the tale
of beldames. Horror shall be dispelled by
familiarity, and contempt shall mock at
the detected imposture. I will pursue
you with an army of persecution, malediction, and ridicule—the horror of the
virtuous, the hatred of the vulgar, the jealous fury of superstition, and the awful
resentment of justice. You shall find
what it is to drive a soul to despair. I will
pursue you from place to place. I will
chase and scatter you over the earth; on
no part of its surface shall you rest; at no
depth below it shall you be safe. Human
                                    power

power shall urge you to the limits of this
world, and the vengeance of religion
shall pursue you to the next. Ha! ha!
what an ideot have I been. Yes! 'tis
a glorious thought—to be revenged of
you; to dash your sceptre of iron, your
scourge of scorpions, from your hand,
and to wield them against you; to deliver myself; to deliver the world; to
do a service to heaven. Methinks I
breathe a new element. The ground on
which I tread bears me up since I have
conceived the thought. The very activity of motion, the energy of pursuit will
be congenial to my nature, and a relief to
my spirits."

The stranger listened without resentment, and paused long before he answered. "Unhappy boy! you grapple
with a chain of adamant. You may run
to its utmost extent, but what will that
avail you? I hold it in my hand. I
have measured its length, and numbered

every link. If you were capable of reason, would you not perceive that this
restlessness of mind, this appetite for
vehement struggle and rapid pursuit,
is but the oppressive sense of unaccom-
plished destiny. You feel that you have a
task, of which you imagine inventing another will destroy the remembrance and
the responsibility. You are approaching
a precipice with silent but gradual swiftness; and you imagine that short devia-
tions, and momentary sallies, will alter
the direction, or intercept the fall. Do
you not already perceive your power of
resistance diminishing? Do you not perceive your excursions are shorter, and
your progress more perceptible. Recollect, when to mention this subject,
was only to excite a torrent of rage and
malediction. Now you can definitely
talk of its enormity; and the next step
will be to consider that enormity as
modified and palliated, till you contemplate

plate it with horror no longer. Recollect,
that when the former thought of it tinged
your dreams, you would awaken with the
force of horrible conceit, and practise
every expedient of childish fear to sleep
no more that night. You dreamed of it
to-night, yet no waking consciousness of
horror broke through your slumbers; no
cold dew gathered on your brow; your
teeth did not gnash, nor your limbs
heave and quiver; your waking was the
effect of accident—of an extraordinary
accident. Recollect (and acknowledge
the power that reads your heart) that
your intended persecution of me is
prompted by an irresistible desire to discover the motives which prompted my
suggestion of the action; the means that
would have been applied to its accom-
plishment; nay, its very form and circumstance, all horrible as they are. Such
is the purpose with which you would
pursue me; and how absurd to depre-

2   cate

cate the contemplation of what it is the
burning and inward thirst of your soul
to satiate itself with the knowledge!
What we desire, from curiosity or fear,
to contemplate, we will soon be habituated to; and what we are habituated
to, soon ceases to be revolting. Thus
you impose on yourself by the very
means you take to avoid imposition.
Your flight from evil is circular, and
brings you to the very point from which
you commenced it. The impulse, upon
whose tide you float so triumphantly, is
ebbing in its pride, and will bear you
back to a depth and distance greater
than even that you have emerged
from."

"Mother of God!" said Ippolito, "I
see I am lost." He staggered and gasped. "Human force cannot contend with
this enemy. You are something which
thought is unable to reach. You blend
the familiarity of human temptation with

the

the dark strength of the fiend. I am weak and cannot contend; I am weary, and amazed, and all strength has failed me. Had I the power of an angel in my arm or my brain, what would it avail? I stand before him naked and helpless as infancy. I think, and he tells me my thoughts. I deliberate, and he anticipates my resolution. I move, and my motions are measured and bounded. I fly, and my flight is overtaken and arrested. Night cannot veil, nor the bowels of the earth hide me. I look upward, and the shadow of his hand is over me. I look downward, and I am thrown before his feet."

He mused in the stupor of horror, and murmured inwardly, "If the great blow to which I am urged, could deliver me from this; if it could be struck, and all this terrible siege he lays to my soul, cease with it—would it not be well?"

A dark

A dark smile passed over the stranger's face, as the last words were spoken. Ippolito burst into rage again, as he noted it.

" Devil, I see your triumph. You think I am parleying with guilt; you think you see the balance held with a trembling hand; you hope that despair has driven nature from her hold, and fixed her black banner in the very centre of her works. No; your infernal wisdom has deceived you. You are deep in the mysteries of iniquity; but your knowledge becomes foolishness when it has to deal with a human heart. You might as well predict the tossings of an earthquake as the struggles of a high-principled soul goaded to phrensy. I am indeed strongly beset. The enemy has had power over me, such as is seldom given him over man. These thoughts are often with me. My powers are shaken

by

by a thousand impulses to evil. But hitherto I think I feel my actual abhorrence of guilt is undiminished. I think so. If I admit the thought of it more frequently and patiently, 'tis not because I am reconciled to it; but because—— no matter; it is better not to think of the cause. I am sure I shall be upheld —I trust so; yet I am dark and lorn. Evil is gathering round me like night, night unbroken by a single ray of light. I would willingly cleave to nature and to my fellow-men. I would call to them for comfort; I would lay hold on their hands for help; but they reject and abhor me. This is one of the fiend's subtlest devices; this is the very pith of his dark power. Yet still I am not cast down. I stand, though sore shaken. Yet, Oh! when shall I be able to curse him, and bid him depart?"

"There is no need. I am gone; but what will that avail you? The power you dread

dread and deprecate is within you, where
its gradual workings shall lead you to
the very act for whose mention you curse
and proscribe me. I attest night and
this vault, the witness of untold things;
I attest these mouldering bones, and this
dagger, on whose blade the gore you
shed is yet visible—three months shall
not elapse, till you do the deed, whose
visioned horrors were disclosed to you
in the chambers of our secrecy. My
task is now finished, and my office has
ceased. When next you behold me it
shall be in another form, not to predict
your fate, but to witness it."

As he said these words, with the
solemn sadness of human feeling, he
slowly retreated. The unhappy young
man was stung to madness. For a moment all was mist and cloud around him.
When he raised his eye again, the stranger was scarce visible in the dark distance.
With a cry of despair, Ippolito rushed
                                        after

after him. In a moment he was at the extremity of the passage. Here several others branched off, losing themselves in the darkness. In none of them could the stranger be traced by sight or sound. The very light he bore had disappeared. It was impossible that, in a few moments, he could have traversed passages of such length. But Ippolito had long since ceased to judge of him by the measure of man, and now plunged into the passage immediately opposite him with the blindness of desperation. No object was visible, as he glided along, but the hoary and frowning arches of the vault ; no sound was heard but the echoes of his steps, half-heard in the thick, damp air.

He had proceeded with a rapidity that left him no time to think of the distance he had traversed, till he was checked by actual weariness, and then perceived, for the first time, that of these winding passages

passages there seemed to be no end. His mind was in too tumultuous a state to recognise this circumstance, further than as it was connected with the length or difficulty of the pursuit. He was like a man, who, waking from a fearful dream, seems still to hold conference with forms of fantasy, peoples darkness and vacancy with shadowy crowds; and is scarce recalled to the objects of life, by discovering that all around him is solitary and silent. It was this deep stillness, this interminable darkness, that first checked Ippolito in his pursuit. The stranger, his appearance, and his words, seemed to him as a vision, a shadowy imagery, that floated on the vapours of the vault. That he could have disappeared thus suddenly and entirely, was a contradiction to his actual presence; and Ippolito, almost distrusting his senses, began slowly to look round him to discover

ver some means of extrication from this maze of passages.

From the moment he looked around him with this object, the length and darkness of the vault became intolerable. He would have been delighted to discover the slightest change in his progress; he would have been delighted to observe the walls more rugged and fractured, or the ground more uneven.

At length, the objects around began evidently to assume a different aspect. Large masses of stone, rude and dark, projected from the walls and roof, as if they would crush the passenger. Around some of them Ippolito observed dusky and stunted weeds were entwined; and once he thought a pale reflection wandered through a chasm over his head, as if light was stealing on him from the world above. Still his progress appeared endless.

He

He now walked on with steady swiftness, not admitting the suggestions of
the hour and place to overshadow his
mind, or benumb his exertions. [Mov-
ing, with the rapidity of one who was
approaching a definite object, while his eye
vainly hung on the darkness to discover
one, sometimes stung with an impulse to
return, he would pause till the perplexity
of the passages wildered his brain in the
effort to retrace them.] Thus he passed
on, dreading to look behind, and scarcely hoping, as he looked onward. In
this state of mind, he suddenly found
his progress checked by a wall that terminated the passage. Neither door nor
window was perceptible in it. He examined it with his lamp, and at length
discovered a grating that, almost decayed with rust, ran for a considerable length
in the wall, parallel to the ground. From
its form and direction, Ippolito conjectured

tured it had been a part of a door,
that was now inclosed in the wall.

Here was something like a means of
escape, though in other circumstances, it
would rather have resembled an obstruction ; but Ippolito, with his natural impetuosity, believed that nothing could resist his strength, stimulated by danger,
and already felt himself liberated from
this dungeon of famine and darkness. As
he laid down his lamp, for the purpose
of examining the bars, he perceived
through them a light so faint and remote,
that he almost believed it a star. As he
gazed on it, it became more distinct,
and he at length perceived it was a light
in motion, though by whom it was borne,
or through what space, it was impossible
to discover. As it flung a tremulous and
misty gleam through the thick air, he
could see after some time, a flight of steps
at a vast distance, that wound beyond
the sight, and of which partial fragments
appeared

appeared through chasms at a still greater,
feebly tinted with the moving rays of
the light. And now as it advanced down
the steps, he could see it was borne by a
tall, dark figure, who preceded another
still more obscure, bearing in his arms
something that was enveloped in white.
They descended from a vast height at the
extremity of a vault, over whose extent
the torch as it approached, threw a tran-
sient flash without exploring it. As the
vast masses of shadow varied with the
motion of the torch, Ippolito thought he
could discover objects that resembled the
furniture of a place of sepulture scattered around the vault before him ; but
the light was too faint and partial to give
them distinctness. The figures at the
other extremity had now descended the
steps, and entered the vault. One of
them laid down his burthen for the purpose of adjusting it, and while the other
held up the torch to assist him, the strong
light

light that fell on his visage, discovered
the stranger! The other was in the habit of a monk.

He resumed his burthen, and was proceeding with it when the stranger producing a dagger, fastened it in the monk's
girdle, pointing with appropriate gesture
to the object in white, and giving him
the torch he bore, retired up the steps,
where Ippolito could see his dark figure
gliding past the chasms, through which
they wound, and sometimes bending from
them, as if to mark the motions of his
agent below.

By what means this mysterious being
was present in every scene of horror, and
active in every purpose of mischief, (for
such the present appeared) filled Ippolito
with new wonder. He seemed to glide
from place to place, like the very genius of
evil, with a dark suggestion for every
mind, and a dagger for every heart.

The monk proceeded wiih slow steps'
across

across the vault, till he was nearly under
the grating where Ippolito stood. The
paleness of guilt and of fear was in his face.
As he held the torch low, to direct his
steps over the broken pavement, Ippolito
could distinguish it was strewed with the
memorials of the dead. He stopped
where the ground was recently disturbed,
and a stone appeared half raised from it;
and seating himself, while the torch burned on the ground, withdrew the covering
from the burthen in his arms—Ippolito
discovered a female form, folded in a
shroud, whose relaxed limbs and pallid
face resembled those of a corse. The
monk looked around, though not a sound
was near, and then unsheathing the dagger, surveyed it wildly.

Ippolito no longer doubted that the object in the shroud was living, though it
seemed determined she should be so no
longer. The monk now raising his hand
tremulously, and half averting his face,
                                    seemed

seemed to wind himself up to the blow.
Ippolito, in an agony of rage and horror,
struggled with the barrier between them,
and uttered a cry so terrible in the conflict, that the assassin, dropping the dagger, remained petrified with fear; his fixed and strong eyes not daring to seek the
direction from whence the sound had issued.

Ippolito grappled with the iron in a
phrensy of rage; bar after bar, loosened by
age, and shaken with supernatural force,
gave way. The stones in which they were
fixed yielded along with them, till an aperture was formed, through which Ippolito
forced himself, and leaping downward a descent of which he did not feel the depth,
burst into the cemetery. The monk, whether
in the confusion of his fear, or determined to effect his purpose before Ippolito
could descend, had struck at the female
with his dagger, but with a hand so uncertain, that it scarce rased the skin; he

then fled, bearing with him the torch,
which however he extinguished in his
flight, and fled up the stairs, his dark garments fluttering through the apertures
above.

Ippolito supported the lady in his
arms, he perceived that she breathed.
The feelings that her beauty might have
inspired, were repelled by her helplessness and her danger, and Ippolito bent
over her with solicitude merely fraternal.
To escape from the cemetery, was the
first object of safety; but to do this it
was necessary to wake his companion, and
procure some information from her; for
he had no knowledge of the place, or of
the direction to which the steps might
lead. All attempt however to wake her
was in vain. " This is not the sleep of
nature." said Ippolito, " some pernicious
means have been employed to reduce her
to this state." He looked around him
in consternation; the steps at the other
                                    extremity

extremity of the vault, appeared the only
mode by which he could escape from it;
the rest were buried in shapeless darkness. The lamp which he had left in the
place from whence he had descended,
threw a faint and shadowy light from
above, which threatened every moment
to expire. There was no time to balance means and expedients. He raised
the lady in his arms, and pursuing the
direction the monk had taken, began to
ascend the steps. He looked around in
vain for direction or assistance; the steps
were broken and irregular, and but for
the dim light that still issued from the
lamp at the other extremity of the vault,
had been utterly dark.

Ippolito knew not whither they led; it
might be into the very centre of danger—but no choice of directions was left
him, no other means of flight from the
cemetery were visible. As he still ascended, wondering at his own safety, he

s 2   could

could distinctly hear the steps of the assassin retreating before him, of which the
sound was sometimes lost in the echo of
doors closing, and in the rush of wind
that accompanied their opening. The
light that still burned in the vault, was
now too remote to afford him assistance;
he saw it but at intervals, as it twinkled
through the chasms; but above him, a
light almost as faint issued through an
opening. Several steps were yet to be
surmounted; he collected his declining
strength, and with one vigorous bound
reached the summit of them.

Pausing for breath, he now looked upward; the light issued through a trap-door
in the roof, which the monk in his flight
had neglected to close. Part of his habit
which still clung to it from the struggle
of his fears in effecting his escape, as-
sisted Ippolito to ascend through it with
the only arm he had at liberty, the other
supported his still insensible burthen.

On

On emerging from it, he looked around him—he was in a cloistered passage, that appeared to belong to some ecclesiastical building. Through the windows, dim and few, a faint moonlight was poured on the checquered floor, the clustering pillars, and the pointed arches of the roof. Far to the left, Ippolito thought he could still distinguish the dark figure of the monk as he flitted along, though his steps were no longer audible; and still further a gleam as of distant lamps, trembled through the obscurity, warning Ippolito to shun the direction, where, as there were probably inhabitants, there was danger. With only this conjecture to direct him, he immediately turned to the right. The passage terminated in a door, feebly secured; but as Ippolito laid down the lady to force back the bolts, he looked behind him with an eye of wonder, to mark was there no sound of pursuit or of danger following them.

Exhausted

Exhausted as his strength was, he found some difficulty in removing the fastenings of the door; it opened on a covered walk, through whose pillars, that still bore the form of cloisters, he beheld a garden on which the moonshine flung its rich and tremulous flood light. On Ippolito, panting from the vapours of a dungeon and torches, no object could have had such sudden power of refreshment and renovation, as the beams of the moon, and the breezes of night.

As he supported his companion, he perceived with delight, that the current of the air had recalled her spirits; she spoke not, but her limbs heaved, and her eyes unclosed, though without a ray of intelligence. As he now hastened with her through the vaulted walk, he distinguished all the features of the building to which the passages were attached. The high tufts of pine, and larch, and cypress concealed the lower parts of the fabric; but

but above them he could see the row of
small convential windows, with the antic
carvings of the battlements above ; at
their extremity, the great staircase window, stained with a thousand colours, that
gave their rich, romantic tingings to the
moon-beams, and the trees that waved
around it ; beyond, features still more
characteristic of the structure appeared ;
the niched and figured walls, the angles
of the buildings surmounted with crosses
of grey marble, and further still the
spire of the convent rich with the fantastic profusion of gothic embellishment.

As he still gazed, though he hastened
onward, he could see tapers gleaming in
different parts of the building ; and once
he thought he beheld a figure passing
among the shade at the opposite extremity of the garden. The walk which he
had traversed, by this time, terminated in
a portico, whose light pillars were connected by trellis-work, and mantled over
with

with luxuriant shrubs ; he crossed it, and
beheld before him an aperture in the
garden wall, whose fragments lay scattered around, through which he beheld
the open country in all the magic of
moonlight. He darted through it with
an impulse which annihilated weariness and fear, and found himself on a
rising ground, whose gradual slope, skirt-
ed with tufts of arbutus and magnolia, led
to the brink of a stream, whose waters reflected the turrets of the convent. Ippolito
hastened to the bank, and depositing his
unconscious charge beside it, sprinkled
her with water, and unfolded her vesture
to the air.

While she slowly recovered her intelligence and speech, Ippolito gazed on her
form, lovely even in the semblance of
death. Her long, dark hair that fell over
her face and bosom, like the foliage of the
cypress over a monumental marble, informed him she was not a religious ; yet
the

the building from which he had borne
her, was evidently a convent. Her first
emotions on recovery, which were terror
and surprise, as Ippolito had expected, he
endeavoured to calm, by the most respect-
ful assurances of safety and protection, de-
livered in a tone so humble and soothing,
as inspired her with a confidence her
strange circumstances opposed in vain.
When at length her perceptions became
clear, and her language collected, Ippolito supplicated her to inform him by what
means she had been involved in a situation so strange, as that from which he had
rescued her; of which, however, he
took care to suppress the circumstances
he judged too terrifying to be repeated
to her.

At the mention of the cemetery and
the convent, the lady shuddered, and, apparently too much agitated to answer his
inquiries, fell at his feet, and with a torrent of tears, avowed her innocence and
                                    her

her helplessness, and implored him to protect her from the horrors prepared for her by the persecutions of mysterious enmity, leagued with the oppressions of religious cruelty.

Her appeal was made in a language now little understood—the language of chivalry; of which no other ever possessed the power, when addressed by a beautiful and helpless woman, to a young man, noble and brave. Even at that period, this language was much disused; and though Ippolito felt its energy in every fibre of his heart, yet he could easily observe, that the manners and conceptions of the lady were utterly remote from those of ordinary life. He raised, and assured her, with impressive fervency, that while he possessed a weapon or an arm to wield it, no power should molest her; that he would defend her with the zeal of a lover, and protect her with the purity of a brother.

1   He

He then, while he conducted her along the bank of the stream, casting around his eyes in quest of some means of escape, of safety, or concealment, again implored her to explain the circumstances that had led to his discovering her.

The lady shrunk from the familiarity of a conference. Her timidity faltered in every accent, and shivered in every limb. She scarce accepted the assistance necessary to support her steps, and in vain endeavoured to raise her eyes to his, and discover if they confirmed the confidence his words inspired.

" I ought to trust you," said she; " nay, I must trust you; for I am destitute and defenceless; but if you are indeed a cavalier of honour, as your demeanour and voice bespeak, conduct me to some matron-relative, some female protector; and, till then, pity and forgive the fears of one, timid by nature, and

and by habit ; fears' that scarce give me breath to thank you for my life."

Ippolito was distracted by this appeal, which he could neither answer nor resist.   " Lady," said he, " I am wretched to afford you protection so imperfect. I am a wanderer myself, and all the safety I can promise you is borrowed from your innocence, and my own courage. I am, like you, a lorn and luckless being, without friend to appeal to, or assistance to claim."

The lady was again in tears as he spake ; but they seemed excited by a cause different from that which her last had flowed from.   " It is his voice," said she, with impressive emotion ; " it is his very language.   Are all men unhappy ? or are the brave and noble only persecuted ?   You, cavalier, are but the second i have ever seen, yet your language is exactly like *his*, whom I would I had never, never seen."   " And why, Signora ;"

nora;" said Ippolito, "is he unfortunate?"
" He said so." " What is his name?"
" He told me never to disclose it, but
that it was noble. I know but little myself of ranks or titles. Are you noble,
cavalier?" " There are few names more
illustrious in Italy than that of Montorio," said Ippolito, forgetting his habitual caution in the pride of the moment.
" Montorio!" shrieked the lady, in the
wildest tones of joy: " Oh, then, I am
safe. I must be safe with you. He is
a Montorio too; and, though he is unfortunate, he is the bravest, the noblest,
the loveliest"—" What, what is his name?"
said Ippolito, eagerly. " His name is
Annibal." " Annibal! how came he
here? He was at the castle of Muralto.
Where is he now? Wherefore did he
come, and where has he gone to?" " I
know not," said the lady, mournfully;
" but he is gone where I never shall see
him

him more. They who separated us will
never permit us to behold each other
again. Oh, that I knew where he was.
I think, I almost think I could fly to
him." "Lady, all you utter is mystery;
but there is, I fear, no time for any thing
but consulting our safety; if, indeed,
there remain enough for that. The
moon is setting; and I see tapers gliding about at the windows of the convent." "And hark, by that chime the
bell will toll for matins in an hour.
They chaunt their matins an hour before sun-rise. I see the vigil-lamp burning in Mother Monica's turret. Oh, Signor, where, or how shall we fly?"

To discover this, Ippolito debated, if
tumultuous anxiety can be called debate,
in vain. His horse he had left behind him
at Bellano, to which he knew not even
the direction. Of the country into which
he had emerged, after a subterrene passage,

sage, he could not be supposed to know any thing; and his companion, though a resident in it, was equally ignorant. All she could inform him was, that she had heard in the convent, Puzzoli was at no great distance from it. This, though contrary to Ippolito's topical conjectures, gave him, nevertheless, some definite object to pursue, though it supplied no means of attaining it.

As they wandered along the bank in quest of some track that communicated with that they intended to pursue, they descried a small boat, that was moored in a thick bed of rushes and watery weeds, and fluctuated lightly on the tide of the stream. " This is fortunate !" exclaimed Ippolito; " we shall be safer from discovery on the water, and shall probably reach some obscure fishing-hut in the windings of the river, where it will be easy to procure assistance without suspicion or delay."

The

The lady's reluctance to venture in a bark that had only one oar to navigate it, was overcome by her more immediate fears; for at that moment a sound was heard, which, she believed, was that of pursuit, issuing from the convent. Ippolito, who thought otherwise, concealed what he thought, lest the aggravated terrors of his companion should render her unable to proceed. They hastened thro' the willows and osiers that hung over the bank against which the bark was beating; but, as Ippolito was reaching for the oar, his companion called to him to observe an extraordinary appearance in the trees which suddenly seemed to bend towards the river, and then retire again, while their branches quivered with a strange vibration. Ippolito looked up for the confirmation of his fears, and, at the same moment, the convent bells rung out a quick and terrible peal, and its spire and turrets rocked with a motion perceptible in the reflection of the water.

The

The lady, screaming with horror, clung to Ippolito, who, combining in the moment, calm reflection with the fullest sense of danger, assured her they would be safer on the water.

As she yet hesitated in the distraction of fear, Ippolito sprung into the boat, and, extending his arms, implored her to embark while yet the ground supported her; but, as she attempted to follow him, the stream suddenly receding, flowed backward to its source with such rapidity, that Ippolito, when he recovered his sight, no longer knew the banks between which it was flowing. Around him all seemed in motion; the shrubs, the trees, the rocks, gliding past him with the undulating swiftness of a fluid; while, before him, the tide on which he floated, separating from that below it, left the bed of the river, black and bare, heaving up, as if the waters from beneath were rushing upward, with wreath-

ed

ed heaps of foam, that sparkled to the meteorous and misty sights with which the air was filled.

Amid the tumultuous sounds of mischief and terror, that now arose on every side, he listened with feeling agony for the voice of the unfortunate female, from whom he had been severed; but all power of discrimination was lost in another agitation of the river, which rushed into its former current with a velocity that left every known object behind it.

As he was borne along, Ippolito could see the turrets of the convent, of which he knew not whether the rent and tottering appearance was owing to the vibration of the air, or to the real injury they had sustained; but no vestige of his companion remained.   The ground on which he had stood appeared to be converted into a marsh, in which were only seen the up-turned roots of the willows

and

and osiers, nodding where their branches had waved a moment before.

The confusion was now general. Amid the concussion of rocks, the crash of buildings, and the hollow and tumultuous rushing of the earth, Ippolito could distinguish a thousand piercing tones of human distress, more terrible than all; the objects from which they issued, he was spared the sight of; but every murmur of inarticulate terror, was associated with the images of social or individual calamity in his imagination. He was still borne on with irresistible rapidity, till a third concussion checked the current with a shock so violent, that Ippolito was obliged to grasp the stern of the boat for safety. The stream moved to and fro with uncertain undulation, while a deep murmur trembled beneath its waters, and eddying whirls of a blackish hue boiled upon the surface, spirting out globes of foam and sand, and bodies from the river's bed,

then

all sunk and subsided. [The river resumed its natural course and level ; and the slender bark glided on in safety between the banks where solid and firm-seated substances had changed their places and forms with the levity of the atoms dancing in the wind.] Ippolito now employing the oar, navigated his boat with all the dexterity in his power, but such still was the fluctuation of the river, that he found himself unable to make either shore ; the current still bearing the boat onward with a force he found it fruitless to contend with.

In spite of the recent and dreadful commotion he had witnessed, Ippolito found it impossible to withdraw his feelings from his own situation, so strange and forlorn. Of all who contended with the terrors of the elements, who had so little to fear from danger ? for who had so little in life to hope or to pursue as he ? The rived earth, and the heaving flood had swallowed many a being that night,

night, whose dying thoughts clung to life with the energy of hope, and the fondness of desire; while they had spared one, who would willingly have sheltered his head from the dark conflict that beset it, in the gloomiest grave their chasms presented.

The inextinguishable persecution of the stranger, the jealous malignity of society, the gloomy presages of an irresistible fatality, and that mistrust of our own power; that sinking of soul which anticipates the issue of long and sore temptation, began to settle over his mind, making it night within him. He had fled from Naples to avoid the presence of his mysterious tempter, he had met him in the solitude of deserts : he had pursued him, and found him again in circumstances, of which no conjecture could furnish an explanation; they were separated again; but where might he not appear as suddenly as in the vaults at Bellano, or the cemetery of the convent ? Distance

tance of space, or strangeness of hour, were no obstruction to him; he might emerge after a subterranean journey, at Puzzoli, or appear again at Naples. But one expedient presented itself, the same which under similar circumstances had been suggested to Annibal, that of flying to another country. To abide the fixed and regular assaults of the stranger, was not tolerable even to thought, as its continuance would not only expose him to aggravated suspicion and danger, but to the greater mischief of familiarized guilt, at which he shuddered, for he had already begun to feel its influence.

The morning now began to pour a pale light through mist and fog on the landscape, and Ippolito looked back on the events of the night, as on the business of years. That a few hours only had passed since his arrival at Bellano the preceding evening; and that into those few hours, so many circumstances should have

have been compressed, almost exceeded the belief of reflection. As objects became stronger in the strengthening light, he discovered that the ravages of the late shock had been partial, and almost confined to that part of the country he had quitted; all around him seemed tranquil nd uninjured. At a distance he beheld along the banks, the huts of fishermen, scarce peering from among the tufts of the thick embowering trees, that love a watery soil, and here and there the sails of their early barks flitting on the distant waves, like the pinions of the white fowl that skim their surface.

He now endeavoured to moor his boat on the shore opposite to that he had embarked from; and at length, though destitute of any skill in the use of the oar, succeeded. He debarked near a small cluster of huts, where he procured the necessary information with regard to the distance of Puzzoli, from whence he resolved

solved immediately to return to Naples; and there make the necessary arrangements for passing into France. He had some faint idea of communicating his project to his brother Annibal, who seemed like himself, the thrall of a wayward fate; but of whose wanderings he knew nothing, except that he was no longer at the castle of Muralto.

While in this hamlet, a horse was procured for. him with much difficulty His soiled, though splendid dress, and his mingled air of grandeur and distraction, excited a curiosity, which he was compelled to appease by a plausible fabrication. As he endeavoured to utter this with fluency, a sting of anguish and proud shame darted through his whole frame: he remembered the stranger's prediction of his gradual immersion into vice and falsehood, and cursed the power that rendered an habitual violation of truth, a part of his existence.

A thousand times in the bold movements

ments of an open heart, he was about
to avow the truth, till he recollected
that it might be attended with many
evils, but not one advantage; and that
in his present progress, it was less necessary to consult his heart, than his
safety. He was informed when, to repel
inquiries, he began to inquire himself,
that the concussion of the earth the preceding night, had been felt but partially;
that the river had undergone some extraordinary fluctuations; but that they were
in daily terror of some great shock, such as
those they had lately experienced, usually
precede; and that they had understood
Vesuvius had been unusually turbulent
for some time. "And these are the
omens of my return," said Ippolito, as he
set out for Puzzoli.

The day was now advanced, and he pursued his way with the guarded and vigi-
lant firmness of a man who is prepared
for danger and interruption. He looked

T around

around with an eye, which habitual fear
had fixed in sternness, for the form of the
stranger, or some other portentous shape
to rush across his path, or glide dimly before him. His spirits seemed collected
for their last effort; their energies were
patient and stern, prepared to resist without violence, or to submit without desperation. Bodily weariness combined with exhausted solicitude, to produce that deep
and unbreathing stillness of soul, in which
the acting powers are not extinct, but
in repose. It was that frame into which
every mind sinks after violent struggles
and repeated defeats, and which usually precedes the last conflict it is able
to support—it was that frame of which the
force is indeed great, but the continuance
doubtful; and the defeat, if there be one,
total and decisive. It is too simple and
absolute for variety of expedients, or re-
newal of contest; its impulse is single
and collected; if it fail, it fails with-

I   out

out hope, and without effort—it was that frame, in which he whose intent was to deceive, would be least willing to encounter his victim. It resists the visions of imagination, it questions even the representations of the senses; but its gloom is a balance for its strength and capacity; it doubts, it resists, but it despairs.

No object occurred in the way to Puzzoli; those that presented themselves on his approach to the city, were in unison with his mind. It is a magnificent theatre of ruins. Antiquity has impressed her bold, gigantic charactery on their remains; she seems to sit among them like a sovereign, at whose feet distant ages and departed nations pour the tribute of their former greatness in their tombs, their temples, and their palaces. They lie scattered as around her footstool, in confused tints and shapeless grandeur. The great Domitian-way filled him with awe as he entered it; he felt the interests

that

that agitated him, disappear like the vicissitude of the life of an ephemeron, at the bare thought of the myriads that had trodden that way since its erection, with thoughts as tempestuous as his own, who had passed away without leaving a trace in the history of mankind.

The temple of Jupiter Serapis, and the ruins scattered around it, detained him till the heat of the day becoming intense, and operating with his sleepless and eventful night, of which he had only dozed a few moments in the turret-chamber at Bellano, he eagerly turned to the first inn the street presented, and after a slight refreshment, threw himself on the bed, and endeavoured to repair his strength for future encounters.

On awaking, he found evening had arrived; and a secret and half unconscious dread of returning to Naples, induced him to determine the remaining for that night at Puzzoli. He wished besides to discover

discover whether the suspicions enter-
tained of him were universal; if there
was no place where he could appear in
safety and innocence; whether the polished and enlightened habits of a city,
might not promise him protection from
that superstitious malevolence, to which
he had been exposed in the more remote
and savage parts of the country. He arose
therefore, and went out, but with dejection in his countenance, and distrust in his
heart. His eyes wandered vacantly over
the many objects of curiosity and delight
that encountered them; but hung with
supplicating and intense solicitude on
every human visage that passed him.

In an Italian city, the great church and
its avenues are usually the places of
principal resort. As Ippolito slowly, and
with agitation ill-concealed, passed through
one of those, two persons of ordinary
appearance followed him at a distance
he judged suspicious, till he observed
they

they were conversing on indifferent subjects. " 'Tis true," said one of them, " so extraordinary a circumstance has never occurred within the walls of Puzzoli; I could not have been persuaded of it, had I not witnessed it. It outdoes all the miracles ever performed within the walls of church or convent—it is a few steps from the confessional, in the principal aisle, and just beneath the window which bears the blazonry of the Mirolo family." The other assented to the singularity of the circumstance, and added, that he concluded no stranger could quit Puzzoli without visiting the great church, and beholding with his own eyes, so remarkable an object.

Ippolito, easily excited by the mention of the marvellous, and glad of the relief which an object of curiosity promised, repaired immediately to the great church. The antiquity and vastness of this awful structure scarce arrested his

step

step as he entered it; he passed on to
the principal aisle, and discovered a
group collected round the spot the person had described. A boding of some
dread, disastrous thing; some evil unmea-
sured and unexplored, darkly hovered in
his mind as he approached them.   He
resisted its effects with the feeling of a
man, who conscious that something terrible is approaching him, and determined
to meet and encounter it, receives the
intimation of evil as an appropriate and
natural presage, and is confirmed, not repelled by it.

As he advanced, he observed they were
gazing in different points of view on an
inscription in the wall, of which the characters seemed to have been traced in
blood.   The group gave way as he drew
near; he raised his eyes—the characters
were large and legible.   He beheld with
horror the very lines which were inscribed over the portal of the subterrene
chamber

chamber at Naples, which *then* surrounded
with more terrible imagery, he had scarce
noticed ; but of which he *now* recognised every impression with a tenacity
that appeared to have slumbered in his
mind till that moment.   All caution, all
power, of reflection forsook him at once.
It seemed as if the lines were visible in
their real character to him alone—to him
alone it seemed as if they were charactered
with lightning that seared his eyes.   In
the excess of ungovernable horror, he
turned around, and fiercely demanded,
" Who had done this, by whose means it
had been placed there ?"   The spectators
stared aghast, till one of much suavity
of address advanced, and inquired what
had discomposed him.   Ippolito in the
hoarse and breathless tones of passion,
repeated the question.   " That inscription," said the stranger, " has not been
lately placed there."   " It must have
been," said Ippolito in the wildness of his
emotions,

emotions, "it is but lately that I beheld
it in another place myself. Every movement around me seems to be conducted
by witchcraft—how may this have been ?"
" Your knowledge of the place where you
last saw, or imagined you saw it," said the
stranger, gravely, " may assist you to form
a probable conjecture on the movements
that brought it there, without doubt."

Half recalled by this speech, yet
still confused and distracted by this
unexpected witness of his secrets, Ippolito made an imperfect apology for his
vehemence, and added, " That the sight
of circumstances so extraordinary had
disturbed him." " They are indeed extraordinary," said the stranger. " Are
you then acquainted with them ?" said
Ippolito relapsing, and staring wildly at
him. " Am I known even here ?" The
circumstances relating to yonder inscription are undoubtedly extraordinary," said
the stranger, "but how far you are interested

terested in them, I cannot presume to
say." " I implore you to relate them,"
said Ippolito, " heed not me, or my interruptions; I am a wild, unhappy being; I am feverish from fatigue of body
and mind; heed not what I may say, or
how I may look as you repeat them. I
am innocent—in spite of those damning
characters, I am innocent. The stranger
half shrinking from his wild, appealing
glances, proceeded in his account.

" This cathedral church, Signor, is of
high antiquity, and frequently memorials
of the classic ages, and perhaps of others
more remote have been found within its
walls. The inscription before you," (the
stranger need not have referred to it, for
Ippolito was unable to remove his eye
from it) " is of such remote antiquity,
that it is supposed it was originally graven
on the stone before the building was
erected, as there is no tradition of its re-
cording any event since that period; it
                                        is

is therefore concluded to have been a fragment of ancient stone, accidentally employed in the first construction of the church. There have been many conjectures on the subject of its meaning, but it is unfortunately in a language which the literati of Europe are utterly unable to recognise. The words you see are barbarous, though the characters are Greek. The most probable conjecture I have yet heard, is founded on the two last words, κοτς, ομπηετς. Ancient authors have acknowledged that these words were employed in the Eleusinian mysteries; they have also admitted that they were words barbarous and unintelligible to those that used them, but were supposed to have some secret reference to the mysterious purposes of that institution. Is it not probable therefore that the whole inscription is the admonitory formula of the mysteries of which the words were admitted to be foreign; but of which the
characters

characters would in transcription be probably Greek, as those before us are? but while the learned had their conjectures, the superstitious had theirs also. There was a tradition connected with these characters, that whenever the fate of a distinguished family in Naples was approaching, the wall of the aisle of the great church at Puzzoli would weep blood. This was repeated from age to age with the partial wonder of imperfect credulity, till lately, when a circumstance occurred that revived its recollection.

It was about a month past that a stranger, tall and closely muffled in a dark habit, arrived in Puzzoli, and immediately repaired to the great church. It was the time of vespers : the stranger planted himself opposite this inscription. The congregation assembled, vespers were performed, the congregation dispersed, the stranger stood unmoved !" (The speaker, during his narrative, kept his eye intently

tently fixed on Ippolito). "It was the vigil of St. John the lesser; the service and offices were renewed every hour of the night, and mass was performed at midnight. Numbers of ecclesiastics came from other churches to assist, and the faithful were passing and repassing at the different hours of service the whole night, so that probably every inhabitant in Puzzoli had successively the opportunity of seeing this extraordinary person, who remained in one posture, silent and motionless the whole night, gazing on the inscription. Towards matin service, one of the lay-brothers going to extinguish the lamps which burned dimly in the dawning light, observed as he passed through the aisle, that the stranger had departed; and as he proceeded to replace the tapers which were nearly extinguished at the shrine yonder, he suddenly was heard to give a cry of horror, and exclaim, That the wall of the aisle was weeping blood ! Several

veral monks hastened to the spot. Whether they confirmed the lay-brother's report, I do not presume to say, but it is
certain, that ever since that period, those
characters which were before of the co-
lour of the stone, have retained the appearance of blood.

"Such are the circumstances, Signor,
which you must acknowledge to be sufficiently extraordinary." "Pardon me,"
said Ippolito, with a sudden and unnatural mildness of tone, "nothing to me appears extraordinary." "You must then
be *conversant* with such circumstances,
said the stranger. "Perfectly conversant—oh, there is no telling how familiar
I am with them!" said Ippolito, with a
frightful laugh. "You will then gratify
me by some conjectures on this singular
subject," said the stranger. "It is more
than conjecture," said Ippolito, answering
his own thoughts. "Have you any idea
of having seen the extraordinary person-
age

age I have described, before," continued
the stranger. Ippolito was silent. "Can
you form a conjecture where he is at present," pursued the wily stranger. "He is
here," answered Ippolito, in a tone that
transfixed him. "Here," repeated he,
trembling, and looking around. "Yes,
here," replied Ippolito, with eyes still
fixed on the inscription—"see him," he
murmured, "yes, I see him always; I see
him now, I hear him; blindness cannot
shut him out—I have lost myself, but I
cannot lose him."

The stranger who had at first raised his
eyes in wonder at Ippolito's unqualified
confessions, now examining his countenance, beheld it fixed in the fiery stare
of madness. Improving this appearance,
according to his own conceptions, into
demoniacal possession, he retreated with
the precipitation of fear, unnoticed by
the wretched young man, who was utterly
careless

careless of the construction put upon the expression of his misery.

He continued for some time gazing vacantly on the wall, and at length sunk against it, in helpless stupefaction; but it was a stupefaction merely of the senses. The operations of his mind were active and acute; he counted every drop of the tempest that was poured out upon him; as the lightning blazed around him, he seemed to dissect its fires with a prism, to concentrate its burnings, and measure their aggravated fury.

The prediction which he applied to his family, whose peace and honor would be for ever blasted by the deed he was tempted to perform. The appearance of the stranger (for he had but one archetype in his mind, for all beings of mysterious appearance and agency) and the obvious, though inscrutable connexion between the characters on the wall, and those he had seen in the vaults of the scene of blood

at

at Naples, rushed on his mind with a force condensed and complicated, and for a a while swept away all power of resistance.

He hung over them with his mental powers benumbed and impassive. He saw them as it were with a mental eye glazed and opaque, that can suffer a body to touch its very organ without feeling it. The intellectual frame, shocked by violence, had folded up its fine texture, and no further assault could compel it to a capacity of suffering. Real and proper absence of reason succeeded; substantial forms faded from before his eyes. He thought the persecuting *stranger* was again beside him forcing into his hands a dagger, which he endeavoured to refuse. The stranger, with a terrible smile, desisted, then retreating a step, held up the dagger, and pointing to the bloody drops which stained it, waved it over his head. The dead and crusted blood dissolved as he moved it

it, and dropt slowly on his face and
hands ; he shuddered in vision, and struggled to wake to free himself from the
terrible imagery. He awoke and felt it
still ; he started—looked around ; his
hands were bedropt with blood ; he touch-
it—it was warm, it flowed from his temples, which as he fell against the wall,
had been wounded by the pediment of
a tomb, and now streamed with blood, unfelt. He wiped it away without a groan,
and quitting the church, hasted back to
his apartment at the inn.

Here he strode about for some time in
agony of thought. The persecution that
hunted him, was aggravated tenfold by
his personal feelings and character : too
noble minded for the bare admission of
a criminal thought, and too impetuous for
the slightest restraint on his actions or
movements, he saw himself invested by
the most noxious characters of a criminal, and circumscribed in every motion
by

by his inexhaustible pursuer. He had
contended, and his struggles had only
wearied himself. he had fled, and his
flight had been measured and accompanied; he had endeavoured to retire from
the conflict in silence, and he had been
rouzed again to phrensy, by fresh in-
stances of the presence of his impassable
tormentor. To sit down in sullen despair, was equally hopeless. His pursuer
was not content with negative malevolence, he contended with him when he
resisted, he excited and goaded him, when
he was passive, he followed him in his
motions, and he was present with him
when he was at rest. There is no thought
more overwhelming than this; it disarms
the soul of every power of resistance,
yet leaves it nothing to hope from submission. "Oh, that he were human!"
Ippolito exclaimed, in the bitterness of
his soul, "that he were an assassin, and I
a lone and naked traveller in the depth of
a moun-

a mountain-forest; that he were an inquisitor, and I a prisoner in his grated and airless dungeon; that he were an earthly tyrant, and I the meanest of his slaves who had incensed him, and stood before him, surrounded y the ministers of torture; then I could measure the power I had to contend with, and prepare my own for resistance; then I could know exactly to what they could extend, and where they *must* terminate. I could image to myself that point where exhausted cruelty could not compel another groan; where nature would mock at the impotence of power. Oh, that he were even of an order of beings above me, whose powers could be recognised and limited; then I might know how far his commission to punish might reach, and insult him with its imbecility. Definite misery cannot be intolerable to an immortal being. Though he pursued me with the rage of the dragon, I would yet know

know that the key of his pit was kept by an angel; though his commission were to last a thousand years, that thousand years would be to me, but as yesterday. But how can I contend with an inaccessible enemy, whose power is undefined, and whose duration is unimaginable? I know not yet if he be man or demon. His goadings and suggestions drive me to phrensy; to resist them is becoming impossible, and to obey them, is to devote myself to destruction, body and soul."

The echo of his loud and agitated voice at this moment coming to his ear, he suppressed it; and at the interval, he thought he heard voices whispering at his door; he stopt, and listened; for fear had made him suspicious of trifles. A voice then articulated, " This must be his apartment--that was his voice." After a moment's pause, another whispered, " He is silent now—did you mark his words?" Several other sentences were uttered in suppressed

suppressed tones, and he then heard step
retiring through the passage that led to
his room.

He hastened to the window, and saw
three persons of ordinary habits pass into
the street. It was a dusky evening in the
close of autumn; he could neither distinguish their persons nor their faces. He
was recalled from his conjectures, by the
voice of his host, who passing near the
door exclaimed, " I cannot conceive who
they are, unless they may be ministers of
the Inquisition?   St. Iago be my protector.   The sight of them makes me tremble from head to foot." He then passed
into a hall adjacent to Ippolito's room,
where others were apparently assembled,
and eagerly repeated his suspicions and
his fears to them.

The whole company were in commotion. The name of the Inquisition operated
like that of pestilence or the sword
amongst them. " Alas," said the host,
" what

" what have I done, that they should honour me with this visit ?"   " Perhaps this
visit is meant to some of your guests,"
said a strange voice, " do you know who is
at present under your roof."   " You are
the only stranger," said the host, " and
you, Signor, look too like one of themselves, to be in any dread of their visit."
" Are you sure of this?" said the other
voice, " Is there no stranger under your
roof but me?"   " Santo Patrone," said
the host, "sure enough there is a strange
cavalier in the house ; but he has remained in his chamber since he entered
it, and I had quite forgotten him."   " Has
he remained alone ?—*that* appears suspicious ; you should observe him." " Observe him ! not for the world ; I would
not take the full of this room of gold ;
and watch a heretic, a criminal of the Inquisition ! How do I know but the very
sight of him would make me as bad as
himself ?"   To this wise observation the
other

other assented, apparently with a view of aggravating the fears of the simple host, which were now extreme and oppressive. " Alas," said he, " what an age is this for good catholics to keep inns in! It was but lately, an inn-keeper at Celano, as innocent as myself, lodged a cavalier, from Naples, a strange man, who, they say, never sleeps at night; and of whom things are told, that would make the hair of a good catholic stand upright." " Have a care," repeated the stranger, " that the same person be not within your walls at this moment." " Jesu Maria forbid," said the host, crossing himself. " If he be under your roof, you are answerable for his appearance," said the stranger. " It cannot be he," said the host, eagerly, vindicating himself from the imputation, " for these plain reasons—" Here he enumerated several circumstances relative to Ippolito's appearance; every one of which tended to confirm what he meant to disprove.

"

" I tell you," said the stranger, exalting his voice, " he is within these walls. Look to him, as you will answer it to the most holy Inquisition."

For some moments after this terrible sentence, the whole company seemed stunned into silence. Ippolito, partaking of their sensation, remained listening, rather from an incapacity to exclude the sound, than any positive effort of attention.

" Who was he that came among us?" said the host at length, in a voice of fear. Every one alike disclaimed any knowledge of him. Some withdrew from the spot he had just quitted; others looked fearfully towards the door. All agreed that he had entered unperceived; that he had mingled in the conversation before they knew he was present; and that he had departed without sound or visible motion.

VOL. II.   u   They

They then began to examine the few words he had uttered; to compare their descriptions of his appearance, and their ideas of his real character and purposes, till, almost petrified with fear, they scarce ventured to raise their eyes to each other's visages, or to trim the lamp, which the imagination of each had tinged with vivid blue.

At length, their consultations took a less abstract turn, and they jointly determined on the expediency of apprising the holy Office of the character of their guest. But Ippolito, obeying the impulse of nature and despair, with a bold and rapid movement, threw open the door between the rooms, and stood amongst them. The group at this time were the host, the females of his family, their confessor, the monk of an adjacent monastery, and some Campanian travellers.

" I am

" I am Ippolito di Montorio," said he, with a disarming voice; " but I am not the monster you dread." In the energy of the preceding moment, he had conceived an appeal of resistless strength and eloquence; but his powers of utterance failed him. He tried in vain to collect the scattered images; they swam darkly before him; their force only oppressed and stifled him. He stood with extended arms, and a form whose expression, with the female party at least, amply supplied the place of elocution.

The party, astonished and dismayed, remained silent, stealing, at intervals, a glance of doubt and fear at the spot where he stood. Their silence chilled and repressed the unhappy Ippolito. With violence he could have contended, and with remonstrance he could have reasoned; but what was to be done with hopeless silence?

At

At length, the flush of his first impulse utterly fled, and his spirits dispersed and weakened, in a faltering voice he addressed the host, intreating him not to accredit the wild and unauthentic suspicions of the vulgar, nor lightly to admit charges so terrible against a being, to whom no means of purgation were allowed, and against whom no definite proof could be urged.

His ardour augmented by what he mistook for the stillness of attention, he proceeded to call Heaven to witness his innocence. He attested every saint that he was a firm believer, and a good catholic. " This is indeed," said he, " the time for me to cleave to God, when all his creatures desert and abhor me." He told them his sufferings arose from a dark and untold cause, that was locked within his own breast; " But those," said he, " who do not solicit confidence, are not

therefore

therefore to be excluded from compassion."

He was proceeding with the increasing warmth which our own vindication seldom fails to inspire, when he was checked by a deep and universal murmur of detestation. Wizard, infidel, and " Eretico damnabile," were echoed from every mouth. " I implore you," said Ippolito, struggling with emotions that made utterance painful, " to retract those horrible words, or at least to reflect on them. Be not so inconsistent in inhumanity; be not so wanton in persecution. Did I possess the powers you ascribe to me, would I stand here to plead for reputation and honour to such a tribunal? Would I supplicate beings from whom I never expected to hear a sound myself but in supplication? Would not my resentment shiver you to atoms? Would not my *sport* scatter you to the winds? Would

5   I not

I not myself mount on their wings, and
fly to regions where persecution would
not reach me ?"

"Stop your cars!" cried the host in
horror ; "he is uttering some spell. He
talks of the winds as familiarly as of a
horse. Signor, whoever you are, I implore you to quit my house. Only quit
it before the roof falls on us, and then
you may mount the first wind you meet,
and ride to the devil on it too if you
like, with my best prayers for your speedy
arrival." "Oh !" said Ippolito, descending, in his distress, to the plainest language;
"talk not, I conjure you, of driving me
from your house. I have often afforded
shelter, but never asked it before. The
protection of your roof is but little for
a son of the house of Montorio to beg ;
but misery is humble. I feel if I am
driven from your doors no other will be
opened to me. It will be the sealing of

2   my

my fate. I shall cease to have strength
for any further conflict, or spirits for any
further appeal. Will you be the first to
raise the outcry of savage pursuit; to
blast the victim of imaginary infection? I
claim the common privileges of a traveller. I am spent and overworn with weariness. Many days have past since I have sat
at a domestic board, or stretched myself
on a quiet bed. My wanderings have been
restless and incessant."

" So they may well have been," said
the monk, who thought it time for him
to interpose: " Fac, ut illi similes sint
rotæ." " Sit via eorum cæca ac peri-
culosa, angelus autem Domini profliget
eos."

" Do not," said Ippolito, with patience
almost exhausted, " do not overwhelm
me with this blind and sottish severity.
Ye have but one standard to judge of
criminals by, and ye make it a bed of
Procrustes, to all alike. Ye have but one
formula

formula of execration, and you fulmi-
nate that without thought or discrimination. Is there no difference between
offenders? Are there no gradations in
evil? Is suspicion to operate like conviction, and is conviction itself to exclude humanity? Do you reckon as
guilty alike, the stubborn villain, from
whose barred and brazen side your
shafts rebound as they would from a
rock, and an erring brother, to whom
the bare glance of a reproachful eye is
as iron that enters into his soul? Do
you reckon lost alike, him who has gone
down so deep into the gulph, that to
follow him would be to sink along with
him: and him who yet shivers on the
verge, and who can be pushed from his
hold by despair?"

"If you repent, and make expiation
for your enormities," said the monk;
"the church is an indulgent mother, and
will

will absolve you on your confession and penitence."

"And is it then impossible to procure the privileges of humanity, but at the price of pouring out your whole soul to men, who can neither judge of its sufferings, nor heal its breaches; who will dismiss you with the cold, professional look of the Levite, but sprinkle neither oil nor wine upon you? Is it not possible that a man may retain his integrity, and yet cherish some secret he cannot disclose? Can you not believe him possessed of resolution to bear up against some sore and inward trial, unless he forfeits that resolution by detailing its exercise? Is there no compassion for the shame of suffering? Is there no garment for the writhings of a naked and wounded mind, to whom the very air and light of day are torture, and who feels it is exposed, not to compassion, but to curiosity? To complain is, to

u 5   me,

me, hateful and uncongenial ; but to
complain to the incredulous, to the un-
pitying, to those who debate whether
you are a criminal or a madman, while
they listen to you—must, must, this be
done ? Or, may I not be reckoned a fel-
low-creature ?"

"By my holy order," said the monk, " he
blasphemes the church and her sacraments."
Ippolito turned from him indignantly.
" You," said he to the females, " have
the habits of women : Oh ! have you not
the hearts ? Judge of me in the gentleness of your natures. I am not what
cruel and bigotted men have told you.
I am like yourselves. I differ only from
others in my sufferings. I am no wizard,
no sorcerer, no heretic. How can you
credit such absurdities of one so helpless,
so supplicating, so persecuted ? I am like
yourselves. I have, like you, a dread of
persecution, a hatred of oppression, a
reputation

reputation to be blasted, a peace to be destroyed, feelings to be wrought to frenzy. Feel these hands I hold out to you; they are warm with life and fever- ish blood. Put your hand on my side. Feel my heart; it is beating, it is burst- ing with agony. I would it were broken this moment" Overcome by anguish, he staggered, he fell backward. A few burn- ing tears fell from his eyes; but they neither gave him relief, nor the power of utterance. "Christo benedetto," said the women, bursting into tears, "how beautiful he is! Ah! madre di Dio, what a pity!" "It is no pity," said the monk. "Satan can transform himself into an angel of light. I have seen him more than once myself, in the shape of a white pidgeon."

Ippolito, swallowing down his tears, sprung, with a convulsive impulse, to the knees of an old man, who had hitherto

sat.

sat silent, and whose mild and venerable aspect seemed to announce an exemption from the resentments of nature. " Father, father," said he, " your looks promise me confidence and compassion. You are already almost an inmate of that world where prejudice and passion are unknown. By your white hairs, I adjure you, if you have a son like me, believe me, acknowledge me, commiserate me. I am innocent, I *am* innocent ; and to leave that impression on such a heart as yours, would be well purchased by the suspicion and abhorrence of a thousand such as those around us."

The old man, who had vainly struggled to free himself from Ippolito's earnest hold, at length exclaimed with vehemence, " If I had a son like you, I would pray to heaven to make me childless. My grey hairs are defiled by the appeal you make to them. I have lived three score and eight years, and I had thought to have

have closed my eyes in peace; but the sight of you has prevented it.   I have lived too long, since I have lived to see you.   I had heard of such wretches before.   They were old, and withered, and miserable, and might almost be forgiven for resorting to forbid len sources to seek from them what nature and this world denied them.   But you, Oh! you, so young, so beautiful, so exalted, what temptation, what excuse, what plea could the destroyer of souls prevail with, to make you seal your ruin, body and soul? Release me; my heart is breaking to see you look so.   Why have you not the visage of a fiend as well as the spirit? I might grow a heretic myself looking at you   Let me go; my blood curdles at your touch.   I said I had lived too long; but I will not think so till I have heard of your terminating your horrid exist-ence in the dungeons of the Inquisi-tion."

The

The old man spake with the energy of virtuous abhorrence. He shook in every limb, and marked himself with the cross wherever Ippolito had touched him; but his failing voice bespoke a lingering of humanity, which his zeal contended with in vain.

Ippolito retreated from his last appeal. The fountain of his heart seemed dried up and sealed. The vitals of humanity were parched and withered within him. He extended his arms, and looked upward. " Then I am outlawed of nature. I am divested of the rights of being. Every ear is deaf, and every heart is iron to me. Wherever I tread, the sole of my foot dries the streams of humanity. I have done; but you, Oh, you! may you one day know what it is to knock at the human heart, and find it shut! May you know what it is to fly from the hell-hounds of superstition, and hear their howl double on you at every winding! May

May you feel, with me, the malignity of men united with that of demons, to chase and scatter you! and may the shelter to which you fly, drive you forth, as you have driven me, to despair!" He rushed out of the house, and ran wildly into the street, reckless of expected danger, and only seeking to subdue the sense of anguish by impetuosity of motion.

"Heaven be praised!" said the monk, "his smooth words did not seduce us to listen to him. He shewed his cloven foot, departing, however." "I saw no cloven foot," said the host, rather angrily. "He went away, to my mind, just like a cavalier in a passion." "Just," said the women; "he did not go away a bit like a sorcerer; there was no blue flame or earthquake; nor did he carry away a stone out of the wall with him." "How!" said the monk; "will you presume to say he went out of the house

like

like a catholic?" " To be sure he did,"
said the host; " and, after all, I shall
have nothing to tell of to-morrow in the
town." " His presence has infected you,"
said the confessor: " will you deny that
he was followed by a track of sulphur;
in which you might see imps flitting up,
and down, like motes in a sun-beam."
" Holy father, be not incensed," said the
wife; " I do think there is indeed a smell
of sulphur." " I begin to perceive it
myself," added the host. " Let us pray,"
said the monk, &c. &c. &c.

Ippolito traversed the streets with rapid steps. Evening was not wholly closed; but he could perceive that his presence every where anticipated the solitude
of night. Children fled from their sports
as· he passed; and the few passengers he
met darted eagerly into another direction.
The influence of the stranger seemed to
surround him, like the spell of an enchanter, converting every human being he met
into

into a silent shadow, and making him a shadow to them.

It was then he felt the extent of his misery. To be alone on earth; to forget the language of man; to lose the vital functions of nature; to be amerced of his humanity; to find " those cords of a man," by which the human race are drawn together, relaxed and severed by a power that was not death; to feel, like the Mexican victims, his heart, the seat of life and sensation, taken out, and held before his eyes, yet panting; to die mentally, yet still feel the burdens and sorrows of the flesh. A deep and utter desolation shadowed over his soul. He loathed life, but knew not how to die.

He still continued to walk, from mere hopelessness of rest or shelter. Night arrived. He loitered on without approaching a door, or addressing an individual. The blast scattered his dark hair;

his

his feet began to falter—when three persons, suddenly surrounding him, commanded him in the name of the most holy Inquisition, to follow them.

This was expected; yet he felt thunderstruck when it actually arrived. To an Italian ear, that name speaks unutterable things. It is associated, in their imagination, with every idea of horror and ruin eternal confinement, undiscovered oblivion, solitary and languishing death, and all shadowed over with a mist of superstitious fear, such as the fancy believes to hover round the cave of an enchanter, and which is suggested by the peculiar mysteriousness of the proceedings of that tribunal.

Ippolito looked wildly on the men, and half-drew his sword; but, after a moment's conflict, folded his arms, and followed them. At this period, the Inquisition was not so fully organized in its several departments.

partments and motions, as it has since been. Its principal seats were then Rome and Naples. In the other cities it only maintained agents, who, with the help of the secular arm, observed, apprehended, and dispatched their several offenders to the principal seats of the office. The present agent at Puzzoli, was a Signor Giberto Angellini, a man of intelligence and humanity.

There was no regular prison in the town; but the number of suspected persons had lately increased so much, that they had been compelled to repair and fortify an ancient structure, that had formerly been a Roman fort, and which stood on a mole on the western shore, whose waves beat against its hoary bastions, murmuring sounds of woe to the sufferers within

Thither Ippolito was conducted. At another hour his mind would have thrill-ed ed and dilated with awe, as the dark features of his prison emerged to his view, in the windings of his long approach to it. The rude, gigantic portal, of a form elder than what was called ancient centuries back; the long perspective of arched passages, over which the torches of his conductors threw a flaring and shadowy light, fringing with deep red the tufts of weed and dusky grass, that wound through their clifts; and shewing the bold irregular shapings and fractures of their unhewn walls; while often, as he passed among them, he caught bright glimpses of the distant sea, quivering in the moonshine; or of the sky, whose deep, clear blue was strongly marked by the black indentures of the walls, whose edges it spangled with stars, finer than points of dew—the dark habits, the gliding steps, and the muffled visages of his guard, giving almost a visionary solemnity to their progress.

They

They arrived at length at a larger and more regular apartment of the building. Ippolito observed, in its dark extent, grated windows, and arched doors, that bore proofs of modern repair. His guard here bowing profoundly, resigned him to a person of solemn appearance, who advanced from the opposite extremity of the hall, and silently lighting a torch at a lamp suspended from an iron chain in the roof, beckoned to Ippolito to follow him.

They began to ascend a flight of stone steps. The cold wind, issuing from a thousand crevices, chilled Ippolito; yet he saw neither door nor window. The ascent seemed endless. His conductor glided on in unbreathing silence. Ippolito stopped. The man stopped also, by way of inquiring, without words, the reason of his delay. " I listen," said Ippolito, " for the relief of some sound beside the echo of my own steps." The man paused for a

few

few moments, as if to convince him no
such relief was to be expected, and then
glided on as before. They now reached
an arched passage, where guards, fully
accoutered, stalked backwards and for-
wards, in silence also. They bowed to
the person who conducted Ippolito, but
at *him* did not even direct a casual glance.
The sullen habits of their office seemed
to have extinguished all human feeling,
even curiosity, the last that might be supposed to linger within the walls of an Inquisition.

His conductor now led Ippolito through
a dark, narrow chamber, to another, more
spacious, but equally gloomy ; and lighting a lamp attached to the wall, and
pointing to a pallet scarcely distinguishable in a distant recess, silently disappeared. Ippolito threw himself on it, and,
reflecting that the influence of the stranger was excluded here, sunk into sleep.

He

He was three days in confinement before he was summoned to attend the Inquisition. During that period, the solitude and silence of his prison; the noise-
less step and mute visage of his guard;
the few and monotonous sounds that reached him from without; the toll of the bell;
the chimes of the night; the whispered
watch-word of the guard; and the hoarse
dashing of the sea at the foot of his tower—
had tranquillized his mind, and poured
into it a still and patient melancholy,
not destitute of vigour, but utterly distinct
from sternness.

On the third day, he was conducted to
Signor Angellini's presence. Through
the passages he traversed, he perceived
day-light gradually diminishing, from the
thickness of the walls, and the narrowness
of the grated apertures. It was almost
twilight, when they reached a low door.
One of the guard touched it with a staff
he held, and it opened. Ippolito was
led

led into a room hung with black, and lighted by a lamp. The inquisitor and his secretary were seated at a table at the upper end. The guard withdrew. There was little of the grim formality of an inquisitorial examination observed, save that Ippolito was seated opposite the agent, the prisoners of that tribunal not being permitted to stand during the examination.

When the inquisitor raised his eyes, he seemed involuntarily struck with Ippolito's form and expression: and surveyed his wild and woe-tinted countenance with a feeling, Ippolito thought proscribed within those walls. " Be so good, cavalier," said he, " as to inform me whether you bear the name of Montorio?" " I did not know," said Ippolito, " that it was part of the business of this office to inquire the name." " In this case it is necessary," observed the inquisitor, " as part of the depositions laid before

before us refer to the actions of a person named Montorio, and part state, that you are that person; this point, therefore, requires the first consideration."

Ippolito had heard much of the subtlety of the proceedings of this tribunal. He determined to make no concessions he could avoid, and to give no information he could with-hold. "If your information be accurate," said he, "you need not inquire my name; if it be not, it becomes you to seek from a more authentic source. I shall not disclose my name." "I must then proceed as if you had," said the inquisitor; "that is the rule of our office in such cases; but I must observe, few are thus anxious to conceal a name they have done nothing to dishonour." "To dishonour it," said Ippolito, with dignity, "would be to avow it in such a cause; to prostitute it to the refutation of absurd and malevolent charges." "You are then acquainted with the nature of the charges urged against you ?" said the inquisitor, with surprise. " How is it possible I should be ignorant of them ?" said Ippolito; " they assail me from every mouth, at every step. The solitude of deserts, and the sanctity of churches protect me in vain. They pursue me in society; they haunt me alone; they have poisoned my existence; they have subverted my peace, almost my reason." " If you were conscious of innocence," said the inquisitor, " why did you not apply to the church, or the secular power. No unoffending person can be thus persecuted with impunity in a civilized country."

Ippolito gnawed his lip, and was silent. He perceived that the stranger, with the malignity and art of a demon, had snared him in his favourite pursuit; that he had involved him in guilt, which to conceal, was no longer possible, and to avow, in such a country, was fatal.

" Were

" Were you ever in Puzzoli before ?"
said the inquisitor. "Never." " Did you
witness any remarkable object on your arrival there ?" Ippolito hesitated. The question was repeated. " I saw an extraordinary inscription in the aisle of the great
church." " What was the reason of the
emotions you betrayed on beholding it ?"
" The emotion of surprise was too natural and general to require an individual
to assign reasons for it; many others ex-
pressed the same, whom I do not see
here." " You were observed to use some
remarkable words." " Were my words then
noted by casual observers ?" said Ippolito,
shocked and overwhelmed at this discovery.
" Those around you were not casual observers," said Angellini ; " your motions
and your expressions have, from the moment of your quitting Naples to the present, and for some preceding time, been
in the possession of the holy Office."
At this terrible intimation, Ippolito sunk
back in his seat, and hid his face with his
x 2   hands.

hands. He felt like a man, who, believing he has eluded the pursuit of an assassin, traverses a long and dreary path with hope, and just as he approaches its termination, perceives that his pursuer has only sported with his destruction ; that he has followed him step by step, and is prepared to spring on him as he reaches the last. The inquisitor seemed slightly affected by his appearance, but renewed the examination.

" Had you," said he, " ever beheld that inscription before ?" Ippolito, within whom all power or impulse of resistance began to fail, admitted he had. " When, and under what circumstances ?" said the inquisitor. Ippolito hesitated, but was too dispirited to construct an answer, till the question was repeated with solemnity, " Ask your informer that," he replied, " and his answers will betray another victim to the holy Office ; his confession will unfold a horrible tale."

" He

" He has already unfolded it," said the inquisitor. " What—is it possible that he has surrendered himself to the judgments of the church ? Has he disclosed the mystery of his iniquity ? Is it possible that a vindication awaits me ?" " Of whom do you speak ?" said the inquisitor, " there appears some mistake here." " Of whom !" said Ippolito with vehemence, " of the evil one that haunts and troubles me ; of him who has blasted my existence, who has defiled my conscience with horrid thoughts, who has hunted me from society, and chased me into the talons of the inquisition." " You speak then of one I am a stranger to," said the inquisitor, " my informer was an individual of unquestionable innocence." " It is impossible," said Ippolito, " he could not have obtained his information if he were ; none but agents were witnesses of the transaction." " Have a care," said the inquisitor. " If it be impossible that a witness

witness could be innocent, what are we
to think of you?" " You confound, you
overwhelm me," said Ippolito, " is this
an examination? I say, whatever guilt is
supposed to be attached to me, the person
who informed you of it, must partake;
for where I was an agent, he was the
same; if he is innocent, I must be innocent also." " You accuse me unjustly,"
said Angellini, " I extort no concessions,
I equivocate myself into no unhappy
man's confidence; I desire to abide by
the plain and direct meaning of your
words. And to convince you of the can-
dour of my proceedings, I give you to
understand, that the charges exhibited
against you are of so important a nature,
that nothing but the most irrefragable
documents should substantiate or re-
fute them; I have therefore compelled
the personal attendance of the principal
witnesses, who are not yet arrived. This
I inform you of, lest you should be terrified

rified into a confession on the usual apprehension instilled by inquisitors; that
they are already in possession of every
thing which confession can inform them
of. You have now time to arrange
your thoughts, and prepare your defence.
I only wished by this private inquiry to
discover if you had any wish to be spared
the shame of involuntary confession, and
being confronted with positive testimony. You may retire; I lament your apparent obstinacy. I warn you—you have
to do with a tribunal with whom the he-
roics of affected defiance will avail just
as little, as the sullen retreat of an universal and positive negation."

Touched by this open address, and
wrung by the thought, that the only sentiment even the generous seemed to have for
him, was a doubtful compassion; Ippolito
would have paused, and appealed—but
it was too late; the guard, on a signal
unperceived but by themselves, advanced
to

to reconduct him to his apartment, and the inquisitor and his secretary silently vanished in the obscurity of the chamber.

He was led back to his solitary tower, where he had abundant leisure for the preparation the inquisitor had recommended to him; but he had now no resolution for it. His mind was weary with misery; his powers weakened by continued sufferance, were now relaxed to that frame, which, out of great events and ample ranges of view, selects only the recent and proximate points, and dwells on them with minute partiality. Of his various and eventful life he only remembered and revolved his conference with the inquisitor. But by what means the stranger could reveal the transactions at Naples without acknowledging himself as a principal, or any other person could obtain a knowledge of them, he conjectured in vain. Yet even this state of uneasy debility and helpless fear was not utterly

without

without relief. The varying colours of the sky, and aspects of the ocean, the wild scenery of rocks and ruins, that indented the bold curvings of the shore, and the endless varieties their shapes and hues underwent from the transitions of morn to noon, of evening to moon-light, with imperceptible gradations, too soft for the quaintest pencil, or most curious eye to follow; all these were with him in his prison. The influence of the stranger could not change the eternal forms of nature, nor prevent their gleaming through the high-grated window of his tower. At intervals, he even perused the fragments of Cyprian's strange story, which had been spared in the search he underwent on his entrance into the Inquisition.

As long as the faintest ray of light trembled over the water or the shore, Ippolito lingered at his casement, studiously confining his thoughts to external objects, pleased even to observe the distant

x 5   tokens

tokens of involuntary sympathy, that were paid to his situation, or its imagined tenant. To observe the fishermen pausing on their oars, as they glided round the vast projecting buttresses that propped the rock on which his tower was perched, and shake their heads, as they threw a scarce perceptible glance at its steep and impassable height. When the guard silently lit his nightly lamp, Ippolito producing his manuscripts, would pore over them with unrelaxed attention; not to procure pleasure, but to exclude pain.

Yet some of these excited his sympathy, exhausted as it was with personal claims. They marked out regular periods of life as well as passion, and therefore conciliated a degree of substantial sympathy and vivid belief, not always accorded or sought in such performances.

In the fragments he now perused, the writer seemed to have exhausted every

drop

drop of the bitterest draught ever held to
the pale lip of human affliction—disappointed passion. She seemed to delight
herself with imaging the last distress
that could be now inflicted or with-held,
—that of separation from the object she
had loved in vain. Whether this separation was voluntary or compulsive, imaginary or real, could not be discovered
from the lines themselves; but to Ippolito, they seemed like the struggles of
weak resolution, (such as might be supposed to linger in the breast of a vestal
crazed with love,) torturing itself with
more last looks at an object it could not
accomplish, and could not renounce. The
first of these fragments appeared an attempt to blend the warmth of passion
with that of devotion. Yet the passion
was neither sanctified, nor the devotion
softened by the union.

I.

'Tis past! my anguish'd heart proclaims
  The mortal conflict o'er;
This silence speaks what words can't tell;
  We part to meet no more.

II.

Do not, I pray thee, shed one tear,
  Let no sigh reach my cheek,
Or my o'er-labour'd sense will fail,
  My o'er-fraught heart will break.

III.

I've wound my fainting courage high,
  And struggled hard for breath;
Oh, let me bear away this smile,
  To deck the face of death.

IV.

Is it not near, the blessed hour,
  When, fleshly suffering o'er,
We'll glow with spirits' sinless loves;
  We'll meet to part no more.

But who can tell the last farewell of
passion? It appeared impossible to tear
                                      her

her from this subject. Her mind seemed fixed on a point from which the object never lessened to her view. The next denoted a state of mind strange and rare. It was that in which all the corporeal parts of love have evaporated, and only the spirit lingers behind, to mourn over the remains, in which the decay of passion is lamented, not as a cessation, but a source of woe. In which the total decline of feelings, which have already begun to wax cold and hopeless, is anticipated, in which the " loosing of the silver cord, and the breaking of the golden bowl," is expected with an anguish, which the loss of acknowledged calamity can scarcely be believed to inspire, except in the visionary mind of love.

I.

Good night, good night, my journey ends,
   The night-shades are closing fast ;
But one faint ray prolongs the light,
   Nor long shall that faint ray last.

                           Still,

II.

Still, still while it gleams, must my steps pursue,
    Still rove by that witching ray ;
But not long shall I follow the false path it points,
    But not long shall the wanderer stray.

III.

Light the landscape no more, thou fairy beam;
    But fade in the face of the west ;
And let all be cold as the bed of my home,
    And dark as the night of my rest.

IV.

For when mine eye views thy meteor sheen,
    The way's long toil seems won,
And hope's quick pulse wakes my withered heart,
    And my failing steps urge on.

V.

Thou unnamed one, on whom while I gaze,
    Mine eyes swim in dews of delight ;
'Tis thou art my lone way's setting star,
    In solitude and night.

VI.

But thou whose eye lit my early hope,
    Come, witness its last gleam o'er ;

                              Come,

Come, catch the least, weak, struggling sigh
   Of the heart that can love no more.

VII.

For I raise my eyes to that madding form,
   That once made their senses fail ;
And I twine my languid arm in thine,
   And unchang'd is my cheek so pale.

VIII.

And that soften'd tone, to which rapture danced;
   Its nameless spell is o'er ;
And that eye, to whose beam the day was pale,
   Darts fire and madness no more.

IX.

It is not that thou art less lovely, love,
   Or less bright thy noon-tide high ;
The sense still might bask in thy sunny cheek,
   The soul still be lit by thine eye.

X.

But I am cold, and a deathly chill
   O'er each frozen feeling creeps ;
And, cold, the flow of the fervid fails,
   And, hush'd, the loudest sleeps.

                                     The

XI.

The master-hand wakes their song no more,
   And their sound of accord is low ;
And my wearied pulse is dead to pain,.
   And my severed heart beats slow.

XII.

Then wonder not that my sighs are still'd,
   And the cold tear congeals in mine eye ;.
'Tis nature fails when passion fades ;.
   And love only with life can die..

XIII.

For I have lived till each lost hour
   Has floated down passion's stream,
And loved till Heaven's immortal light:
   Was quenched in thy brighter beam.

XIV.

My time, my health, my mind, my peace,
   Were tribute to its sway ;
And when each humbler offering fail'd,
   I pined my life away.

XV.

Then wonder not, my heart's lost hope,
   At its scanted homage weak ;

                                      But

But read the cause in my sunken eye,
  In my wan and woe-stained cheek.

XVI.

But shouldst thou approach the solemn bed,
  Where fluttering life is stay'd,
To pour its last look on thy form,
  Or for thy peace to plead ;

XVII.

May I not at that hour, when anger is dumb,
  My heart's deep wound unfold;
Oh, may it not fall from my dying lip,
  That tale of horror untold.

XVIII.

Oh no, for ere then will the fine nerve be broke,
  That should raise my closing eye ;
And all that would prompt my trembling tongue,
  Shall be hushed as its last, low sigh.

But the tranquillity promised by the
farewell to passion, was mere temporiz-
ing. She still lingered over the remembrance, and endeavoured to describe the
desolation of life after its spring and hope
                                    are

are extinguished for ever. Compared
to her former feelings, those she was
now possessed with appeared like those
of a departed spirit, hovering over the deserted abode and memory of its human
agency.   Her love darted a spent and
feeble ray through mist and vapour.   Its
direction was unaltered, but its lustre
gone.

I.

There was a ray that lit my life,
   It has sunk in the west so pale;
And once ere mine eyes that sight might see,
   I hoped their sense might fail.

II.

There was a path of pleasantness,
   In which I was spelled to stray;
I would I had died ere I lost that path,
   Though wild and lorn my way.

III.

There was a voice which did discourse
   Sweet music to mine ear;

And

And (oh that I live to hear mine own)
  That voice I no more must hear.

IV.

The ray that lit my life is sunk,
  The voice is stopped with sand ;
And o'er that path forbid, high Heaven
  Doth wave a flaming brand.

V.

And I must wend my way alone,
  Despair's last curse to prove ;
To pine o'er passion's vanished dream ;
  To live, yet not to love.

But these pursuits soon failed to diver-
sify the monotony of confinement. The
repose of solitude soon degenerated into
apathy—listless, depressing apathy. He
began to remit the habits of watching at
the window for objects ; of taking the exercise the limits of his apartment allowed ;
of making those petty provisions against
utter vacancy, that every one makes on
the first apprehensions of it ; but which
                  gradually

gradually decline as its influence in-
creases.

Dreading the total enervation of mind
and body, which the progress of this habit menaced, he almost welcomed his second summons to attend the inquisitor.
There are few who could imagine such a
message would communicate joy; but
Ippolito longed for the sound of a human
voice; for the excitement which human
conference supplies. He longed to try
the powers of his mind, and the organs
of speech, to the exercise of which confinement had made him almost a stranger. The
shadows, that silently presented him food
and light at stated hours, had nothing of
human but the shape.

He was again conducted in utter silence
to the same apartment, from which he
again found the light of day excluded at
noon, and supplied by torches which shed
their smouldering and funereal light on
darker hangings, and sterner visages than
he

he had seen on the former examination.

The depositions which Angellini had collected, had appeared to him so momentous and extraordinary, that he had applied for assistants from the holy Office at Naples, which were granted to enable him to make a more full and deliberate report of the charges against his prisoner, before he was referred to the supreme cognizance of the tribunal in that city. There was more of form on this occasion than the preceding; and more of that appalling preparation, that dark pomp of mystery and fear. Quaint habits, mute assistants, silent signals, and whispered consultations, by which the office obtain an influence over the firmest minds, utterly distinct from the sense of the awe of their authority, or the uprightness and ability of their proceedings.

The examination, which lasted six hours, consisted entirely of questions drawn from the various depositions made before the
5   inquisitors,

inquisitors, relative to Ippolito's supposed character and movements both before and after he quitted Naples. Ippolito collecting the utmost energy of his mind, and inwardly not displeased at the trial of it to which he was summoned, at first objected in a moderate, but earnest manner to the process of the examination. He demanded the names of his accusers. He was informed it was totally contrary to the practices of the institution, to declare them. He then demanded a copy of the accusations, and time to prepare a refutation of them. He was told with this also it was impossible to comply; that if the charges urged against him were groundless, no length of deliberation was requisite for him to disclaim them; and if they were just, the less evasion and delay in admitting them the better; so that in either case, a categorical affirmative or negative was all that was expected from him. This was the sentence

tence of the Neapolitan assessors; but on the representation of Angellini, they consented to let the depositions relative to which he was examined, be read to him before they proceeded.

Ippolito listened to them with a solicitude, (which even his dangerous and disastrous situation could not repress) to learn the various opinions and conjectures excited by conduct so extraordinary as his had been. Nor could he even resist the visionary vanity that inflated him, while he heard himself mentioned as a being whose character and purposes were only to be known by fearful conjecture; who moved before the eyes of men in a cloud of mystery, through which they only caught passing glimpses of a form and movements more than human. The information laid before the holy Office of his conduct while in Naples, appeared to be the testimony of men who had watched it with wonder and suspicion; but

but without sacrificing either their judgment or their senses. They stated generally, that he had been observed to wander out at night unattended, frequently with gestures of gloomy distraction; to proceed to a certain spot, where he was met by a person of extraordinary appearance; that almost immediately on each meeting, they both disappeared; nor could the minutest search discover a trace of their persons, or their direction from that moment. To this extraordinary circumstance they added no fantastic comment, no wild exaggeration; but they strongly noticed the obvious and consequential alteration in the Count's temper, habits, and pursuit, which from being gay and open, had become severe, unsocial, and gloomy. In addition to these were the informations communicated by the servant, who had accompanied him from Naples, and the peasant he had seen at Bellano. These were as monstrous as

fear

fear, falsehood and superstitious malevolence could make them.

The wretch, whose folly had betrayed
him at Celano, and whom he had afterwards
forgiven, and condescended to vindicate
himself to, when they met in the deserted
inn, at Bellano, stated to the Inquisition,
" That his master was a sorcerer; that he
had endeavoured to seduce him to his
iniquitous art; that he had fled from him
to avoid his persecutions; that they had
afterwards met in that untenanted house,
whither the Count had resorted to confer
with the spirits that were known to possess it; that supernatural voices had called
him from room to room, and shapes of
unimaginable horror had crossed and overshadowed him; that terrified at a situation which no human courage could sustain, he had swooned, and just before his
senses forsook him, had seen Montorio
sinking in a fiery cloud through a chasm
in the floor, from which a host of huge,

black hands, armed with claws of griffins, were extended to receive him. The peasant whom he had met when wandering round the building, deposed that he had seen him assume different forms while he spoke with him; that at the end of their conference, he suddenly sprung upon the highest turret of the building, where he appeared, mounted on a black horse, who breathed fire, whose feet were cleft into talons, and whose mane scattered lightnings; that goading this terrific courser with a large serpent he held in his hand, both disappeared, leaving a train of bluish light behind them." If this information proved any thing, it proved that he had not entered the building at all. The inquisitors crossed themselves with devout horror as they listened to it, and Angellini hardly suppressed a smile that struggled with indignation and pity.

Ippolito observed with astonishment, that

that not an article of this information had been supplied by the stranger; nor was there any mention of the terrible transactions of the vault at Naples, which he believed had been divulged by him to the Inquisition, and would have constituted the subject of his examination. As it appeared, however, it must be partially known to them, by the process of the first examination, of which the subject had been the recognition of the inscription, he concluded that its present suppression was only a device of inquisitorial subtlety, which concealed the extent of information, in order either to lead to it by a chain of evidence, it would afterwards be impossible to retrace or disentangle, or to anticipate it by confessions drawn from the prisoner in the course of examination. He resolved therefore to admit nothing but what they already possessed; of which its absurdity was the easiest refutation.

At

At the conclusion of the depositions, he was solemnly exhorted to confess, by the principal inquisitor. "What have I to confess?" said Ippolito, "what mockery of equitable investigation is this? You urge accusations too monstrous for the credulity of an ideot; and you hope by affecting to believe them, to impose their belief on one whose conscience and memory disavow them; to make him doubt the testimony of his senses, and the events of his own existence; or to lead him in the fictitious heat of vindication from imaginary charges, to the mention of real ones." (At this ill-timed observation, he saw the inquisitors exchange looks of grim intelligence; but he was exasperated, not checked by it, and hurried on.) "Confession! Of what use were confession to me now? If I should even convince you of my innocence, can you restore to me its purity and its praise? Can you restore it to me without suspicion,

cion, and without reproach? Impossible. He who has once entered your walls, never can regain the estimation of society—never can regain his own confidence and honest pride. Whether acquitted or convicted, it matters not; he is held in the invisible chains of suspicion for life; the damps and dews of his dungeon form an atmosphere of repulsion around him for ever; the shadow of your walls darkens over him like a curse. Of what avail would confession be to me? It cannot recal the past, it cannot unmake me a prisoner of the Inquisition. Your dreadful policy can neither reverse its proceedings, nor remedy its evils; it rushes through society confounding, subverting, and trampling; but it cannot pause to raise or to repair; and if it could, it were in vain. The wounds it inflicts are mental, and therefore cannot be healed; the brand impressed by irons red from the furnace of superstition, can never be effaced, and ache at every

breath

breath of heaven. No reputation of habitual innocence, no actual evidence of universal integrity, can protect your victims. A single suspicion, a whisper, a look, can dash them from the height of human excellence into the dungeons of the Inquisition; the most abject villain may blast and destroy the most exalted of mankind. Though unassailable every where to the view, the most trivial of his motions, the very *heel* of his moral frame may be reached by the shaft of clandestine malignity, and the wound is mortal. Of what service is acquittal to such a man; is the world into which he returns, the same as that he quitted? No; while he slept in the lethargy of confinement; the vestal fire of his honour, which it was the business of his life to guard, has gone out; and he sees its ashes scattered and trampled on. How are these evils to be anticipated by confession? Confession itself is an engine of mental torture, which none but an inquisitor would

would use ; it is possessing yourselves, under the name of religious authority, of the means of gratifying carnal and selfish curiosity. It is, where your natural forces have failed, to lurk in the *horse of super-stition*, and enter in dishonourable tri-umph. The thoughts and actions of the purest lives cannot bear this universal scrutiny. There is no human being fully known to another ; it is only by partial ignorance, that mutual esteem is pre-served. To the wife of his bosom, to the friend of his soul, to his own consci-ousness and recollection, a man will not dare to reveal every thought that visits his mind ; there are some which he almost hopes are concealed from the Deity. When a man exhibits his mind, he shows you a city, whose public walks and palaces are ostentatiously displayed, while its pri-sons, its cages of unclean birds, its hold of foul and hidden evil are conceal-ed ; or he exhibits it as he would the sovereign

sovereign of that city, when he stands on
the pinnacle of his pride, and looks round
on the ample prospect of his own magnificence, not as when he flies from the resort of men, and herds with the beasts;
when his power is lost in degradation, and
his form buried in brutality.

And why confess to *you* ? What claim have
you from nature, or from confidence for
the demand, or do you ground it upon the
absence of all ?   Are we to repose in you
a trust, withheld from all mankind beside,
because you have less motive of solicitude,
less claim on confidence, less power or wish
of sympathy than all mankind ?   Are *you*
like the ocean, to engulph in silence and
darkness, the treasures intended to be
shared with affection and sympathy ? is
confidence like the ebony, the growth
of subterrene darkness, the nursling of a
dungeon ? No, it is your greedy, furtive,
serpent curiosity, that longs to wind itself
about the tree of knowledge; 'tis the
ambition

ambition of a fiend, counterfeiting the
aspirations of an angel, like the impure
priests of a pagan idol, ye love to prey
on violated purity, that as yet has never
sacrificed to nature or to passion, and to
call it a rite of religion."

He would have proceeded, for the inquisitors listened with the most unrelaxed composure; but Angellini, shocked
at his impetuosity, that offended without
advantage, interrupted him by observing
with severity, " That a vague and rhapso-
dical declamation was no defence; that a
definite charge had been read in his ears,
and that they were prepared to listen to
his vindication; that on the wild expressions he had used, no construction could
be put that could tend either to the information of his examiners, or his own
exculpation." This was said with the
benevolent intention of dissipating the
injurious inferences that might be drawn
from the careless vehemence with which
he poured out his thoughts.

Y 5   " Vindication,"

"Vindication," repeated Montorio, "from what? From charges you do not, you cannot believe—from charges of which my present situation is the fullest refutation. Who can believe such powers as they ascribe to me, to belong to a being whom they themselves hold in durance and dungeons? If I possess these powers, why do I not exercise them for my own preservation? If I can remove the barriers of nature, and sport with the opposition of the elements, why am I here? Have I more pleasure in terrifying a solitary peasant, than in extricating myself from persecution and danger? Why do I not mount in flames? Why do I not cleave your walls at this moment? Do these powers desert their possessor at his hour of need alone? No, it is impossible you can be thus deceived; no habits of suspicion and bigotry could reduce minds to such a level in judgment; it is impossible such weak instruments could impel you

to

to distrust the experience of your senses, the course of nature, and what should be more unquestioned than either—the honour of a noble house ! No, your informers and your information are of a higher class ; 'tis no dream of a lying menial that has brought me here." " You are conscious then of some more important causes which the holy Office have had for their proceedings relative to you," said one of the inquisitors. " I did not say so," said the prisoner. " You implied it," said the inquisitor.

At this observation a new object rushed on Montorio's mind; that of turning his defence into an accusation. He found that it was impossible to contend against the evidence of his dark pursuits they were possessed of; all that could be done, was to make their confession fatal if possible, to the minister of evil who had betrayed and destroyed him. The terrors and dangers of the fate that
probably

probably awaited his confession, disappeared, when he thought of his enemy trembling before the same tribunal with himself; his visionary person and claims, either reduced to a definite and vulnerable substance, or analysed and dispersed to their original element. His natural vehemence, his curiosity, his despair of exclusive vindication, urged him together to this bold movement. The toils that invested him he could neither rend nor unravel; but with a lion-bound, he broke away and bore them with him. " I am conscious," said he, in a firm tone, " that other and more momentous information has thrown me into the prisons of the Inquisition; but I am also conscious, that he who supplied that information, is dyed a thousand fold more black and deep in its implications than I am. If there be guilt, he has been the framer, the prompter, the minister of it. Summon him here, if you can. Confront me
with

with him. Let his business be unfolded
with a solemn and deliberate hand. When
we stand as criminals together; then
will I speak, and tell a tale that shall
amaze your souls. Till then, I shall only
speak to arraign the justice of the pro-
cedure that treats a supposed offender
as a criminal, and an actual one as innocent. He could not accuse me without
condemning himself. Why is he not
then here along with me? Can he alone,
like the Messinean assassin, stab invisible
and unpunished? Can he only shake off the
viper of sorcery from his hand, and feel
no hurt? Can he like the fabulous ferry-
man, convey souls to the infernal regions,
yet never enter them himself?"

Angellini again interrupted him to assure him the conceptions he had formed
of this character, were totally erroneous;
that he was an innocent individual, who
had not even a personal knowledge of
Montorio, and whose only motive in giving

ing information to the holy Office was a disinterested zeal for the Catholic faith. Montorio persisted on the other hand in the most emphatic assertions of his positive guilt. " He is a sorcerer," said he. " He is an ecclesiastic," replied Angellini. "He is a murderer," pursued Montorio. " He escaped with difficulty from the fangs of murder," said Angellini. " He is a fiend," repeated Montorio, gnashing his teeth, " and his office is to betray the souls of men." " His office," said Angellini seriously incensed, " has been to rescue a human soul from its betrayers." " Prove your charges," said the inquisitors, "prove that the person who informed against you, is obnoxious to the power of the holy Office, and here we pledge our faith, that he shall be cited to our tribunal." " Reverend fathers, he knows not what he says," said Angellini. " I know what I say, Signor," said Montorio, " and I also remember what I have said ; I re-

member

member that I pledged myself to prove the guilt of your informer, in the event of your summoning him to your tribunal, and confronting him with me." " And on what information shall we cite him?" said the inquisitor.

Again Montorio was silent from confusion and fear. He found it necessary to criminate himself in order to the bare citation of the stranger. In the moment of his hesitation, Angellini again interposed. " Reverend fathers," said he, " here is some profound mistake. The prisoner is evidently ignorant of his real accuser. Permit me to relate the circumstances under which I received the information on which he was confined; they will perhaps remove his errors with regard to the person of the informer, and assist us to examine this intricate and mysterious affair" The inquisitors hesitated, till one of them reminded the rest, that by doing so they might discover the person against whom Montorio's invectives

tives had been directed, and that the discovery might furnish further matter of
cognizance to the holy Office. They
therefore permitted Angellini to proceed
in his narrative, to which Montorio listened with the breathless, fixed attention of
one whose existence and vital determina-
tions were suspended on the words of
the speaker.

" It is now near a month," said Angellini, " since I was informed, one evening,
that a stranger desired to speak with me on
affairs relative to the holy Office. I desired
him to be admitted. He was in the habit of an ecclesiastic. His figure and face
were remarkable ; but of his voice, I never shall lose the memory of the sound as
long as I retain my senses. The singular
degree of awe, almost amounting to repugnance, which his appearance inspired, was
removed by his entering on the subject of
his business, with unusual promptness and
intelligence.

His

His narrative was extraordinary, but perfectly probable. He mentioned that he had been travelling from Padua to Naples; that his direction was to a convent in the western suburbs of that city, where he had not arrived till the approach of night. That his ignorance of the avenues of the deserted part of the city, combined with the lateness of the hour, at length suggested some apprehensions of his personal danger, which were confirmed when he saw from the projections of a ruinous building which he was to pass, two figures occasionally leaning and retreating when they perceived themselves observed. He could distinguish indeed that their habit and appearance was utterly unlike that of assassins, or indeed any class of men he had before seen in any part of Italy; but he knew not what disguises assassins might assume in Naples, and he felt it was probable there could be no common motive for their

their partial and hurried concealments. In the first impulse of his fear, he dismounted from his mule, and ran to shelter himself under a dismantled arch, which he did not conceive to be connected with the building from whence they had appeared to start. He had hardly done so, when he heard their steps approaching his retreat, and saw their tall shadows projecting from the entrance of the arch. He rushed desperately forward. In the tumult of fear and flight. Little accuracy was to be expected from him with regard to the passages he traversed, or the objects he witnessed ; otherwise perhaps deserving the minutest attention.

His perceptions, he confessed, were only exercised to discover whether the steps of his pursuers were advancing on him. He perceived they were, and sprung headlong forward with the rapidity of one who fears no danger, but the obstruction

of

of his flight.   The steps of his pursuers
gained on him.   He perceived he had
reached a flight of steps, and he rushed
down them without any other object than
of escape.   Occupied only by his fears,
he did not perceive the vast depth he had
descended to, till he was in utter darkness.
Terrors of equal magnitude now beset
him, and he endeavoured to retrace his
former steps, or discover some means of
relief and assistance.   While he was thus
employed, he perceived a faint light in
the vast distance of the darkness that surrounded him.   He approached it through
many obstructions he described with the
strength of personal suffering, but which
I need not repeat, and at length discovered that it twinkled through an iron grating
in the wall of the passage he was travers-
ing;   he applied his eye to it, and beheld
within, figures employed in actions which
suspended every faculty of mind and sense,
as he gazed on them.   In the first impulse

pulse of horror he would have fled; but
after a moment's delay, found himself ri-
vetted to the spot by the very feelings
that at first would have hurried him away.
He remained long enough to observe the
agents and their strange deeds, with that
tenacious and indelible feeling which the
very reluctance of horror impresses on the
mind. He reported them to me with
strong, but evidently real emotion, such
as none but the recollection of actual
objects could inspire. In consequence
of this information, I proceeded with regard to the holy Office, and to its prisoner, as you have seen; I also communicated the mode of his escape from the
vault, and his extraordinary reasons for
laying his information before me, instead
of the tribunal at Naples." "They were
extraordinary," said the inquisitor, "but
fully justified by the event."

Montorio had listened with the pro-
foundest attention; but remained un-
convinced.

convinced.   A secret mistrust of the stranger's agency, bound up his mind as if by a spell of incredulity. He addressed himself to Angellini. " I have little," said he with solemnity, " to offer in support of what I say, but my own convictions.   I cannot be supposed armed with a regular refutation of positions I now hear for the first time ; yet there are no words of sufficient power to express the firmness of my belief, that the circumstances you have just now mentioned, are only a new device of subtlety and malevolence, which I have found exhaustless ; they are incongruous, fictitious, impossible." He paused to search his memory for some circumstance to substantiate his assertions. After a long silence, he said, with a severe smile, " You will form a judgment of the strength of my convictions, and my earnestness to impress them on you, from my being led to confess circumstances no other power could have ex-

torted

torted from me. The vault of which your informer pretended he commanded a view, had neither grating nor aperture; it was on every side inaccessible but to those who visibly entered it. In this point I feel I cannot be mistaken. No lapse of time, no intervention of other circumstances, however numerous or important, can efface from my memory, the few and minute notices it retains of that place. I have counted every stone in its walls, the curve of the arches, the depth of the shadow, the peculiar hue of its blackness, are written on my soul for ever. You see I do not deceive you, when I venture on defences so distinct. Reverend fathers, it is impossible that any being could have approached from without the place, your informer specified. He must have been the instrument of another's ministry—the channel of higher intelligence. I again repeat my adjuration, that you will compel him, from whom you received your information

information, to attend the tribunal of the
holy Office, and confront him with me
personally."

"This incredulity is affected," said
an inquisitor, "we have more than
the bare assertion of the witness for
his extraordinary information ; we have
proof, such as none but the most intimate
knowledge could supply, and such as artificial obduracy will resist in vain. Must
we remind you of the mysterious inscription over the portals of the vault ? Could
that have been recognized and reported
to the Inquisition by one who had never
read it?" Montorio trembled ; he thought
he felt the toils of evidence tightening
around him. "Must we remind you,"
said the inquisitor, in a thrilling voice, "of
the bloody dagger that is for ever shaken
before your eyes, and of the deed its sight
recals and punishes—that deed unseen,
unspeakable, wrought in central darkness,
lapped in the very skirts of the nether
world. I see you tremble—I tremble myself."

self." He sunk back in the seat from which he had risen in the force of speaking; the attendants hid their faces with visible shudderings of fear. Montorio, in broken and inaudible tones, said, with frequent intervals, " I cease to feel for myself—to speak for myself; I have no longer any power of defence or of resistance. I speak without hope of belief or conviction ; but I speak it with the solemn firmness of despair. I am a prisoner without a crime; I am a visionary without intercourse with forbidden things; I am a murderer without the stain of human blood."

He stopped suddenly. A hollow, broken sound succeeded. The inquisitor motioned to the attendants to lower the lamp that was suspended from the ceiling, that they might observe the changes in his countenance. It was then perceived that he had fainted. He was conveyed to his apartment; but the inquisitors

sitors entered into a consultation that
continued till midnight. When Montorio recovered, the operations of his mind
were decisive and rapid. Danger was no
longer indefinite or avoidable; but in
proportion as it became certain, his terrors were diminished, or exchanged for
other feelings. The temper of his soul
became at once rigid and vindictive. His
sensibility of suffering was appeased by
the hope of teaching another to suffer;
and the horrors of the Inquisition only
served to exalt his prospect of revenge.

On the next appearance of his guard,
he signified his wish to be supplied with
pen and ink, and to be undisturbed for
some time, in order to prepare some documents for the inspection of the holy Office.
His request was complied with, and he devoted himself for some days to writing; but
as he proceeded in his task, he was often
checked

checked by suggestions of repentance.
The goaded and unnatural vehemence of
mind that prompts to extraordinary
movements, soon fails us, if their execution be not instant. This occupied some
time; and during that time he often debated the possibility of some interme-
diate measure, often lamented the necessary violence of motion the emergency compelled him to ; and was only
urged to the completion of his task, by
the recollection that he was pledged to
its performance, and that the danger of
confession in his case, admitted neither
degree nor diminution.

On the third day it was completed ;
and he then put it into the hands of
Angellini, who received it with a look
of mournful solicitude, which his judi-
cial gravity vainly resisted. Montorio
gave it to him in silence, a silence which
the other's deep feeling did not permit
him

him to break. He was quitting the room,
when Montorio waved his hand. Angellini heard the sound this slight motion
occasioned; and turning eagerly round
said, " You wish then to speak with me ?"
" No, Signor," said his prisoner, " no ;
I have now neither wishes nor fears.
Let the holy Office be acquainted as soon
as possible with the contents of these
manuscripts." " And for me," said Angellini, with emotion, " you have no
charge for me ?" " Yes," said Montorio, after a pause, " to reflect on the
horrors of that fate, to fly from which
I have plunged into the dungeons of
the Inquisition."

Angellini quitted the room. For an
hour after he left it, the prisoner remained fixed in his seat, his clasped
hands resting on his knees, his head declined, his eyes fixed on the ground,
which he did not see.   The sun set,

and

and it grew dark ; but he perceived no change of light or object.

At length, he felt a step in the room, and dimly descried a figure which stood opposite him.   He saw not whether it was human or not; nor did he raise his eyes till he heard, addressing him, the voice of the *Stranger*.   "You now," said he, repeating the words he had uttered at Bellano, " behold me in another form, not as a forteller, but as a witness of your fate."   Montorio beheld him stead-fastly.   He was now in the dress of a monk, which he wore with the case and freedom of an habitual dress.   " It is he," said the unhappy young man, speak-ing to himself; " it is he, but I will not see him."   " You can no longer avoid it," said the stranger; " here are no re-sources to palliate the deceptions of sense. We are alone; nor is there any human cause or object to hide from either

of

of us the real character and purposes of the other." " I will not look up till he is past," said Montorio, still speaking inwardly ; " this terrible shadow will soon disperse, and I shall be a whole man again." " Look up, look up," said the stranger ; " it is no shadow that stands before you ; it is the form of him who has followed you so long, who must follow you for a term still ; of him, from whom it is folly to fly ; for your flight has only been into the clutches of the Inquisition." " Better a thousand-fold than into yours ; better into the hands of man than of you, whom I will not call a demon, lest I should wrong superior depravity. Yes, I have fled hither ; and therefore it is, that I can bear to behold and confer with you. Look round, and tell me what has an inmate of this mansion further to fear. I stand upon the utmost verge of nature. I shall see or hear my own species no more. I am a

z 3   prisoner

prisoner of the Inquisition for life. I have reached the bare and desolate crag, and the wave of vengeance bursts at my feet. Here I am safe in despair. You did not calculate this last giant-spring. You did not know that life is easily thrown away by him to whom it has lost its worth. You did not know that a soul can wrestle with its chains of darkness; aye, and do deeds with them beyond the pitch of mortal implements. Fool! how I have mocked and baffled you! how I triumph over you this moment! How did you enter this prison? By all that is good I am rejoiced to see you. Hark! I have intelligence for you. I have told every thing to the Inquisition—every thing, by my immortal soul! I am a prisoner for life; I know it; I triumph in it. Better their chains for ever, than yours, in thought, for a moment." " What do you call my chains? I never forged or bound them

on

on you. I unfolded their connexion as
far as was visible to humanity. Mine
is a hopeless task—to reconcile nature
to suffering, and pride to shame. But
weariness will not excuse it. I, whom
you think the sole and voluntary mover
in this business, I am myself impelled
by a hand whose urgings never remit or
rest. The central seat of our mysteries
at Naples; the solitary heights of the
mountain; the vault at Bellano; this
chamber in the prison of the Inquisition—are all but parts of a progress that
is incessant and interminable; though it
mostly holds a direction invisible to the
human eye. I know your folly in dis-
closing your secret to the Inquisition. I
knew it before I entered these walls.
What have you gained by it? The publication of your guilt, the certainty of
your condemnation. Were all the armies
of the earth summoned together to hold
you from the commission of that deed,

it

it were in vain. They would only witness what they could not prevent. To
resist the agency of the invisible world,
you might as well employ a broken reed,
a gossamer, a mote, as the whole pith and
puissance of the earth. To conduct your
steps in silence and without interruption,
I threw over them a veil of mystery You
have rent it open; and what have you gained by it?—Exposure without commisera-
tion, and confidence without assistance."

" I will not," said Montorio, " be
pushed from the proof by words. The
trial-hour is arrived; the power with
which we are to contend is extrinsic and
impartial. I have strove darkling with
you; but the light approaches at last.
These walls are indeed the last retreat
man would fly to; but they will protect me. I feel here a gloomy strength,
a defiance of those devices by which you
have deluded my senses. You cannot
crumble these towers into dust; you
cannot

cannot fight with an institution whose
source is in the power and vitals of the
church." " It were better for you that I
should ; but your ingratitude and obduracy deserve that I should resign you
to your fate." " What is it you mean ?"
said Montorio. " Do you then know so
little of the Inquisition ? Do you imagine that they can believe the tale you
have told—that they will not consider *it*
as an attempt to delude and mock them,
and you as an audacious and obdurate
enemy of the faith. No ; should you
disclose to them all you saw and all you
imagined, they would never believe your
confession, full or sincere; they will
look on you as a hoard of dark secrets,
which can never be exhausted ; and they
will for ever continue urging you to confessions when you have no longer any
thing to disclose. Shelter in the Inquisition ! Yes, they will give you shelter
safe and deep; your bed will be burning

ing coals, and you will be pillowed on pincers and scaring irons. No declarations of ignorance will avail you; and no resources of fiction will shield you from their endless persecution." " There is yet a resource," said Montorio; " I can die." " Die! you know little of the Inquisition. Oh, they have horrid arts of protracting life; of quickening the pulse that vibrates with pain; of making life and sufferance flow on together like two artificial streams of which they hold the sources. They inquire to what precise limit nature can support their inflictions, and precisely to that limit they pursue them; and then remand their prisoner to his cell, to renew his strength for the next conflict. You will waste away in their dungeons, like the lamp that glares on your agonies. You will never, never escape their hands, till you are unconsciously enlarged to do the deed you fled into them to avoid in vain." " This

is

impossible," said Montorio; " the grave will sooner yield up its dead than the Inquisition her victims. Here I am safe. It is a dreadful immunity ; but I welcome it. I will stretch myself on my burning bed. I will gripe the irons of torture, for they will protect me from you. To preserve my life and innocence is perhaps impossible ; but it is at least possible to purchase innocence with loss of life." " You are deceived. It is indeed in your power to aggravate your sufferings by fruitless resistance ; but not to remove their cause. The deed you are fated to do, you may delay, but cannot decline. Respiration is not more necessary to existence, or consciousness to thought. You might as well contend to reverse the past, as to resist the future. Your struggles may work the torrent into foam, but cannot repel its course. The dungeons of the Inquisition, and the summit of a mountain,

tain afford you equal shelter. For proofs
of the power with which I, the weakest
minister of your fate, am armed, I can,
at this moment, bid those bars of iron
dissolve.   I can lead you forth through
every passage of your prison, under the
eyes of your guard, in the very presence of the Inquisitors.   Will you be
wise? Is your arm strong? Is your
heart set and bound up? Will you do
the deed to-night? Within an hour you
shall be on the spot; your path so secret, a leaf shall not rustle beneath
your feet; your blow so certain, no
groan shall follow it.   Shall this be the
hour—the hour of enlargement—aye,
and the hour of fame.   A pestilence,
an earthquake, a volcano live in the histories of men, when sunny days, and
drowsy prosperity are forgotten."

His manner, as he spoke, changed beyond all power of description.   It was
bold, animating, daring; but mixed with
a wild-

a wildness that appalled, with a demon-greatness of wickedness and strength that exalted and terrified. He placed his hearer on the extreme point of a precipice, shook him over the abyss, and laughed at his shudderings. Montorio looked at him for a moment with a fixed but speechless eye, and then said inwardly, "If my passage be only thither, there is a shorter way."

As he spoke, he sprung up with a violence neither to be foreseen nor resisted; and, rushing past the stranger, dashed himself against the massive and studded barrings of his iron door. He fell to the ground. The stranger raised him, and perceived he breathed no longer. He bent over him. He received in his hands the blood that gushed from Montorio's forehead and mouth; and, holding it out, murmured, "Drink, drink, if thou hast any mouth; but do not haunt me with those famished eyes.

Yes, yes, anon I shall sup with thee, and we will feast it well."

As he spoke, his eye fixed on a remote spot in the darkness; and he shrieked in agony, " Oh, hide, hide the scourge—thou seest I am about it."

END OF VOL. IL.

C. Stewer, Printer, Paternoster Row.

GOTHIC NOVELS

An Arno Press Collection

Series I

Dacre, Charlotte ("Rosa Matilda"). **Confessions of the Nun of St. Omer,** A Tale. 2 vols. 1805. New Introduction by Devendra P. Varma.

Godwin, William. **St. Leon:** A Tale of the Sixteenth Century. 1831. New Foreword by Devendra P. Varma. New Introduction by Juliet Beckett.

Lee, Sophia. **The Recess:** Or, A Tale of Other Times. 3 vols. 1783. New Foreword by J. M. S. Tompkins. New Introduction by Devendra P. Varma.

Lewis, M[atthew] G[regory], trans. **The Bravo of Venice,** A Romance. 1805. New Introduction by Devendra P. Varma.

Prest, Thomas Preskett. **Varney the Vampire.** 3 vols. 1847. New Foreword by Robert Bloch. New Introduction by Devendra P. Varma.

Radcliffe, Ann. **The Castles of Athlin and Dunbayne:** A Highland Story. 1821. New Foreword by Frederick Shroyer.

Radcliffe, Ann. **Gaston De Blondeville.** 2 vols. 1826. New Introduction by Devendra P. Varma.

Radcliffe, Ann. **A Sicilian Romance.** 1821. New Foreword by Howard Mumford Jones. New Introduction by Devendra P. Varma.

Radcliffe, Mary-Anne. **Manfroné:** Or The One-Handed Monk. 2 vols. 1828. New Foreword by Devendra P. Varma. New Introduction by Coral Ann Howells.

Sleath, Eleanor. **The Nocturnal Minstrel.** 1810. New Introduction by Devendra P. Varma.

Series II

Dacre, Charlotte ("Rosa Matilda"). **The Libertine**. 4 vols. 1807.
New Foreword by John Garrett. New Introduction by
Devendra P. Varma.

Dacre, Charlotte ("Rosa Matilda"). **The Passions**. 4 vols. 1811.
New Foreword by Sandra Knight-Roth. New Introduction
by Devendra P. Varma.

Dacre, Charlotte ("Rosa Matilda"). **Zofloya**; Or, The Moor:
A Romance of the Fifteenth Century. 3 vols. 1806. New
Foreword by G. Wilson Knight. New Introduction by
Devendra P. Varma.

Ireland, W[illiam] H[enry]. **The Abbess**, A Romance. 4 vols.
1799. New Foreword by Devendra P. Varma. New
Introduction by Benjamin Franklin Fisher IV.

[Leland, Thomas]. **Longsword**, Earl of Salisbury: An
Historical Romance. 2 vols. 1775. New Foreword by
Devendra P. Varma. New Introduction by Robert D. Hume.

[Maturin, Charles Robert]. **The Albigenses**: A Romance.
4 vols. 1824. New Foreword by James Gray. New
Introduction by Dale Kramer.

Maturin, Charles Robert ("Dennis Jasper Murphy"). **The Fatal
Revenge**: Or, The Family of Montorio. A Romance.
3 vols. 1807. New Foreword by Henry D. Hicks. New
Introduction by Maurice Lévy.

[Moore, George]. **Grasville Abbey**: A Romance. 3 vols. 1797.
New Foreword by Devendra P. Varma. New Introduction
by Robert D. Mayo.

Radcliffe, Ann. **The Romance of the Forest**: Interspersed With
Some Pieces of Poetry. 3 vols. 1827. New Foreword by
Frederick Garber. New Introduction by Devendra P.
Varma.

[Warner, Richard]. **Netley Abbey**: A Gothic Story. 2 vols.
1795. New Introduction by Devendra P. Varma.